THE ONE THAT KILLS YOU

C STREET MYSTERY
BOOK 1

RICK ROTHERMEL

ROUGH
EDGES
PRESS

Rough Edges Press
An Imprint of Wolfpack Publishing
9850 S. Maryland Parkway, Suite A-5 #323
Las Vegas, Nevada 89183

roughedgespress.com

Paperback ISBN 978-1-68549-231-1
eBook ISBN 978-1-68549-230-4

This book is dedicated to the memory of author Sue Grafton.
'S' is for 'Story'.

THE ONE THAT KILLS YOU

1

October 7, 1996

He'd never heard her scream.

The final morning together for Ron and Annie Connors started the way their mornings always had...early, with a hot breakfast pastry and a cup of French Roast from the big, noisy brushed aluminum machine on the kitchen counter and some quiet intimate conversation before they began their morning rituals in advance of the start of their busy day.

Ron was a popular figure and a respected name in the automotive aftermarket industry, his companies marketing hundreds of specialty items for the professional auto racing and civilian high-performance markets. He was more famous, though, as a racer. He was a legitimate 'legend' in that sport, famous worldwide for decades for his exploits in numerous facets of motorsports all his adult life and much of his adolescence before that. He still looked a lot like those early photos; his eyes bright, his jaw square, his tan deep and his hair jet black, just starting to silver at the temples—each element belying his sixty-eight years.

Ron had the spoils to show for his efforts and successes.

Trophies, plaques and awards certificates were visible in modest displays in his home and at their various business locations. He was always busy, and he traveled hundreds of thousands of miles yearly. He often wondered if his 'legend' status just meant that people had his number so that they could keep him busy 'round the clock. Still, he knew he'd been richly blessed. He relished each challenge every time the phone rang.

Ron called to Annie that he had the phone when it started ringing that morning, and he stayed on the line as they dressed for their day, as they'd done every morning in the last fourteen years. Now back downstairs in the kitchen looking at the still warm fax paper laying on the counter, initiated the discussion of the sales profile for the storm-ravaged pacific northwest states as Annie entered his peripheral vision. She carried his best suit jacket, destined for the dry cleaners down on Foothill, as she finger-waved and smiled.

She left the top half of the Dutch door open to vent cooler air from the garage into the warm kitchen. In the next two minutes Ron cleaners down the hill as she approached the door to the garage and they finger-waved to one another. She looked as good as ever, youthful and vibrant at 52, with the style and demeanor of a well-kept second wife. Ron absently heard the garage door motor open before her minivan started and backed from the space. Ron was halfway through the discussion of a tire design when he heard the first strange noise from outside. It was an odd sound, really, a shrill cry of pain and shock totally alien to his years of experience with Annie. His mind went blank for a second, then it came to him.

"NO!" he yelled, his mind suddenly filled with dread. "That bastard!" Ron disconnected from his call and started toward the garage, still carrying the cordless phone.

As he crossed the threshold he realized that his handgun was in the console glove box of his pickup at the rear of the property. He ascended the brick steps in his sock feet and crossed the empty space. He saw her idling silver Astro van, drivers' door wide open and lights on, as it coasted backwards until its rear bumper tapped the stone retaining wall at the edge of the driveway. Ron ran across the dark vacant garage space toward the first of the loud, awful 'pops.' His mind shifted into a strange slow-motion as he emerged from the garage.

Then he saw Annie, her mouth agape and running red. The front of her modest beige suit ran red with blood as the attacker shot her again. She jumped a foot as the blast hit her, shattering the van window behind her. She started a slow slump to the ground before she sagged face-first onto the white concrete driveway, beyond help.

At that moment Ron cleared the open garage, his bright white t-shirt and khakis stark against the dark garage opening. He stopped in his tracks and dropped his phone in shock to what he was witnessing as the intruders turned to confront him. For the first time ever he turned from his Annie and ran on leaden feet toward the front of the property. His mind reeled as he struggled for traction on the cold slick driveway.

"If someone heard the noise," he reasoned to himself, "they'd surely call 9-1-1 and help would come to save Annie." He knew better. Goddam his side hurt. That was a rib shattering and he felt each cruel hot rivet as they pierced his left side and both of his calves and his left arm, but still he willed himself forward in a slow wobbly bloody path. After one shot took out his left knee he toppled onto the driveway a few feet from the front gate. As he fell he saw a silent spurt of deep red erupt from his chest. Why didn't that one hurt?

Ron Connors tried in vain during those last eternal, fleeting moments to breathe...swallow...speak...cough...cry...anything as he looked back toward his Annie and the home he so dearly loved. Through the deepening blur, he saw the dark men approach and he saw their arms move. Silent fire erupted from their wrists and then it all went mercifully dark.

That was fourteen years ago, the day that Ron Connors and his wife were murdered.

March 2010

When I was a kid, I had a lot of heroes. Ron Connors had been one of the first. He was a legend and an inspiration for this kid from Jersey and countless others all over the world. He had looked like a movie idol. His dark hair, square jaw and ready smile were the stuff of legend. His race teams had set speed and endurance records in almost every facet of motor racing. The Indy 500, the amateur and professional ranks of drag racing, off-road racing in Baja California and the Bonneville Salt Flats had all seen his teams' efforts and successes before he created some of the best-marketed names in the history of the automotive aftermarket industry.

I'd heard of the brutal murders of Ron and Annie Connors when I was in college. I'd been shocked that such a great man could suffer such a cruel and violent fate. In any event I had no idea that well over a decade later I would be the one tapped to look for a solution to the still-unsolved murders.

My name's Street. A criminologist by training and profession, but I carry a California Private Investigators' license. I live and work in Los Angeles. That's been the fulfillment of a lifelong dream. I grew up in New Jersey, watching afternoon re-runs of all of the old L.A.-based detective series from the '60s and 70s. My one-named heroes coursed smooth, wide, dry streets in flashy convertibles while I was stuck wearing hooded parkas shoveling snow a few months a year. It just didn't seem fair.

As I watched the shows I studied the stories and learned from the characters. I said 'wow' and 'cool' a lot back then and I may have copied a few too many mannerisms. I was really into crooked smiles when I was eleven. I hummed the theme music and I was an expert on which hero drove which car, and how well. I wanted to be just like them. That's what heroes are for. I was twelve years old when I promised myself that sometime, some way, I would live in L-period, A-period.

I went to college and completed a degree in Criminology. Then I went to work for the Atlantic City Police Department while I earned my Master's. Unfortunately, rank and time in service to the Department trumped scholarly pursuits when applied to traction within the ACPD bureaucracy. All that class time didn't keep the brass from assigning me night shift patrol duty and weekend DUI checkpoint posts instead of murder investigations. I did the legwork that solved a couple of knotty murders, but credit went to senior officers. I was 'still learning;' they assured me my time would come.

Still, I hung-in until a few years later, when I hit it big at one of the Atlantic City casinos—a total fluke of winning a pair of double Jackpots during a city-wide slot tournament. Couple of million dollars net, but because of an obscure ACPD regulation, I faced a stern reprimand and a temporary loss of rank. Should I stay on the job and take the grief or just move on?

That decision took about four seconds. Two weeks later I was headed west.

At the end of my meandering 4000-mile adventure, I pulled to the curb on Ocean Boulevard in Santa Monica above the Pacific Coast at dusk. That September evening, I sat on the front fender of my old GTO and watched for the first time as the pale amber sun set over the Pacific Ocean. It was one of the most breathtaking sights I'd laid eyes on. I took a series of photos of that sunset. A while later I had the GTO painted to match the color of the ocean in one of the pictures.

After I got my bearings in the area, I found a house that I liked a lot. I cashed it out and spent almost as much money renovating it to my taste. Then I hung out a shingle, became a licensed P.I. and went to work. I fully realize how fortunate I am: I'm living my dream; I live and work in a city I love; I find myself in some interesting and challenging situations, and the rewards have been many. That particular morning, I was facing a new challenge.

I was sitting on the plush high-backed grey leather sofa in a color-coordinated reception area and gazing appreciatively across the foyer, chatting with Elizabeth Damarow's delicately attractive ash-blonde receptionist—appropriately named Ashley. Eventually, but a little too soon for my taste Ashley answered her intercom and directed me toward the hallway that led to the executive office area of the complex. I walked the length of the glass-walled corridor, pushed open the paneled walnut and frosted-glass doors on the sixteenth floor of the downtown Pasadena office tower that held but a portion of the Damarow business empire.

Sitting behind her massive oak desk in her more-massive corner office, Elizabeth looked to be a little north of sixty and 'way north of wealthy'...a well-appointed mature woman quite comfortable in a position of highly-focused power. Her reputation was that of a tough, innovative and determined leader. I liked that. As I entered, she stood, reached across her desk and shook my hand. Her grip was impressive.

"Mister Street", she smiled, "Welcome! I am, so pleased to finally meet you. You come very highly recommended!" Elizabeth's hair was short, frosted silver and expensively maintained; her makeup subtle and dignified. She wore a pale pink wool suit that probably cost more than my refrigerator. Her delicate diamond necklace and matching earrings set a confident, modest, but really expensive tone that matched the woman's aura perfectly.

"I'm glad to hear that. How long has Lynn been your corporate counsel?"

Elizabeth smiled like a proud parent. "Oh, about six years, but I've known Lynnie since before she was born. Her mother and I were best friends in high school, then Sorority sisters in college. We've been best friends for decades. I was Maid of Honor at her wedding and she at mine. We did all that 'buddy stuff' from about ninth grade on. Lynnie and my son grew up together and I am so very proud of her. Not to discount, of course, that she has proven to be a world-class attorney as well."

I smiled at the reference. "It's good to see that we agree on that. She has given me referrals to several of her clients and we have become good friends over the last few years."

"She speaks very highly of you." I was glad for that. Formalities and introductions dealt with, the questions started. "So tell me Mister Street, what do you know of my late brother, Ron Connors?"

This was my natural territory. "The man's a legend. I'm a big-time 'car guy'. I have hundreds of back-issue car magazines in my library at home. Through the decades he was featured in hundreds of them and he's on more covers than I can count. I studied his exploits in detail when I was a kid. He was a true hero and an inspiration to me and countless others like me. I was shocked when I read of how he and his wife died."

"We all were. It was just devastating! It still is, in many ways. I miss him terribly! She picked up her delicate, porcelain coffee cup and held it a couple of inches from her lips as she asked, "What do you know of the investigation into his murders?" She sipped her coffee as I answered.

"I was aware of it from the start, but I studied it after Lynn first mentioned it. The prime suspect is a former business associate, a Ray Cole from down in Orange County. He and Ron were partners in a motorsports promotions effort in the early half of the nineties. They had similar businesses catering to different aspects of stadium-based motorsports. Ron had off-road truck racing; Cole promoted Motocross. They combined efforts and for a while and the arrangement was initially successful for both."

I cleared my throat and continued. "At some point it all went sour. The partnership split up and the matter went to arbitration. Ron came to the table with superior organization and better legal representation, and he won big. The court's judgment cost Cole almost everything he owned, after which Cole pretty much 'lost it'. He threatened and on occasion promised revenge. A while later, Ron and his wife were murdered. Cole has been the prime suspect since Day One. He claims innocence of the crime and ignorance of the circumstances. All of the larger fingers still point in his general direction, but dead-bang evidence has yet to be presented. He remains free and unindicted, though in greatly reduced circumstances."

Elizabeth had listened intently and seemed to tick off the elements as I spoke. "Well said, Mister Street. I'm impressed with your preparation. We have employed several other private investigators over the years, and they have proven to be disappointments. Ray Cole is still a free man. Frankly, I have no interest in employing another slacker on the payroll. You sound well-prepared and studious as Lynn said to expect. I am confident that you will do quite well.

She smiled as she spoke. That's usually a good sign.

Now it was my turn. "Thank you for that. I won't waste my time or your money. I try to work quickly and efficiently, and I have been told that at times I communicate a bit *too* much." Just the facts, madam.

Her eyebrows raised a bit. "That's good to know, Mister Street."

I always try to clarify one 'style element' with my clients, up front. "I do have to mention one thing about my methods. I start a situation like this by taking a very wide view. I look at every possibility and element from any realistic vantage point. Your sole focus from the day of the crime points at Ray Cole as the sole possible suspect. I will have to look beyond that. If my findings lead in a different direction, is that going to create a problem?"

Elizabeth took the query in stride. "No, it won't. I have great confidence in your abilities and talents, Mister Street. Your methods are up to you. Find what you can find and bring it all to me. I will look at everything."

Elizabeth gestured toward a tall white box on a table near my seat. "That package contains our topic material from day one, including local and national news coverage and, as you requested, the reports from all of our previous investigators. Copies of any available police reports and photographs are included as well. There is an index of the materials on top. There is a lot of information for you to digest. Your initial retainer check is on the top. I trust it is sufficient."

I spread the envelope and looked at the check. It was inscribed with my name, always a good sign, and as well as a couple of digits and a few zeroes that complied with the amount I had quoted Lynn. I slid the check, in its envelope, into my inside jacket pocket, then I moved the box to the floor in front of my seat.

Elizabeth spoke as I moved the package. "We have substantial property holdings, business resources and professional alliances in southern California, Mister Street. You are welcome to use any of them as you see fit in your work. Just call my office when you need assistance." I nodded my appreciation as she continued. "You are also aware that we are offering a substantial reward for the proper final solution of Ron's murder. You could become a rather wealthy young man. Please do not hesitate to contact me with any developments and concerns." I was being dismissed. Powerful people have a way of doing that. She rose and we shook hands one final time. "Good luck, Mister Street. I look forward to working with you."

3

I left the Damarow offices a few minutes later, retrieved my GTO from the parking deck and considered my status. I now had a box containing a wealth of information at my feet, a *really* healthy check in my pocket—close to my heart—and countless questions in my head. To forestall at least one of the questions, I let the car idle for a few minutes and keyed the phone as I 'went to the source'.

Lynn Noel had been a friend since my third day in L.A. We had met purely by accident as I trolled for information regarding professional licensing in the Golden State. She had been instrumental in getting my business permits, my California State P.I. license, and my concealed weapons permits through her connections in various city government offices and law enforcement in the L.A. basin. In appreciation, I had done various investigative efforts on her behalf while I served my apprenticeship as I familiarized myself with the ins-and-outs of the snoop business in the Golden State. Time went on and my referrals became meatier and less errand-oriented. Each of us also enjoyed the other's company and sense of humor, and we teased one another with 'great energy.' The friendship may have been helped by her appearance. Lynn Noel was simply a California classic—tall and tan, blonde and blue.

One of our better 'saves', a year prior, had rescued the kidnapped son, age nine, of a prominent record industry executive. That case had put Lynn on the front page of the L.A. Times for a solid week. Her business had jumped with her new profile as had mine, and our mutual respect and camaraderie had jumped along with the profits. I decided to ring her up that morning early in the process to get an opinion or two, glean some information, and pass on my thanks.

She answered her cell with her usual energy on the first ring. "Hey, C.! I just got an e-mail from Elizabeth. She adores you! I am so glad that worked out."

"Well, thank you for the referral. That woman loves you like a daughter, you know."

Lynn responded, "Yes she does, and I love her as well. She and my mom have been friends since they were teenagers. There was just so much loss in Elizabeth's life through the years, I know it has taken a toll on her. I try to stay as close as I can. Do you think you can help her?"

"I hope so. She mentioned that you and her son had grown up together. He is the one who was killed, right? What can you tell me about him?"

"Ricky? Sure. Well, Rick was about eight months older than I was and we were best friends until he was fourteen or so. When his hormones kicked in, we couldn't be friends as much. He thought himself an operator at that point and I was wise enough to steer clear. No teen mommy I!"

"He was a handful?"

"More likely a roving hand, trying to get a handful."

I chuckled. Lynn's way with words was often entertaining. "Ah. I see."

"Yeah, my folks had me on the fast-track early on, and the cool older kid in the jacked-up F-150 didn't cut it."

"I would certainly expect you to aim higher than a mere pickup truck. I see you at roughly Aston Martin level."

"Oh, at least!" Lynn made no secret of her fondness for the finer things in life.

"Good for you. So, when did you last see Ricky?" I knew what answer to expect.

"Let's see. It was at a Thanksgiving dinner party at Catherine's new home at the time, in Laguna, down in Orange County, before he went missing early that next year. There was a huge family-and-friends get together and all our family members were there. I had just gotten engaged so it was a big deal."

"And Ricky was justifiably jealous?"

"Quite! But I know that Elizabeth understood, as did everyone else there that day, that the rest of us had grown the hell up. Ricky was still about fifteen between his ears. He and I were friendly enough, but I think he and I both realized that we had nothing in common. He left Elizabeth's house early that day, just after dinner, and I doubt anyone noticed his absence at all. That was the last time I saw him, ever.

"Good reason for that though, everyone was probably blinded by the glare from your engagement ring. That is one serious rock!"

I heard her smile, and I could tell that she had raised her hand. "Yeah, it is, isn't it? I lucked out. I married a jeweler!"

"Well, yeah, but think of that poor guy. He got stuck with a *lawyer*. Eeeewww!"

Her voice went all smoky as she replied. "He did indeed. But she has great legs."

"Yes... she does. I have noticed that. Rather often, actually." We both laughed. "So, I thank you again for your referral and your generosity. It is always appreciated." Returning to one of her favorite topics, I asked, "Now, when can we get together so that I can get your referral fee taken care of?"

"Double-double, animal style, with well-done fries at In & Out in your GTO, right? I'm tied up until the weekend. We can go with James. Call me."

"Shall do. So nothing else on Ricky?"

"No. He's just another throwaway, a willing and unfortunate

victim of the drug culture. I'm still sad that it happened that way. He probably would have been a great guy eventually."

"Understandable." Information gleaned, it was time to go. "We will talk soon. I'll keep you posted on my progress. Tell hubby hi for me."

She turned cheerful with a "Shall do. See ya!"

I closed the phone, put the cell into its slot on the console, snicked the shifter into first gear and soon entered the sporadic flow of Pasadena surface street traffic. I made my way to the southbound 110 freeway, then to the clogged downtown interchange, then north on the Hollywood freeway. It was a slow half-hour till I 'offed' at Melrose, headed toward gastronomic adventure and eventually, home.

Each of my fictional heroes had his own tools, habits, methods and quirks for establishing the proper inertia toward the examination of the situation at hand. Over time, I have developed mine as well. I start each case study parked at the curb near one of my favorite informal dining spots in L.A., clearing my mind over an uncomplicated lunch. That day it was a couple of chili dogs, pickle spears on the side and a Coke from Pink's—a genuine authentic cultural landmark just off Melrose in the un-glitzy flatlands of old Hollywood. After I stood in line for twenty minutes—Mondays are always busy at Pink's—I sat and read. My meal was spread across the passenger's seat and console of the GTO as I began to peruse the assorted printed material and news clippings.

Elizabeth's archives were comprehensive and well-detailed. They provided an excellent window into the events surrounding Ron and Ann Connors' murders, much of which I had been unaware. There were background histories and biographical notes on Connors, his wife, and any witnesses, business associates or personal acquaintances mentioned. The study of the base information continued after I arrived home as I reviewed several hours of coverage that had been provided on DVD. The proper study and digestion of the material would keep me busy into the wee hours of the next morning and several thereafter.

I had figured that this would be a long, complicated investigation with tons of detail, so I needed one of my better organizational tools to help keep it all straight. Late in the evening that Monday I went to the garage and retrieved two six-by-eight-foot clear acrylic sheets. One had dozens of horizontal lines on it, the other was 'clean' with a colored border. I hung them from the chains hanging from the hooks in the exposed beams at the 'office' end of my combined office/den. This created a pair of event boards upon which I would chart the progress of the investigation.

I drew an initial timeline on the 'clean' board and added names of the principal players to the lined board. Then I spent a couple more hours reading, trying to accurately map the places and the players and define the opposing teams. I finally fell asleep on the couch about 3 a.m.

Before seven that morning I rose and made a big sloppy breakfast of scrambled eggs, custom-ground sausage, wheat toast, fresh peach preserves and French Roast coffee. I keep trying to drink coffee, but it's one of very few things that I have problems with. This blend was fairly strong, but it seemed to agree with me.

During and after the feast and cleaning the kitchen, I spent the morning on the phone to all corners of the nation talking with or leaving messages for any business associates mentioned in the archival material. By noon that day my fifteen inquiries had brought eighteen responses and eight more referrals, each reinforcing the carefully developed and consistently maintained opinion that Ron Connors, in his personal and professional dealings, had been the salt of the earth. He was sorely missed by a great many high-quality people. A further course following names and events lasted into the evening, Tuesday, before I called it a day. I now had a list of references eight pages long, most all of them verifying the others' glowing assertions.

Carefully managed public entities like Ron Connors and his companies have ways of covering over bad news regarding their brand. After a stalled investigation early in my career, I had developed a ritual of fact checking my clients' histories for negative vibes. I had on occasion turned down jobs because of negative findings. Few people and fewer companies are absolutely flawless in their reputation, but from my findings so far disproof of major positive elements of Ron Connors' sterling integrity was not gonna happen. There had been periods of fluctuating finances, and occasional short-term loans had been granted and repaid, but accounts always squared in the end with no long-term negative trends. No surprises or blindsides would come from the Connors' side of this investigation.

After spending two days with my face in a computer screen I spent that evening with my nose in a new novel. One of my favorite mystery authors, Robert B. Parker, had released his latest volume a few weeks before and I had wanted to catch up. I polished off the book in a little over five hours and was reminded again that I would never be as cool as 'Spenser'.

By early the next morning I had gathered my notes categorized the facts from the provided material and listed all the questions that came to mind. It was time for a road trip.

It was a little after eight on that sparkling Wednesday morning when I suited up in my casual 'detective clothes'—a pair of black Rockport walking shoes, dark grey wool slacks, a pale blue oxford shirt and a medium grey sport coat tailored to accommodate my recently-adopted shoulder holster—before I hit the freeway, travelling opposite the oppressive late-morning rush hour traffic. For L.A. residents, travelling against the grain of morning madness is a great victory, especially when the other side of the median looks like a parking lot.

Montego Hills was an aging but still quite stylish hillside enclave a dozen miles east of Pasadena. I drove the eastbound San Bernardino freeway all the way to the 605 then cut north to the 210's parallel surface four-lane, Foothill Boulevard. West for a mile then north again into the gated community. A mile and a half up the hill on the wide smooth street the Connors estate was a rambling beige brick and white stucco, single story ranch style home perched on level ground near the top of the hill. The property had been retained by one of Elizabeth's holding companies and had been maintained, with few exceptions, in the condition of the day before the shootings. It was a snapshot of sorts, a time warp, maybe a shrine kept by my client. And while it was a fine property in itself, my knowledge of the events that had occurred there made it a little creepy around the edges.

I idled past the tall vertical slat dark grey wrought iron gate into a well—manicured two-acre property. A pleasantly plump fiftyish Hispanic man wearing a new pair of blue denim overalls approached me as I parked the GTO in the morning shade of a stand of pepper trees on the outer side of the driveway.

"You are Mister Street?" He spoke with a well-styled accent.

"I'm him." We shook hands after he removed his faded cloth-trimmed gardeners' glove. I handed him a card and he read it, then he looked at me.

"I am Jorge." He spoke the name with an 'H' for the 'J' and a rolling 'R' that I would never even attempt. "It is good to meet you. Ms. Damarow e-mailed me Monday, told me to prepare for your visit. Make yourself at home, look around and come to the back when you are finished. We should talk." As I closed the car door he retreated to his work.

The property was impressive. Every element pertinent to my concerns was perfectly maintained in the condition prior to the murders. The Damarow and Connors corporate entities often housed out-of-town staff and business associates for extended periods at the spacious home as Ron had done for decades during his lifetime, but at this time the home was unoccupied. I was free to roam and examine the area uninterrupted. I crouched in the shrubbery just inside the wrought iron fence as the police crime reports said the killers had done. From that perch there was a commanding view of the house and the garages from which the Connors would eventually emerge.

Crime-scene actuality photos from the day of the murders established that the killers had been well-hidden from the street in front of the home by the thick shrubbery just inside the fence. One of them had dropped the partial wrapper of a king size Snickers candy bar in the flower bed. The inventoried wrapper, pictured in the Sheriff's department evidence files from that morning, had shown no identifiable fingerprints—the shooter had worn gloves. The wrapper itself had been misplaced or discarded a year after the murders. Had today's DNA technology been available thirteen years ago, that item may have been used to help identify one of the killers.

I read to myself from the L.A. Sheriffs' Department Initial Crime Report, included in my box of stuff, simulating the words that the supervising detective would have heard from the patrol deputies as he arrived that morning. Later revisions had sanitized the report of conjecture so I valued the initial raw text in that first report.

The crux of the matter was that as Annie Beverly Connors had backed her silver 1997 GMC Sprint minivan from her garage at six-fifty that morning, two gunmen had run from their concealment at the front of the property, taking her by surprise. They had dragged her from the driver's seat of the van, thrown her against the side of the vehicle and shot her seven times, mortally wounding her. Tire tracks through blood on the concrete indicated that the driverless van had coasted a few feet until it stopped against the retaining wall.

Ann's cries had alerted her husband inside the house. He had ended his long-distance call and ran through the garage toward the sounds of his wife's distress. As he emerged from the cover of the open garage, he saw his wife take the last of seven rounds from a second shooter, these from close range. Bloodstains on the side of the vehicle indicated that the petite woman had been lifted off the ground as the shots went through her and shattered the van's side window.

At some point, Connors dropped the portable phone he carried and had begun tracking toward the front of the property. He was instantly pursued by the shooters. By the time he had fallen ten feet from the wrought iron front gate he had taken seventeen shots, the final two close range fatal rounds to the face.

The Connors' next-door neighbor, Pasadena optometrist Frederick Keegan—since deceased—had been walking the length of his driveway to pick up his morning copy of the *L.A. Daily News*. He had heard the sounds of the attack and had called 9-1-1 from his portable phone as soon as he reached the safety of his kitchen. The copied recording of the call provided evidence of the volleys of gunshots and an indication of the types of weapons used. As is often the case it was disturbing to hear.

The attack was over in two minutes. Crime scene photos showed that Ron Connors had expired laying across the width of his driveway at a point ten feet inside the fence, facing the house. The shooters had broken the beam to activate the sliding gate at the street end of the driveway, then they had retrieved their bicycles from beneath the trees just outside the fence and had ridden down the hill. The first of the Sheriff's deputies responding to the 9-1-1 call sped uphill within a minute of the broadcast of the call. That first deputy probably passed the shooters as they coasted downhill through the early morning mist.

I looked at the site from every realistic angle as I read the report. I snapped a few fresh images with my camera to use for reference on the event boards at home, hoping to chronicle the visual differences made over the last thirteen years. Shrubs and trees were larger and the driveway itself had been resurfaced in a snow-white concrete. After fifteen minutes at the front of the property I walked toward a nicely terraced rear yard. Its main features were a large oval-shaped custom pool, a larger paving-stone patio and a low-slung single-story guest house with deeply tinted floor-to-ceiling windows and beige trim.

Jorge waved as I rounded the side of the house, motioning me to join him at the large canopied glass-topped table on the patio between the guest house and the pool. We sat and he pushed a tall frosty glass toward me past a large bowl of oranges, some as big as grapefruit. He smiled and said, "My wife makes sun tea every morning, Mister Street. I hope you like it."

I took a sip of the coppery liquid and found it to be pretty stout stuff, not the sugary glop I expected. "This is excellent, Jorge! My compliments to your wife." I selected an orange from the bowl and began to peel it as I asked, "How long have you and your family lived here?"

"I helped Ron oversee the construction of the main house back in the early '80s, so, a long time. This area was practically wilderness back then. This was the only house within a mile. My wife and I both worked for Ron and we raised our sons in this house. Ron treated me as an equal. We were part of his family and we were friends. He was like a part of our family as well. We have some great memories here."

"It's a beautiful property. I'm surprised that the house and grounds haven't been altered in thirteen years. You take excellent care of it."

He grinned at that. "Thank you. The upkeep is a lot of work. The inside of the house has been modernized quite a bit. We had some plumbing work done last week. The only real visual change is the white driveway surfacing. We could still see the bloodstains on the old concrete years after the murders. My wife asked that those changes be made."

"That's understandable. I have been told that you were not on the property at the time of the murders."

Jorge' shrugged. "That is true. I had driven down the hill to the garden store and the pharmacy. Our sons were home from school with fevers and bad colds. We had been up with them all night. I was glad to leave for a while." He looked sad at the memory. "My wife was in the back of the house with them, so she heard nothing until she came outside hours later."

"I know you've been asked, but did you see anything unusual here that day?"

"Nothing here at all before I left but let me tell you what I did see." He took a deep breath. "I left about 6:30 that morning. I went to the garden store first for a bag of peat moss. That stop just took me a few minutes, and the pharmacy didn't open till eight, so I stopped at the little diner down on Foothill for breakfast. I was sitting in the car, waiting to listen to the weather report when this pickup truck backed into the space in front of me. A few minutes later the driver was met by two men on bicycles."

He reached for his glass of iced tea and took a sip. "The three of them went to put the bikes in the bed of the truck. The driver had backed a little too close to the front of my car, so when he dropped the tailgate it hit the hood ornament of my old station wagon. The driver saw me sitting there and walked over and apologized. When I looked at the two cars, I saw that he had the damage, not me. He had a little dent and some chipped paint right at the top of the tail-gate. It was no big thing. I told him to just forget it. They loaded the bicycles, he closed the tailgate, and covered the bed and the bikes with a tarp. Then all three of them piled into the truck and they left." I didn't give it another thought. I had my breakfast. I went to the pharmacy. I took my time and then I came back home and found my friends Annie and Ron shot to death and about fifty policemen and helicopters up above. It was awful."

"Did you give your statement about the diner to the officers who were here?"

His reply was almost plaintive. "I tried, Mister Street, but to them I was just some Mexican, and I really wasn't here at the time of the murders so in that moment they weren't interested. I can't really blame them, considering what they were dealing with."

I knew he had important information for me. "But you did get a good look at the driver, his passengers, and the truck, didn't you?"

"Good enough."

"Tell me about them."

"The driver was a gringo. He was tall and thin, and he had a scraggly moustache. He looked really tired. His hair was all messed up, like he had driven a long distance with his window down. He needed a shower and a shave at the very least. The bike guys...one was Mexican, the other was white and he was older. They both wore the elastic caps that pull down..." He motioned, pulling his hands down over his face.

Getting a sense of the terrain, I asked, "These knit caps—do you think they were toboggans that are worn on top of the head or were they ski masks with the eye holes that you pull down over your face?"

He answered quickly. "They were ski masks with the eye holes. Both were black or dark blue."

Now we had some momentum. "Got it. Now do you recall anything specific about the driver or the passenger? Tattoos, scars, piercings, hair color, identifying marks of any kind?" I'm big on ink, as they can lead to identifying gang affiliations.

Jorge scratched his chin and frowned. "The driver of the truck, he had a shabby moustache like I said. He looked really tired. The Mexican took off his cap as he got into the truck, he had a devil-face tattoo on the back of his head. His head was shaved, the hair just starting to grow out. The older white guy kept his cap pulled down. I couldn't tell anything about him. Neither of the passengers said anything at all. I could tell the driver was the one in charge."

I smiled. We were making progress. "Okay, you paid a lot of attention to the people, now tell me about the truck. Being friends with Ron all those years, I know you looked at that."

"Yes. It was the smaller Chevy, new at the time with the round front end. It was dark blue, new or almost new. It had a nice set of aluminum wheels and the tires had the letters in white. Oh, and there were the lines on the side, like Ron's race cars." He paused for a moment. "Is any of this of any help to you, mister Street?"

I had to smile. "Jorge, my friend, in my business there is no such thing as 'too much information'. This all helps. If you think of anything else, give me a call, anytime." We talked for a few more minutes about his memories of his friend Ron and how generous the Connors family and estate had been with his family. I finished my sun tea and maybe the most perfect orange ever picked, then we shook hands and I walked back to the car.

Jorge's account of the events of that morning provided just the start of what would be a mountain of new information for me to consider. My scenario for the Connors murder was starting to fall together, but there were many gaps in the story. Many questions would fill spots on the event board back home. The background information I studied for hours-on-end had raised many more questions than answers. Since I was close to the source of the matter, I decided to make another stop and fill in a few more blanks.

The Los Angeles County Sheriff's Department's East County substation in Montgomery Park was a few miles south of Montego Hills and a couple of miles east of the 605 freeway. At street level it was a low-slung processed block structure behind a parking lot filled with bland, unmarked, cop-spec black, charcoal and dark-toned Malibus and Crown Vics. The tall wall that surrounded the rear of the complex was topped with maybe a mile of spooled razor-wire, a hint of the hospitality afforded the guests invited through the sliding vehicle gate. An invitation of that sort usually involved a ride in the back of a sedan with lights on top after an admonition to 'watch your head'. My five years as an A.C. cop had seen many drives through that style of facility perimeter.

Once past the front desk I walked the aisles till I found the corner office of a chiseled veteran Deputy. We shook hands and I settled into the chair across from his desk position and read his blue embossed nameplate: Wallace Clinton. His light blue dress shirt and dark red necktie offered the only color in the beige painted room. "Call me Clint," he'd said. "So, you're Street." I nodded in the affirmative. "You may not recall, but we crossed paths a couple of years ago. I testified in the Gates estate matter and you had done the forensics study on the deaths. That was nice work. You cut to the chase and cleared up some questions for us." He picked up a can of Red Bull and took a sip.

"I thought I remembered your name from somewhere."

"It's not that hard to remember. You don't meet too many people named after two southern politicians. It wasn't planned like that, it just kinda happened." He returned the can to his desk. He spoke in the clipped terms of a practiced, well-trained lawman. "If you'll indulge me for a minute, I need to conform with a bullshit rule from Sacramento. Are you packin'?"

I pulled my jacket back, showing the empty shoulder holster. "Shiny new H&K P2000, safely packed away in the trunk of my car in the parking lot out front."

"I appreciate that, Street. What about the backup just above your left ankle?"

"Good eye. Little 22 left over from my cop days in Jersey, locked in the same trunk of the same car in the same parking lot."

"Good enough. Don't shoot anyone on the station property. I hate the paperwork." He grinned a warning.

"Done. Reason I'm here, I'm told that you were lead 'suit' on the Connors double murder case from thirteen years ago."

"Yeah, that was my first gig as team leader. I'm hoping the damn thing will go to court before I pull the plug next year."

I looked at him and guesstimated. "Thirty years and out?"

He nodded, "Twenty-five, actually. My wife is a computer tech, and we have a home-based business and that has worked out well. We also have a new daughter, a real surprise at my age, so me being home will solve a problem or two. It's my third marriage, and she's the first one says she likes having me around so I figure I should play along."

"Good for you." Back to business. "The Connors' deaths—is there anything that jumps out at you after thirteen years?"

He smiled as he started his answer. "I'm gonna sound like an old lazy cop here, Street. To me, the former business partner is the most obvious doer. He is the one who flew over the Rose Bowl in a helicopter with a loudspeaker trashing Ron Connors during a stadium race event. He's the only one who lost his ass in a sudden business split, and he's the only one known far and wide to have threatened Ron Connors every chance he got."

"That's true."

"See, to me it's always the same with these high-profile crimes: the first person we think did it, probably did it, open and shut. I mean c'mon...O.J. did it, Robert Blake did it, Scott Peterson did it, the Menendi did it, Phil Specter did it, Charlie Rathbun did it, on down the line. First name up is the best suspect, 95% of the time."

He and I agreed about that, and from his examples only the Spector case was a 'maybe' for me. "I'm looking at the murders for Ron's surviving sister. I read your actuality reports. Nice crisp work, by the way. I'm interested in the background information concerning Connors' activities prior to his murder. I see there is reference to another trial in which you were a witness. What can you tell me about his nephew, Rick Damarow? He was killed a little more than year and a half prior and it was mentioned at length in the workup.

He frowned as he answered, and he motioned for me to close the office door.

As the door shut, he started. "Oh, I remember it quite well. That was part of our background on the Connors killings. Young Richard was your basic spoiled rich punk. He wanted to think the edgy life suited him, so he decided he'd be a drug dealer for a while. Kid needs a hobby, right? He got a little action out here and down in the O.C. He made a little money, got on the radar of the Santa Ana drug cops once or twice. He probably thought it was an easy gig so he decided to step it up a bit and come out here and play with the big guys, including some out here in the suburbs of the badlands."

He took a sip of Red Bull and continued. "No problem for him at first, but these guys weren't just trust fund brats out here slumming. They were serious. They watched him, they took his money for a while, and they played along with him, like a house cat with a gecko. At some point he crossed their arbitrary line. The thought at the time, and I still do, that he undercut their prices or took some of their business. At that point they took great offense to his very existence. They followed him to a Norm's restaurant over in Corona, they abducted him, they took him to locations unknown and beat on him for a while. Then they shot him in both knees to emphasize their point, then they dropped his skinny ass out of an airplane from 2500 feet."

Clinton Wallace was on a roll, and he was a good story-teller. "This eliminated their primary problem, except that a road crew foreman out near where the body fell had an excellent set of field glasses and he got the plane's wing numbers. Turned out the plane had been rented from a feeder airport in our jurisdiction. A few months later I went to court to verify the plane rental for the preliminaries. At that point it was just leg work but I did keep track of the developments in the case after I testified so I have my own opinions about it. The Prosecutor did a great job with the information she had to work with. Slam dunk!

I had a question for him. "Curious about something. How do you know he was shot in the knees first? I would imagine he landed in a heap."

"He made a big wet puddle of goo with some bone powder and a few fingernails and an eyeball or two but there was another element. The killers had wrapped his legs in a big black trash bag. Maybe they didn't want to bloody-up the rental plane. He landed head-first but below the waist he was fairly intact except for the blown-up knees. His billfold and California ID and Drivers' License were intact. His car keys were in his pocket too, inside the trash bag. Still a mess, but it made our job easier. One of the CHP guys found the car three days later down in Corona."

He had filled in a couple of important blanks for me so I asked for more. "I notice that your description of the killers or abductors in the Damarow matter is always 'they'. There was only one conviction. Any thoughts on that? Any ideas on how many people were involved? Who got away?"

He smiled. "Good ear, Street. I have no idea how many people were involved, but I know there were three people, two willingly, in the cabin of that plane. Most of this happened over in Riverside or San Bernardino counties, right on the border of the two counties, so it's not our deal. Had I been assigned the case I would have dug further." He paused. "You've never had the pleasure of meeting the kid who was convicted. Arnie Sutton was your basic slacker, mostly just a blank stare. There is no way an airhead like him could establish, manage, and grow a sophisticated operation like the one he was involved with. Someone else, someone far smarter, much quicker and far more attentive was calling the shots. Sutton was a follower, pure and simple.

That last statement would become very important to me in the next few days.

I redirected my questions. "Let's go back to the Connors. Did your Department look at any property surveillance footage from the area of the Connors property that morning? That's a wealthy area, and I see camera perches everywhere up and down that street now. Was it that way back then, too?"

He thought about that for a few seconds. "There were a few cameras in use back then, not as many as there are now, of course. We looked at every one of them and found nothing of any evidentiary value. There were a few blurry frames showing a couple of guys rolling down the hill on their bikes as a patrol car sped up the hill. We already knew that. There were bike tracks under the trees just outside the Connors' front gate. The site officers took plaster casts of them. To date that has gone nowhere. Had we happened upon a magic bullet, trust me, Street, we would've acted on it."

"I spoke to the caretaker of the Connors' property an hour ago. He had left the property at 6:30 that morning. A little later that morning at a diner down the hill he had an exchange with the driver of a late model, at the time, Chevy S-10 pickup and two bicyclists just a few minutes after the shootings. His account would seem to tie directly back to the crime. Were his observations ever a factor for you?"

"I remember him. Nice guy. One of my men talked to him that

morning as he returned to the Connors property. We determined that his departure that morning probably gave the shooters their point of entry. When I talked to him, I could have told him that exact thing. I saw no reason to make him feel guilty about his innocent action. Trust me, man, these guys were determined. If he hadn't given them their way in they would have found another way. As for his information, we took it, we looked at it and we put it in the mix, but it didn't lead anywhere."

That sounded reasonable. The conclusion nudged my actions to their logical end. "Do you have the contact information for that Prosecutor? There are elements of the Damarow trial that I am curious about. What was the sentence for the guy who was convicted?"

He was consulting his Rolodex, old school style, wrote on a yellow Post-It note, tore it off the top of the pad and handed it to me as he spoke. "Sentence was a richly deserved 25-to-life dealt down from an LWOP." He looked at me as he spoke. "As we discussed earlier, I still think there's another doer out there somewhere, but you have to deal with the realities at hand and move on to the next scumbag, right?"

"Comes with the badge." I closed my wire-bound notebook and rose. "Thank you for your time, Clint. I may be back in touch with you as this thing develops."

"No problem, Street. Call anytime." He stood and walked around his desk. "Quick and concise. Were you ever on the job?"

"I was. Five years, Atlantic City P.D. I came west to see the sun."

"Atlantic City? How does someone from there end up all the way out here?"

"I may have had little choice in the matter. My dad told me that I was brought home from the hospital at age two days in a bright red, four-speed, Ram Air III '69 GTO with a Beach Boys tape playing in the 8-track. Muscle cars, surf music and classic rock were part of my life since day one and that all happens best out here."

"I can dig it." Stay in touch."

I turned my cell phone back on as I left the building. As I

walked back to the car, I checked for messages. While I had talked to Clint, Jorge' had called with some new information. I stopped back at the Connors property on my way back to town. An excited Jorge' met me at the front of the property as I drove in. "Mister Street! Thank you for stopping. I found the information for the truck I saw at the diner that morning."

I looked up at him and asked, "The license number?" Hope springs eternal.

He was excited at his revelation. "That's just it! The truck didn't *have* a license plate. It had a cardboard sign on the bumper inside a red plastic plate frame. Both were labeled, 'Sunset Motors' in Jarupa." Another 'H' for a 'J'. "And in the rear window there was the red square paper like when you order a special plate. Ron did that with every car he bought. The number was '10'."

"What about the truck itself?"

"It was newer at the time, the smaller Chevy pickup with the smaller window behind the door. It was dark blue, and it had colored lines like Ron's race cars. It had a set of fancy chrome rims and nice tires with the white letters. It looked sharp." He looked down at the fence. "Oh, and let me give you these." He hefted a large clear plastic bag filled with huge oranges over the window-sill and handed them off to me. "You seemed to enjoy the oranges this morning and we grow many more than we can eat." I laid them on the passenger side floor.

"Jorge you are officially 'The Man!' Thank you very much, please stay in touch."

6

May 28, 2004 — Atlantic City, New Jersey

When he arrived home that day, she was waiting in the driveway, sitting in the new Miata he bought her the day after he'd won the money. "You'd look good in that!" he'd said. Then he'd done some other things involving money before they'd decided that they wouldn't continue together. She'd driven away crying that evening.

That was a week ago. She still looked good in the car.

Now she was exiting the car, yelling at him. "Street, damn you, you cannot do this!" She stood next to the grey-primered GTO, waving papers at him—the mortgages for two homes, hers and her parents'.

"Well hello to you, too," he said as he walked around to get to his kitchen door to enter his house. "How're things?" He stood aside to invite her in; she wasn't having it.

She stood on the porch. "Street you can't do this. You can't just pay off two mortgages as you head out of town. It's not right. It's too much."

He stood in the doorway and looked at her, short of breath, his mind wiped almost blank from seeing her again, but he was still pissed. He held his ground. "Y'know, Ange, you signed out of my life almost a week ago. Your choice. And at that time, you pretty much gave up your influence over what I can and cannot do with my money. I told you at the Casino that night, "Now that I have money, I'm gonna be like Elvis. I'm gonna pay off mortgages and buy new cars for people who matter in my life. Hell, I'm closer to your dad than I am to my own and I know that after the layoff he could use the help. You and your family have been better to me than my own folks have been and it's my gift to them and to you, even if you no longer want the whole package. You're stuck with it, just not with me anymore."

He realized that he had let his anger come to the surface. He looked at her. She was beautiful...she always would be in his eyes. She was crying, and she said nothing. Out of pure frustration, and to further make his point, he said, "You're welcome."

She didn't make a move toward him, nor he toward her. He left the door open, turned, and walked back into the house. She didn't follow him. Three minutes later he heard the Miata start and drive away. They would both hurt for a long time after that.

7

It was still early as I drove back down the hill from the Connors property, so I consulted Clint's yellow post-it-note and called the prosecutor in the Damarow kid's murder case. Circumstances had changed somewhat in the years since the trial. The former assistant DA was now in private practice, her office in downtown Riverside. I asked her to meet me for lunch. It's a proven fact: Lawyers never turn down a free meal.

We met at a Chilean restaurant in downtown Riverside. The rich aroma wafting from the place was astounding. I was greeted at the foyer by a petite, attractive, well-dressed woman who introduced herself as Catherine Gadsden. Judging from her facial features and her long jet-black hair, I guessed her to be in her mid-thirties. We settled into a booth at the rear of the dining room and she was already fielding questions. As we looked at our menus she asked, "So you're a real live private detective, like Jim Rockford, Thomas Magnum, and Joe Mannix?"

I played it straight. "Pretty much. We're all cast from the same mold, y'know. I do try to keep my personal cliché count within reason. Let's see...I get in fewer fist fights than Joe Mannix, I don't sponge off old rich guys like Thomas Magnum, and I can fling a car at least as well as Jim Rockford. No evil twins or dead girlfriends have appeared recently, I have never solved a difficult case in an hour, and I deny any willing use of plaid. Other than that, we're all practically identical."

"Cool!"

"You're into old TV cop shows? I'm surprised."

She smiled. "Oh, my husband loved them. After he died eight years ago, they were a comfort to me. Odd, huh?" She tapped her ear. "I just wish I could get the theme music out of my head. Lalo Schifrin lives!"

I laughed at that. "He does indeed." Her keen observation of the principally obscure brought a smile to my face. I have few allies in fandom of obsolete TV. "Oh, we're gonna get along fine."

And we did. We talked about anything but business for a half-hour as our lunch was ordered, served, and quickly devoured. This restaurant was epic.

Catherine pointed at me with her fork as she attacked the last of her salad. "You seem to have lived an unusual life. How would you describe yourself?"

"Let's see...six foot-one, 185, light brown and blue, Caucasian, aggressively hetero, relatively comfortable in my own skin...does that help?"

She smiled. "Okay, maybe a little, but you know what I mean by the question."

"Sure. Let me see—first, not bragging, I pride myself in having a good work ethic. When I start a job, I follow a thread and my instincts, or both, to the bitter end, as my clients would expect. Sometimes I even fall asleep in my home office. I also have a respectable attention span, and that has served me well in this work. I hope it continues to do so."

Catherine opened the work topic first. "You were interested in my take on the Richard Damarow murder trial."

"I am. You were lead prosecutor on that trial. You did quite well."

She nodded. "The perpetrator was convicted. That was the sole intent. In that case the defendant was, what's the proper term...I guess 'soulless' fits. He was silent, emotionless, yet still hostile. He would stare at a specific juror until there was a response, then he would stare at another one and repeat the process. He was the biggest thug in the courtroom. He knew it, and he wanted everyone else to be convinced of the same. When the verdict came down, he just shrugged it off. Sorry to say I saw the same corrosive attitude many more times in that job. I'm glad I left it behind, for several reasons." She paused for a second. "You're working for Elizabeth Damarow, aren't you?"

"I am. How much of a role did she have in your trial?" I suspected the answer I'd hear.

She frowned as she answered. "Really, not much of one. It was *really* annoying. I think she had written her son off sometime before his death. She no longer wished to concern herself with the tawdry aspects of his wayward life, so the details of his death were beneath her concern as well. I have to tell you, I received dozens of letters, some quite poignant, from surviving family members after a trial. Elizabeth Damarow would hardly acknowledge our presence. She treated us as employees instead of legal professionals intent on convicting her son's killer"

I countered, "Ron Connors was a big part of your case against the Sutton kid."

She brightened at the mention of his name. "Oh, Ron was great. He went to a lot of trouble and expense hiring the detective who traced Rick's movements and researched his associates. Then they had Arnie Sutton arrested. Both Ron and the detective testified and gave slam-dunk testimony. Ron spent three hours on the stand, and he was great. Sutton's joke of an attorney tried to trip him up but Ron just 'owned' him. He was merciless, almost mocking toward the defense. The jury just adored him. I may have prosecuted that trial, but Ron Connors won it."

"The detective did well, too, I understand."

"He was excellent! Sometimes, you guys—investigators, come across as arrogant and detached, and there are times when they just don't have much to say other than the rote material of their reports. This guy was pitch perfect. He and Ron were a great team. They made my job a lot easier." Now she looked enthused at the memory.

I was glad for her perspective. "That's great! Was there anyone in Sutton's corner? Friends? Family?"

"I'll check my notes, but I know it was sparse for him. I know his parents had recently divorced. His mother was there most of the time; his dad came once for a couple of hours. He just stared, looking like he wanted to kill the kid with his bare hands. It was clear he was disgusted by the while matter. There was also a girlfriend, a cute blonde, maybe nineteen or twenty, and she was maybe four months pregnant, just starting to show. I don't think any of his outside friends attended at all, but that's not unusual. See, even back then the Riverside County Courthouses had a strict ID check policy. Even a casual druggie is smart enough or sufficiently paranoid to avoid a warrant check or casual attendance at legal venues."

She continued, on a roll, as I finished my iced tea. "The defense attorney was a real piece of work as well. He has a lot of drug arrest clients and all he ever does is tread water. He brought up a few character witnesses, all of whom were quickly neutralized and sent packing by, well, me!". Catherine smiled her widest.

"You had fun with it."

"I never thought of it like that at the time, but yeah, I did. I was young in the job, and a little nervous at first, but I brought it around soon enough. It was a good early 'win' for me. Sutton was such a caricature of a thug that I didn't have much resistance. I overplayed the closing a bit, made a couple of other rookie mistakes, but once I reached cruising speed it was great. The end goal was achieved."

I offered, "There was a sketchy outline of the Damarow trial in the background information I received, but I'd like more specifics. I know I'd like to get some face time with the detective that Ron hired. Would you have his name or contact information? I have many questions."

Catherine said, "I have it at home. I'll e-mail it to you. He was quite good. I think he was based in the Santa Clarita valley. Bongelli really went after him but the detective held his ground. He was impressive."

"I need to talk to him. I read Elizabeth's account of the trial, but it really wasn't thorough. I'm a stickler for details in matters like this and I still need to fill in some blanks."

"I'll get that to you. Bongelli accused him of being a mercenary but the guy never lost his cool. I was impressed."

"It sounds as if you are not a fan of the defense attorney." I had finished the last of my braised beef as the waiter approached. I signaled for the bill, and he presented it as he cleared our plates.

Catherine shook her head and chuckled. "Vinnie Bongelli. Oh, he's a local legend and practically a monument to niche marketing for the shallow end of the legal profession."

"In what way?"

"He defends drug cases only, so he has a large and steady clientele of mean but gullible clients, especially after the onset of the meth culture out here. He's made a lot of money in recent years by being on retainer to his former defendants who are already in prison. Figure that one out! His nickname among his clients? Bongelli the Bong."

"Cute. How can I get a copy of the trial transcript? I am starting to wonder about a connection between this trial and the Connors murders. I'm just spit-balling, of course, but knowing is better than not knowing. I hate loose ends and I want to follow a hunch or two, see where they lead."

Catherine seemed to brighten at the prospect. "Tell you what. I have to be in L.A. tomorrow for a deposition. I have a transcript of the trial on my old computer discs at home. I'll make a copy on a memory stick and I'll bring it with me. This might also be a good time to find out where Sutton is currently housed. Bongelli tried to mount an appeal for a sentence reduction a couple of years ago and it might be a good time to check up on him. Anything else I can do? You have captured my interest."

"And you have captured mine. Let's do this: open a standard client account for me, and do some research on my behalf, help me get the facts sorted out on this thing. I'll cut you a check, put you on a retainer. You know far more than anyone else about this matter and you'll be a great resource. I have to meet with Ron Connors' son and Ray Cole tomorrow. If I find what I'm starting to suspect, I'll need some help digging into the histories and architecture of this thing."

As we rose from the table Catherine said, "I do have one last question. What does the 'C' stand for?"

"It's the first letter of my first name." I smiled as we walked toward the restaurant's foyer.

She laughed. "Ooh! Okay... I'll call as soon as I get that file transferred and we will talk tomorrow." We shook hands and went our separate ways outside the door. I'd learned a lot that day in the Inland Empire and had made some great contacts and allies.

I spent the evening studying more from Elizabeth's archives and using the pertinent findings to modify the time-line and cast of characters on the event boards. It was a long night.

8

January 7, 1995

Rick Damarow was rarely nervous, but this particular evening he was nearly beside himself. He had always seen himself as a lucky guy. He was young, handsome, wealthy and confident, and since he had climbed into the tight-knit little world of SoCal drug trafficking he was finally making serious money on his own. Early that afternoon he had gotten a call from Arnie Sutton, right hand man to Grant Carty, a major mover in the business. Arnie had asked for a meeting that evening, eleven p.m., at the Park & Ride on the I-15 in the foothills just south of Temecula. Carty was a big deal. This could be really good.

Rick backed his finely-polished 'Arrest me red' '90 Camaro IROC Z into a space at the far south end of the almost empty paved facility, up the hill from the entrance, with a good view of the area. He'd seen that cautionary step on TV once. It seemed to make sense to know the lay of the land and if necessary have a good escape route in case stuff went sideways. Soon after he positioned himself, a tricked-out '90 Ford Bronco 4x4, bronze in color and lifted, wearing some killer rims and tall Dick Cepek knobby tires, rolled into the lot. Rick watched, then flashed his headlights in recognition of the familiar truck. It rolled toward the Camaro and stopped a dozen feet away. Its lights doused and both doors opened.

Rick recognized Carty and his friend, half-brother Arnie Sutton, as they approached. Arnie had been Rick's first contact with Carty two years earlier when he bought his first pound of herb. Now the pair walked toward the Camaro. Young Damarow rose through the open T-top, exited the car and approached the pair, palms open to assure them that he was a visitor on their turf where their rules ruled.

Rick spoke first. No one shook hands.

"Arnie! How you doin' man?" he looked past the younger man toward Carty, an authority figure in the trade, then back at Arnie as he started to speak. Carty didn't look all that imposing that evening; he looked tired and annoyed.

The younger man looked calm as he answered, "I'm fine, Rick boy, but Grant says we gotta talk."

Rick looked back at Carty, who spoke, all business, "Yeah, Rick Damarow, we do. Tell me something. Who, specifically, told you that you could deal herb out in Lemon Grove? I need a name, bro."

Rick held his ground. "No one 'gave it to me', Grant. I answered an inquiry and I started doin' business. Nobody stepped up to tell me not to. What's the problem?"

Carty had turned, surveying the surrounding property and looking at the Park & Ride entrance. "Well, here's the thing. Rick. That's our turf. You need to go somewhere that's NOT our turf." Grant was looking at Rick straight-on, with a cold stare. "You get that? Do you understand that I could cap your stupid ass right here? Two shots, base of the skull, drag you to the edge of the pavement right over there? No one would find your body till it started to stink!" He stepped forward and spoke louder now. "Now tell me... do you want me to do that, Rick, or do you want to get back into your pretty little red car, drive out of here and never let me see your skinny white ass ever again?" He snapped his fingers for effect. "Which one, bitch? Right now! Which one?"

Rick Damarow was taken aback by the threat, but he didn't flinch. "Hey Carty! Chill back, bro! Sorry if I stepped on ya! Not my intention, ever, y'know? No disrespect intended, guys! I'll stick to the O.C.! I know that turf better anyway."

Now Grant exhaled through a tight grin. He stepped forward again. Now he was less than a foot from Rick's chin. His voice was hardly above a whisper as he hissed, "Here's the thing, you fuckin' prima donna... I don't really want you in the business at all. We don't need no amateurs in the mix. You need to find another hobby," louder, "Now!"

The threat made Rick angry and more defiant. As Carty took a step back, Rick responded, "I wasn't aware that you were making the decisions for everyone in the industry, Grant. I'll take that under advisement."

Grant stared at Rick for ten seconds, then he looked back at Arnie. Finally, he turned on his heel and started walking back to the Bronco. Arnie looked back at Rick as he angled toward the open door of his Camaro and mouthed the word, "Careful." Rick regained the driver's seat, nodded his acknowledgment to Arnie and watched as the Bronco backed away and retreated toward the exit ramp. He sat for a few seconds, trying to cope with a case of the shakes.

9

Neat as that first day on the road had been, my travels the next overcast morning started nearer to my true element. I rolled into the parking structure of the Petersen Automotive Museum in the Miracle Mile of Wilshire Boulevard. Arriving a few minutes before ten, I parked the Goat on the first level of the parking deck, locked it, and walked to the Foyer. As I showed my membership card to the receptionist, a tall 40-ish guy wearing an expensively tooled leather jacket approached. He moved with the relaxed manner of someone with means.

"You're Street?"

"I'm him."

"Tony Connors. Ron's son." We shook hands and chatted for a minute before we began the slow trek through the intertwined histories of the automobile and its role in the development of the metropolis of Los Angeles.

"So have you been here before?"

"Many times," I said. "It's one of my favorite places in Los Angeles. I'm an Executive Member. Bob Petersen was one of my heroes so this was one of the first places I wanted to see when I arrived in town five years ago. He's the only billionaire I ever met."

"Bob was epic! He and dad were very close. This place is a perfect tribute to him. I think you and I may have attended some of the same events here. It's good to put a name to the face. What is your work, exactly? I wasn't clear when we spoke on the phone."

"I'm a licensed Private Investigator. I do a lot of criminology studies. I consult for small-town police departments and I do legwork for attorneys. I give expert witness testimony and I consult on criminal behavior. I study the sequencing of pertinent events regarding crimes. I also seem to look at a lot of old unsolved crimes, some many years old, like your father's killing.

Connors looked directly at me, his eyes slightly narrowed. "That's my father's *murder*, Mister Street. Cold-blooded and brutal. I'm still raw about that. I hate that it has become such a generality instead of the horrific event it really is."

"Understandable."

"You're working for my dear Aunt Liz?" His inflection didn't hide his dislike for her.

"I am. I gather you're not her biggest fan," We had ambled through the history of the first third of the twentieth century and were now standing in front of an authentically-rendered Packard showroom, circa 1932.

Tony grinned as he started to explain. "You may eventually find that Liz is strictly a one-of-a-kind lady. She and dad were very close. She was quite fair with me in the estate settlement but we're not friends now, by mutual declaration. I am said by her to be highly emotional and overly sensitive. She has this all-business mindset that pushes even the most basic human emotion and family loyalty completely out of the picture. You know she even kept dad's house? Who would ever think to do that? Two people *died* there. I'd blade the place flat!"

"I was out there yesterday. If you aren't aware of the history it's a beautiful property, but if you know what happened there it has a bit of an 'O.J.'s mansion' vibe to it at first. Why is she keeping it?"

"I think she called it a 'write-down' for estate valuation, or something equally cold and impersonal. Probably a fancy name for depreciation. Who knows? I don't care anymore. I can't go near the place."

"Understandable. So, tell me about your dad."

"Simply," he paused out of emotion and clenched his chin as he resumed speaking, "He was the best man I've ever known. He will never be properly credited for many of the things he did for people, in and out of motorsports. He would go to the wall for you time after time, even if he barely knew you, and he was the most loyal and generous racer ever."

I countered, "He certainly had a way of dealing with the media. All those magazine covers? That was unheard of at the time. He was a PR genius!"

Tony was adamant. "He paved the way for countless people, Street, in so many ways. He set the highest standards for behavior and event promotion decades before the John Forces and the Jeff Gordons, even predating the prime years of Richard Petty. He injected warmth and personality into the team owners and drivers' positions and as a result he helped make motorsports palatable to the general public. Good as the stars of today are, he was just as good, and he did it first."

I listened and agreed. "He was a hero of mine from my childhood. I don't think I ever heard a negative word about him." I looked at Tony as I asked, "How were his business affairs? Did he have any perceived rivals? Any enemies? Was there someone with an old grudge? Some of the people I know of in motorsports have strong opinions and long memories."

We stopped near the top of the escalator in front of a display of historic hot rods and early model custom cars. "Street, my dad was 'old school'. Hell, he probably invented 'old school'! He started when he was a kid, back before most of these cars were built. Back then racers would argue, maybe toss a wrench or a fist or two. I remember more than a few desert race sessions, there'd be guys just *pounding* on one another, rolling around in the mud. You'd think they were trying to kill each other. An hour later, it's over. They're back working, side by side, wrenching on the same car.

Disagreements? Sure. They'd toss it around, they'd work it out, and they'd move on. Later on, business could be a struggle at times. It was easier for a while after Cole came on board."

I'd wondered about the non-Elizabeth spin on the relationship. "They got along at first?"

"Famously. For three and a half years it was good. Each of them took care of his own share of the events, combining common elements like advertising, and venue rental and prep. Modifying a stadium for those weekend events takes three days and requires hundreds of loads of topsoil. That's a big money outlay before they see penny-one from the gate. The events were very successful and both of them made a lot of extra money for a while."

Tony cleared his throat and continued as we walked. "Their lifestyles were different, though. Ray was high-rent. He liked flashy cars, big houses, and big goofy jewelry, and he had a really hot, younger wife. We knew he had a big budget going out, but he was down in Orange County between sessions, so we weren't in each other's faces all the time. We found out eventually that everything he displayed was rented or borrowed or heavily mortgaged. Nothing he had was really 'his'. By comparison, dad owned everything he touched. We were so accustomed to that management style, we may have been a bit inattentive to Cole's issues."

He shifted his stance a bit. "So, one Wednesday morning in late '95, this guy shows up at the Dad's event office, delivering a small package for Ray, asking for cash. He's supposed to meet Ray, who of course is not yet in attendance. This is no big deal at first, but this guy is insistent...he wants what he wants, right? But with no advance warning any business would call for approval first and issue a check. The receptionist went to Ray's office to make the call and get a counter check for his account, but this guy was *not* having it. He loudly demanded four thousand dollars, long green, for a neatly-packaged quantity of prime grade cocaine."

I did the math. "That'd be enough for a possession-for-sale charge if he was pulled over for a busted taillight, and certainly enough to cause your dad serious problems if the delivery was traced to his business location."

"Yeah. And dad had dozens of friends in law enforcement. He'd been an honorary LA County Sheriff Deputy for decades. He'd taken their training and was familiar with the current drug laws. He heard the disturbance as he walked through the lobby, determined the cause and he flipped out. I had never seen him that angry. He went into a purple rage. He called his attorneys that morning to dissolve the partnership immediately. So as Cole came in that day, a couple of hours late, of course, the contents of his office are being taken to the parking lot in big grey trash cans. He was out on his ear."

I asked, "Cole was aware of the rules when he came on board? Just an errant delivery guy caused all this?"

Tony smiled as he answered. "Oh, yeah! Cole signed off on all the rules. He had totally concealed any drug use or involvement. None of the usual coke freak bull shit—no spending an hour in the bathroom, none of the tweaking, none of the telltale signs that would tip us off. Dad had always resisted doing business with obvious users and he put morals and ethics clauses in his legal and partnership agreements. Those were the only 'instant outs' in the whole document.

Tony was on a roll now as we stood in front of a display of Bob Petersen's favorite Ferraris. "So, with the dissolution of the partnership came the audit. Turns out Cole had been cooking his books and there was a shortage of about three million-two, and the money had been disappearing for two-plus years. This was near the start of the season, so the accounts were light anyway, but his end of the coffers were almost bare. So the partnership is gone, and the suit was filed. Dad made a generous offer to settle the matter and leave Cole with a little money, with a five-day time limit for agreement. Cole refused and he made a weak counter-offer that didn't fly. We responded with another 'counter' but Cole took too long to make a decision. He let it get into the court system where the legal team fast-tracked it. Our side won big. Soon Ray Cole didn't have two nickels to rub together. The 'hot wife' took off eventually and took her money with her; she had a modest family fortune and had 'divorced well' in previous episodes."

"Yet another blow to Cole's ego. All of that still didn't shut him up?"

"No, not for months. I think his attorney finally dropped him and he just got tired and went away. His wife had filed for divorce by then, and she came out okay, but she let him keep his precious boat. He had a beautiful eighty-foot cruiser that he used for fishing trips and coast cruising. We suspected that he'd paid for the boat with the money he dropped from his accounts." We had walked into the display of TV and movie cars...lots of Batmobiles but Joe Mannix's '68 Dart GTS and Lt. Columbo's Peugeot were nowhere to be seen. Bummer.

Tony went on.

"After the 'fall' he lived on the thing, off the coast somewhere. With no cash flow, he couldn't afford the slip rental. The repo guys knew where he hung out; so he was scarce in most of those places as well. He would hit a Marina once in a while to refuel but he usually just stayed out of sight. Being remote, cut down on the number of threats he made toward dad, so it was a good idea for all involved."

I worked the calendar. "This was what, eight months before your dad's death? You don't think he had any money at all?"

"About then, yeah. Whatever he could scrape together went out as fast as it came in, and he probably used the boat as his ATM because eventually it was repo'd."

I speculated, "So if he hired shooters it would have been a low-buck deal."

"So it would seem."

"Okay." I still had my doubts. I changed the subject. "So, tell me about your cousin Ricky."

"Ricky? Man, you really do your research, don't you?" He smiled and looked at me. "Rick was maybe the first indication of our eventual issues with Elizabeth. Dad loved Rick, treated him like his own kid. He and I were practically inseparable until he was sixteen or so, then he took a hard left turn. He got a girl pregnant, wrecked a couple of new cars, and got into casual drugs. Good old Liz, though, she always looked the other way. She always believed all his bullshit excuses and she kept him on a fat allowance. Money was always her lanyard. Maybe she felt guilty about the divorce or something, but whatever stunt he pulled, he always got a pass from mom. My Dad showed far more concern for his welfare and his actual progress toward manhood than she ever did."

He cleared his throat and continued. "Kids need restrictions, and Rick desperately needed guidance or discipline or at least a strong male role model. Liz couldn't be bothered with the edgier elements of male adolescence. Dad tried like hell to be an influence. We even took Rick to Baja one year for the races down there. He seemed to love it, and he was a big help to the crew. Unfortunately, there were stronger influences at work. Flash forward a couple of years, he's left us behind and he's wrapped up with a seriously bad crowd. Perhaps he didn't realize he was in over his head, but they sure as hell did. They played along with him until he wore out his welcome, then they 'offed' him."

"What about Ricky's dad?"

"Not in the picture. Liz divorced him decades ago. She had all the money, so she had better attorneys and she got sole custody... worst thing that could possibly have happened to that kid. Jerry's retired now, lives in Vermont. We get a Christmas card every year. He and Ricky had been out of touch for years."

I presented a fact. "Your dad hired the P.I. who traced Rick's killer."

Tony nodded. "Yes, he did, after Liz refused to do so. They argued about that for a week. Dad stepped up, spent a pile of money, and eventually got the desired results." He smiled. "You guys don't come cheap."

I shrugged, "Some of us don't. The detective found Arnie Sutton, had him arrested, then he and your dad testified at the murder trial."

He grinned at the memory. "It was epic! Imagine the best Perry Mason episode ever. The detective testified first. He was good. Then dad took the stand and knocked it out of the park. Afterwards he was as proud as if he had won the Indy 500. One of my last, best memories of him was at the victory party the night the verdict came down. Oh, and just to be clear, your client was not in attendance that evening."

"Your dad sounds like the man I imagined him to be. This has been great."

We had made an entire lap of the upper display floor of the 'Pete'. Tony stopped in front of a pearl yellow front engine Top Fuel dragster, a legendary drag racer from the mid-'60s. Its original pilot was an acknowledged pioneer in professional drag racing.

"Let me illustrate this, Street. You see that car? My dad saw something in that driver back when he was just a kid. He gave him and his crew shop space and technical help, free of charge, to build that very car. He taught them how to tune it, then he taught the driver how to keep it off the wall. That same guy, with that same team, using that exact same car, won Top Fuel Eliminator at the NHRA Winter Nationals at Pomona just three months later. That kind of sudden success was unheard of back then, and it still is. That driver has become a legend in the sport. He listened and he learned, and he worked hard, and he added a lot of luck, then he built on those early successes and became one of the best-known names in motorsports. He's wealthy now, and famous beyond his wildest dreams. Make no mistake, Street, he did the heavy lifting, but dad gave him that initial push."

He paused, his eyes now moist. "Listen to me, brother." His voice was thick with emotion. "Decades later, even with all that fame and fortune, that man still loved my dad. He cried genuine tears at the funeral. He and dozens of others would have stood in for Dad and Annie that morning. He and hundreds of his peers attended the funeral and each of them was sincere in their emotion. Dad and Annie were loved by countless people and any of dozens of the most powerful and famous people in motorsports would have taken their places."

Now he was agitated. He exhaled heavily and stated an opinion that affected the direction of my work for the coming weeks. "You asked me earlier, Street, my opinion of who would have commissioned these murders." He pointed at me for emphasis. "Here it is: No serious racer, no enthusiast at any level, rivalry or no rivalry, grudge or no grudge, love, hate or indifferent, would have hired someone to kill Ron Connors. You, my friend, are looking for someone who doesn't even remotely understand or identify with the racers' mindset."

I couldn't've asked for a better conclusion to our conversation. "Thank you, Tony. This has been great. I appreciate your time. We will talk again soon." We shook hands one final time, and I left the Museum minutes later.

10

An hour later, after creeping southward on the 405 freeway through the expected LAX clot and observing the traumatic effects of a broken median-strip sprinkler head on the normal flow of south-county freeway traffic, I took the Seal Beach off-ramp. The extended drive had given me time to consider my new respect for someone who had already been a hero.

My next stop would not have the same results. I was set to encounter Ray Cole, who had agreed to meet me at a halfway point for both of us, at one of those great SoCal time-warp destinations. Seal Beach is California beach town perfection. It displays wide smooth streets and has been maintained with a strong sense of history. Main Street offered excellent aromas from great food and great visuals, all day, every day. Three Irish bars in two blocks? That's Main Street, Seal Beach. As I drove west toward the beach, I could almost see Frankie Avalon foot-racing David Hasselhoff across the broad, flawless white sand beach. Okay, that would be weird.

I parked at the Municipal lot at the base of the pier, couple of spaces downwind from a decrepit early '80s Cadillac Eldorado with a tattered vinyl roof cover and flaking paint. I recognized a weathered Ray Cole from the pictures in news coverage in Elizabeth's archival material. As I thumbed the key fob to lock the GTO, he approached me.

"You're Mister Street? I'm Ray Cole." He extended his hand. "Pleased to meet you." His handshake was weak. He turned to the GTO. "Man! That is one great car! It's a '68 right? A 400 motor?"

"No, it's a '69. Different grille and taillights than the '68. This one's not stock. I had it rebuilt a while back. It has a big-inch stroker motor, a 'Vette six-speed, EFI, a tubular four-link rear suspension on a bagged Art Morrison chassis, Vintage Air, eighteen-inch American alloys with Nitto rubber, Recaro seats, and a few other bits and pieces. It's my 401k substitute." I had explained this to an oblivious Ray Cole. His blank gaze heightened my suspicions.

He had made a lap of the car and stopped at the drivers' door. "I had a coupla Trans Ams back in the late '70s, the Bandit cars? Wrecked one of 'em."

"You're why they're rare."

"I reckon. When I get back up I wanna get another one, do it up right."

"There are plenty of them out there. They're not getting any cheaper though." I looked at him as we walked toward the base of the municipal pier. He looked old and tired in every way. Stooped slightly at the shoulders, he carried a few extra pounds in his middle, and he walked with a pronounced leftward limp. His hair was mussed from his trip up the freeway next to an open window. His skin was pallid and his eyes showed red. He wore a pair of faded and oil-spotted khakis, a stretched and tattered maroon short sleeve knit shirt that whispered 'thrift shop' and a pair of sweat-stained deck shoes. I asked, "How're things going for you?"

As we walked past the police department substation at the base of the pier and climbed the half-dozen steps to the pier, he explained, "Well, y'know, it is what it is. The L.A. county DA is gonna make another run at me before long and I am sunk. I'm down to the nubs. I got nothing left. Gotta borrow my dad's old piece o'shit Caddy and live in the back bedroom of a twelve-wide house trailer. Have I come down a ways or what?"

I didn't feel like attending his pity party. "I understand much of the downhill slide is of your own making."

We had stopped at the south-facing railing a quarter of the way up the pier. Cole looked out toward the ocean for a few seconds, then he turned to me. "Yeah, I guess I deserve that, Mister Street. I had it all. I did it all. I was damn good at my work, then I let it get away from me. I lost my wife, my business, my properties, my cars, my boat, just ever'thing. Now if I got half a shot, I could come back strong though. I really could."

I was already running short of patience for Cole's litany of personal gloom. "Let's get to it, okay? You and Ron Connors had a joint venture for a while, then it split up. He filed suit and won big in court. The settlement cost you everything you owned. You made a lot of threats. A while later Connors and his wife were shot dead in their driveway as they left for work. A lot of people, including the L.A. County Sheriffs' Department and most of the southern California law enforcement and legal communities assume that you commissioned the hits."

Cole straightened a bit, took a deep breath and looked at me. "Mister Street, I swear by the God I worship, I had nothing to do with that man and his wife dying. I respected Ron for decades and I adored his wife. She was a real sweetheart. We did some things together and we had some success, and we made a lot of money together for a long time. I wish it had lasted a lot longer. Then some things went sour and I just lost it. I was a mess back then and God damn it I'm sorry! I'm still payin' for some of my bad shit from back then. I prob'ly won't outlive some of it. But you listen to me. I may be a lot of things, and I'm not proud of a lot of 'em or where I am today, but I did not murder those people!"

"No one ever said you pulled the trigger, Cole. Many people are convinced that you hired the killers."

He was louder now, his teeth clenched. "I did nothing of the sort! I was already dead broke by then. I was livin' on my boat, tryin' like hell to keep my wife from walkin' out on me! We heard the news that day as we came into port and we both knew that I'd be the first sonofabitch they'd come lookin' for."

I could match his volume if not his emotion. "Okay then, who did it? Do you have any ideas? C'mon, Cole, who, other than you, was making threats against Connors to anyone who would listen? Name another sworn enemy." I paused a second then continued, "Sorry, but from my vantage point there was no one else making threats. You're it, pal!"

Cole stared toward the ocean. He sounded weary and resigned as he responded. "Hell, I dunno! Ron had a long and complicated career! He had a hunnert things happening at the same time and I wasn't involved in 98 of 'em! You got access to his business records? Audit ever'thing! You'll see I wasn't his only problem!"

I'd had my fill of Cole for the day so I called him on his pronouncement. "Cole, I'll give you one shot. I'm looking in several directions on this thing. If I find anything that leads directly away from you, I'll give you a heads up. You'll pardon me if I don't hold my breath waiting for that to happen." I looked at him one last time. "Have a nice afternoon." I walked back to the car, totally unimpressed.

11

It was a few minutes after 6a.m. The sun was just starting to lighten the eastern horizon when the blue pickup pulled to the curb a hundred feet up the hill, past the rambling hillside house with the big fence. The driver had studied the Thomas Guide map books and had made several trips through the neighborhood in previous weeks. Today he had taken the longer route across the top of the foothills instead of driving through the formal entrance off the main drag at the bottom of the hill.

The driver turned to his passengers, the older white man in the front passenger seat and the Latino in the jump seat at the rear of the cab. "Awright guys, get inside the gate and hide in the flower bed by the fence like I tol' ya. When one of 'em comes out, go do 'em. The other one will follow. They always leave early in the morning. Do both of 'em and anyone else comes along too. Then you get on the bikes and boogie down the hill. I'll meet you at the diner there at the corner. You talk to no one, y'unnerstand?"

The older white guy answered, staring hard at the driver, "Gotcha boss. You just be sure you're there." Both passengers left the truck, removed their bikes from the bed and walked across the street to the area under the trees by the fence. The sun had just begun lightening the sky and their dark blue clothing rendered them nearly invisible.

A few minutes after 6:30, the front gate started to motor open. The gardener's light blue '66 Chevelle station wagon rolled through the gate and started down the hill. By the time the gate started its return trip to close, the two gunmen were already inside the fence and secreted in the massive flower bed just inside the fence.

The white guy, a dozen years older than the Latino, tore the wrapper on a king-size Snickers bar and took a bite. He squeezed his right knee as it throbbed from an old work injury. This cool damp air did him no favors. If this asshole paid as promised he'd try to get that place down in Chula Vista, the one with the hot tub. That'd be nice.

Almost twenty minutes passed before the double garage door at the side of the house motored open and the silver minivan started backing out. By the time the rear wheel cleared the threshold of the garage, the two men were halfway across the driveway. The Mexican kid yanked open the drivers' door and tore the woman from her perch as the van rolled backwards. She screamed in shock as the gloved hand closed around her forearm.

12

Later, as I approached the onramp to the 405 back to L.A. my cell phone rang. The caller ID told who was at the other end. "Catherine! How did your dep go?"

"I don't know yet, Street. It's been delayed, as usual. I don't go in 'till 2:30. But I have some news for you. Can you go to Chino this afternoon? I found out that Arnie Sutton is back down here. His attorney is trying for a sentence modification that I wasn't yet aware of. His attorney has him starting at 3 p.m. but you can talk to him starting at 2:30 if you want."

This call was great news on two fronts. I was not only furthering the work at hand, but I was also being taken seriously by my operative. "Ooh! You're good! I didn't expect to have to go to prison so early in the process."

"One does what one can, Street. Your name is already at the gate. The warden there is an old friend. He's Phil Ritchey. Good luck!"

"Thanks! I'll see you tonight." I closed the phone and set it aside and took the next onramp to turn back south to the 91 freeway toward Riverside county. Eighty minutes later, after a trip out the perpetually clotted Riverside freeway including a forty-minute creep session thanks to some kid driving his donor cycle under a trash truck just west of the Imperial Highway exit, I sat in the idling GTO at the front gate of an industrial-looking suburban prison complex. After my name was checked off, I drove onto the crowded parking lot and tried to find a spot with some potential of shade.

I found a suitable space, locked the car and set the security system...hey, this place is full of criminals! I removed my back-up piece and its holster from my left ankle and put it and its holster along with my shoulder rig and pistol into the metal box bolted to the floor in the corner of the GTO's trunk. I'd had it installed there years before to facilitate travel through the many gun-restricted communities in SoCal. Made sense at a prison, too.

The front entrance to the prison complex was an easy eighth mile from the parking lot. The facility just looked 'governmental' at this point. It could have been anything from a sewage treatment facility to a junior high school...a *really* rough one. As soon as I was signed in and 'wanded' I was ushered into the Warden's office. The thin, middle-aged bespectacled man rose from his desk and extended his hand as I entered.

"Welcome, Mister Street. I'm Phil Ritchey. I run this place. I understand you're working with Catherine Hallowell." We shook hands and took out seats on the appropriate side of his government-issue metal desk.

"Might you mean Catherine Gadsden, the attorney from Riverside?"

"Sure. That's right. I was tight with her older brother. I know her by her maiden name."

"Nice meeting you. Catherine had mentioned your name. Thank you for seeing me on such short notice today. On her behalf I'm requesting a visit with one of your tenants."

"Ah, yes. Our Mister Sutton, first name Arnold, transferred here two weeks ago as a result of his attorney's pressure tactics on the Corrections Department and the power structure of the Prison Guard's union in Sacramento. What a piece of work that clown is!"

"That's the one." I passed him my credentials and he looked at them as he spoke.

"Well, any confidant of Cath's passes muster with me, no problem. Might I ask the specific reason for the visit?" He passed my credentials back to me, settled back in his chair and took a sip of his coffee.

"I'm looking to develop some background information regarding his original conviction. He had an accomplice who didn't get nailed in that deal, and I suspect there may even be a connection to a number of other crimes, both earlier and later. That's not all. There may be some link to other inmates from this or other correctional facilities around the time of his initial incarceration."

He squinted slightly. "What do you need from, me?"

"Perhaps just some information. I'm working a hunch, looking for some kind of a connection between your inmate Sutton and the Connors murders from a while later that year. Sutton was sent here after his murder conviction thirteen years ago, September 22, 1996, while he waited for his transfer up north. Ron Connors had funded the private investigation that led to the arrest and had testified at his trial. His testimony knocked it out of the park. A few weeks later, Connors and his wife were murdered at their home. We are wondering if somehow Sutton helped source a couple of shooters from the ranks of parolees from within these walls. I would like a list of parolees from the time of his arrival to October 21, 1996. Can you get that for me?"

He wrote the dates after I repeated them. "That's what you need? Consider it done. Records from that far back will have to come from the State, so no telling how long it'll take, but I will access them and we'll see what turns up. All of our computers are steam powered so it might take a while."

"Understood. I was a cop for a few years, I can wait. Just get it to me when you can." I passed him one of my cards. "E-mail's on the bottom."

"Is there anything else you need?"

"I'd like to get a look at his financials. We know he's getting money from someone."

He pursed his lips then responded. "Well, there we have an issue. Out of respect for his privacy and as a response to a nasty lawsuit a few years ago, I can't give you direct access, but I will take a peek myself and pass any pertinent information your way as a sign of my respect for Catherine. Will that work?"

I smiled as I rose from the chair. "Swimmingly."

"Tell Catherine 'hi' for me. Good luck with Sutton." We shook hands and I left the office. Five minutes later I made my way through the ranks of cubicle-bound minions of officialdom. I was led along a Lysol-smelling, camera-surveilled, gray painted concrete floored corridor by an officious, crisply uniformed guard. As we passed the tall, open casement windows I could smell the food being prepared in the nearby kitchen. The aroma was bleak. I was glad I wasn't a guest at this Inn. As we walked, I asked the guard, "Do you have any interaction with Sutton?"

He looked straight ahead as we walked. "No interaction because I'm a guard and he's not. I wouldn't expect a lot, though. He's been inside for a long time. Most of these guys take a set after a while. He hasn't had to make a critical decision in what, thirteen years? He thinks he's a big deal. We don't have to agree." He looked at me as he opened the door to the meeting room. "Like I said, I wouldn't expect much."

I followed him into a twelve-by-twelve-foot room, lit by fluorescent lights inset to the acoustic tile ceiling. He took a seat at the door. As a non-attorney I had no expectation of confidentiality within the facility walls. Arnie Sutton was led into the room and his handcuffs were unhooked. He turned his chair backwards and rested his chin and his wrists on the back of the chair. He showed attitude before he spoke a single word. He wore a ratty looking goatee and displayed indecipherable prison tattoos on his neck and face. I tried to read the ones on his neck and gave up when I read 'born to loose'. The ink included an indecipherable name or title over each eyebrow. How classy can one guy be?

When he spoke, he affected the manner of an inner-city tough guy.

As I took the seat opposite him, he asked, "Wassup? So, who you, boss? Watchoo need?"

I slid a blank card with my name and e-mail toward him. His lips moved as he read it.

I answered him, "I'm him. I'm looking at the technicalities surrounding your trial. I'm just trolling for some information, Arnie."

"Yo homes, like...what's in it for me?" Prison attitude. Ya gotta love it.

"Well, maybe just think of it as your most recent contribution toward increasing the intrinsic value of mankind, Arnie. I just have a few questions then I'll leave you to the wonderment of your surroundings." I raised my eyebrows and looked around the room. I watched his facial expressions. Both of them. He was baffled.

"Makin my day, boss. Ax away."

I jumped right in. "So tell me, Arnie, who piloted the plane when you killed the Damarow kid? Your VISA card rented the plane, but the FAA credentials given for the rental didn't match any legitimate ticket."

The smirk of a controlling fifteen-year-old appeared. "Hey, bro, we lied. So put me in jail!" He paused and looked at me. "Hey, wait..." He laughed at his own joke.

Words have great value if you listen. "So it was a 'we'. There was someone else with you flying that plane. Thanks for that."

Sneering, confident on his own turf, he looked at me as he answered. "Jus' one o' my bros, boss. I got lotsa mufuggin' bros."

Mild insults, complex sentences and topic changes seemed to be the way to keep this little creep off balance. "That's okay Arnie, I try not to be critical of alternative lifestyles. Have you talked to your daughter lately?"

"Huh? How you know about her?" he leaned forward again.

"Your girlfriend was in the courtroom during the trial. She was pregnant, just starting to show. Birth records in San Diego county name you as father of a baby girl born almost thirteen years ago. I hear the girlfriend was kinda hot." I looked at the surroundings. "It must be really depressing going from that to...well...this."

That got his attention. He backtracked and blushed a bit. "Naw, boss! I straight! I got a 'ho' comes in once a month, takes care o' business." He smiled, "I tear that 'ho' up! Y'know what I mean?" Now he was making sweeping motions with his hands, 'hood' style.

I had tried to suppress mental images as he spoke. "Yeah, Arnie, good for you. Word has it you get healthy bank here. Do you still have outside income or did someone pay you to take the rap?"

He took that in stride. "Lawyer does that for me. He takes real good care o' me. Lotsa others too, boss."

"Oh, for sure! He's a real prince! And yet, here you still are, wearin' orange, lookin' at grey, all day, every day. Go figure! Hey, maybe he'll get you on parole by the time your daughter gets her Master's degree. You could be the only proud dad with face tatts at the graduation ceremony!" I tried to smile my most ironic smile.

That slowed him down a bit. "My little girl. You seen her? She what, twelve, thirteen now? Prob'ly looks like her mama." His tongue skimmed his lower lip as he spoke.

That did it. I could sense Arnie taking the low road regarding his daughter. No birthday pic for him. "No, not yet. Do you know where she and her mom are living now?"

"I unnastan' they over near Vegas now, near where her people retired. They was teachers. I try ta call ya with her number, I got that in ma crib." He was lapsing into adult conversation for a few seconds. That didn't continue.

"Nope." Phone calls from a state facility cost a fortune. "My e-mail's on the card. Just use that. So do you stay in touch with your mom? Your dad?"

He returned top punk dialect. "Sheeut! Naw, boss! Not if I see him comin' first. Him an' me, we not exactly friends, y'know what I mean?" He had emphasized his dad. That factor would soon be important.

I looked at Arnie. My patience was gone. This was getting old now, and predictable. "Sutton? Three things here. You're a thirty-five-year-old pasty-faced white guy with the worst ink in the history of mankind. You're not a thug, or a homie, or a 'bro'. You're not from the hood. Try talking like a grownup to another grownup sometime. It'll do you a lot of good. Two: I'm not your boss. And Three: After you say 'Y'know what I'm sayin' half a dozen times nobody cares what you're sayin'."

Oblivious, Arnie just stared at me. "Huh? Oh, that. Gotcha boss."

"So c'mon, Arnie, man up. Concentrate for a few seconds. Who helped you when you dropped the Damarow kid from that plane? He was taller than you are, he weighed more than you did. There is no way you could wrestle that inert body from the cabin of that plane and keep it in the air as well. The right words now could get you out of prison before you're eighty! Whatever deal you made with these people, you're well past paid up. Those accounts are square!"

This lit him up. "Dude. Lissen up. Yo, I got busted f'dis shit thirteen years ago, you think I give a shit about it now? I'm in it, doin' my time, straight up, an' I ain't givin' up any o' my boys! I do' need no cop comin' in here getting' in my face, getting' in my binness!"

I sat and listened to him prattle on for a few seconds, then I spoke. "Okay, Sutton. So be it. You're right where you belong. This is what you do best. It's just your speed. Bongelli passes you a few bucks every once in a while, just to keep you fat, dumb, and happy. You're less than a rounding error for him. If that's all you ever want from life, have at it. Be my guest."

His blank stare told me all I needed to know. "You have a great day." I rose from my chair and walked toward the door and the guard. Seconds later we entered the breezy hallway. As we walked toward the offices, he looked at me and said, "Told ya." He smiled, then said, "Be sure to sign out at the Warden's office. Have a good day." He broke off and went to his cubicle as we entered the office wing. Moments later as I entered the men's rest room, I stepped sideways to allow room for a portly, balding, well-dressed man as he exited. When I entered the wardens' outer office to sign out, I asked the guard at the desk, "Did Sutton's attorney just arrive?"

He consulted his clipboard. "Lessee...yessir. Vincent Bongelli, Riverside, attorney for Sutton and three other inmates. He and Sutton are trying for a sentence modification hearing in a few weeks." He lifted a blue Post-It from his desk and read it. "Brass just gave me this, says he may have the information you asked for late tonight or early tomorrow."

"Thank you, and thank him for me, too. Tell him there's no real hurry. I appreciate the courtesy."

Outside the walls I sat in the sweltering car with the A/C on high. I tried to find a local talk show or an all-news station or maybe even NPR on the radio—anything to help me regain the IQ points that I felt I'd lost during my session with Sutton. My eyes settled on a well-polished pearl black AMG Mercedes coupe parked two slots away on the other side of the aisle. I checked my messages on my cell, found none, then I snicked the Hurst shifter into first gear and drove toward the 71 Freeway, windows powered down to cool the interior as I traveled.

I arrived home a little after four-fifteen and went to the office to update my files and amend the information on the event boards. After a half-hour I went back outside, moved the GTO to the shade and started my weekly ritual of cleaning it up before the evening out. Top to bottom, front to back, it was part of a long-standing practice that sometimes doubled as therapy for me. A little after five-thirty I heard Catherine's red Trailblazer drive in. She parked near the garage. She stepped out and looked to where I was cleaning the GTO.

I switched positions so I could watch her. She looked good. Her official courtroom attire was a dark blue wool suit with a skirt that was cut just high enough to keep the viewers' attention, at least if the viewer shared my sense of style in females and their attire.

I called to her. "How did your deposition go?"

She stepped back, loosened the last button on her blazer, removed it, folded it neatly and laid it on the seat of her truck. "It was okay. It took a while, but I expected that. The hard part for me is the trip into L.A. I am losing my nerve for that. There is a video deposition program in development, I'll sign onto that when it's complete. It'll save a lot of time and mileage." She walked toward the car as she spoke. "How did your visits go?"

"Tony Connors was great. He is his fathers' son. I like him. Cole's a loser, though I do get mixed signals from him. He has a hard time dealing with the fact that his troubles are of his own making. I almost feel for the guy...almost. Sutton is a weird useless little creep, rightly housed behind tall walls with razor wire at the top." I looked at her and smiled. "Thank you for that reference. I also learned that prison tattoo artists do not employ spell check."

She frowned at that. "Good eye. So how is your alternate theory of the Connors' murders progressing?"

I tried to sound confident. "It's still in development. There are elements still MIA and I'm looking for something that will tie it all together. I'm always open to suggestions."

"Don't look at me. I'm new to speculative criminology."

I considered the term. "Wow. I like that. Is that trademarked?"

She smiled, "No. Use it in good health."

I wiped the last of the detail spray from the fender of the GTO and stood to look at it one last time. "There. Done! Poor old car took a real beating in the sun and heat and all the traffic today. I spent a small fortune on paint and body work on this thing, I'm trying to make it last."

"It's like a work of art. What is it?"

Okay, I get a lot of questions about the car. "It's a Pontiac GTO, a 1969 model. It was my dad's car when he was in college, and my folks brought me home from the hospital in it at age two days. My dad kept it as a work car for several years but sold it to buy a minivan when I was four years old. Flash forward twenty-plus years, I find a GTO behind a barn during a chop shop raid when I was a cop in Atlantic City. I ran the numbers, determined it was the same car, and I bought it from the seizure auction. I put it back on the road myself, then when I moved out here I had it rebuilt by a pro shop down in Orange County. Same car, new engine, new transmission, new chassis, now upholstery... it's a little like George Washington's ax. The handle was changed, the blade was replaced, but it's still his hatchet, right?"

"I never thought of it like that. I guess you're right."

My pontification continued. "Y'know, L.A. is supposed to be the car capital of the universe, but there's too little variety. I refuse to drive just another leased, silver, 3-series BMW. There's nothing boring about this thing."

She had looked at the car inside and out. "Well, it's beautiful. It suits you well. My old Trailblazer is about done after eight years. I'll be looking for something new before long."

"Let me know when you start looking, I'll give you some ideas." I folded the last of the towels, put them onto their box in the trunk and closed the lid. "End of lecture. Come on in the house, I'll give you the nickel tour." We walked to the patio then past the double doors to the combined office/den.

Catherine walked in and looked around. "Wow! This is really nice, Street. Definitely a 'guy house', but it's not overbearing about it. I'm impressed!"

"Thanks. I like it. When I moved to town and found it, I had this end of the house gutted and remodeled. It's home now."

"It's very nice. This is your office?" She walked around the room, looking at the décor and the furnishings, then stopped at the suspended event boards.

"Yes, it is. As you can see, I've started mapping the Connors murders. I've started the boards to chart the progress. I've put a lot of work in on it in the last week." Now I spoke to her from the adjoining half-bath as I changed shirts and checked my appearance.

As I emerged from the bathroom Catherine put her purse in the desk, opened it and withdrew a white notebook and a white plastic computer flash drive sleeve. She put both on the desk on my desk pad. "Before I forget, here are the trial notes and the court transcript for the Damarow trial, as requested. I need to get the notebook back from you when you're done with it."

"Very nice. Thank you." I opened the desk drawer, withdrew an envelope and handed it to her. "I'll trade you that for a retainer check." I closed the drawer and thumbed through the notebook as she put the envelope into her purse. "I'm impressed. Excellent detail in these. Nice work. I'll get this back to you when we meet again."

Now Catherine had zoned in on the 65-inch flat screen TV and the DVD racks on the adjoining wall in the den. As she walked along the display she said, "Wow! I haven't seen some of these titles in decades. This is cool, Street."

"That's my library. What can I say? I've been popular with eBay vendors and bootleg sources for years. There are about twenty-eight hundred hours on that wall, eighty-odd titles going back to the early fifties, not all of stellar quality. If you see anything you want copied, let me know. I have a great dupe system. I can burn a DVD in a little over a minute. That may be my one acquiescence to blatant illegality."

She turned from the wall and walked toward the desk. "I understand. If the FBI ever comes after you let me, know, I'll represent you." She looked around the room. "I'm impressed. This is all so clean and organized. Well done, Street."

"Thank you." I plucked my leather jacket from the back of the office chair. "So are you hungry?"

She smiled. "Famished."

"Great! Me, too." We walked to the patio doors. I punched in the code for the security system, opened the door, and stood aside for her to pass. "Our chariot awaits!"

13

After years of practice and experience I pride myself on my keen powers of observation. As we left the driveway that afternoon, I noticed the daytime running lights flare on the solo-occupied silver late-model Chevy Malibu sedan parked three houses south on the residential street in front of the house. Street parking was rare in my neighborhood of older homes with wide driveways and big garages. I made a mental note of his presence and kept a wary eye on the mirror as we drove across the Hollywood hills toward our destination, the Daily Grille at Ventura and Laurel Canyon Boulevards in Studio City. After about twenty minutes I parked the car on the westernmost side of the low walled parking lot. We walked across the lot and took the escalator to the second floor then walked to the restaurant on the west end of the upper level.

As we were led to our tables Catherine said, "This is nice. I halfway expected a trip to some hot dog place." She smiled as we were seated toward the rear of the room. I took the 'visibility seat' with a view of the door. When you're being tailed by a guy in a silver Malibu, you can't be too careful.

"I have carefully mapped the reference points for fine, and not-so-fine dining in the greater Los Angeles area. Let's see, hot dogs,

Carneys or Pink's; pastrami, The Hat; chili, Barney's Beanery. Big sloppy burgers, Tommy's. There are about a half-dozen places I like for good authentic Mexican drive-thru but the Green Burrito in Anaheim is at the top of the list right now. I know a lot of the better places for a quick meal of earthy food, but I have a few places like this that I like in case I have to feed an attorney or something. I have a short but impressive list of sit-down eateries, and The Daily Grille is a favorite. I come here a lot."

Catherine looked at me and gave a thoughtful smile. "Earthy... I think that's a good term for you. I am amazed that you can even exist in one of the most politically correct cities on earth without it annoying the hell out of you. From my vantage point it seems you keep everything balanced. How do you keep it all straight?"

"It's probably part luck and partly me being annoyingly selective. My profession allows me to choose my work and by extension I get to choose the people I work with. I turn down quite a few jobs, and I do not entertain the ultra-PC firms or the people who fill them. My referrals mostly come from a Century City attorney who is a really close friend. She knows not to send me into uppity lions' dens on my assignments. She and I see eye to eye on most legal and cultural issues, but she gets to assume the role of a starchy Century City attorney because she's good at that. She likes those people more than I do. I avoid those situations entirely, if at all possible. It's far healthier that way."

Catherine looked at the menu as she spoke. "You've thought about it a lot." The waiter brought us our menus. "What's good here?"

"I like the crab cakes, myself, and the salmon is excellent, but everything else is good, too."

"Have you had the Chicken Caesar salad?"

"Yes. One day last week for lunch. It was splendid." The wire basket holding the fresh bread was set on our table. The aroma always made me twice as hungry as I had been before. I suspect a plot.

"Well...I am quite hungry. I want something solid. I'll try the chicken parm and a house salad. Iced tea to drink, please."

As the waiter wrote on his book, I added, "And I'll have the crab cakes and a Caesar salad. Iced tea here, too."

"Good choices," the waiter said as he hurried away.

As I split and buttered a warm roll, Catherine opened the non-work conversation. "So when you were a little kid, what did you want to be when you grew up?"

I chewed a section of the roll while I composed my answer. I swallowed after a few seconds and said, "Best, most specific answer, 'Living in L.A.' I grew up on classic rock music and muscle cars. I built scale model hot rods during summer vacations and the first magazine I ever bought with my own money was the May 1983 issue of HOT ROD. I liked surfing even though I was really on the wrong coast. I asked for a surfboard for Christmas for three years in a row before my folks took me seriously. My dad thought I was nuts. All of that was due to the west coast media influence."

"So, in your adolescence you adapted the mythical California lifestyle as your ideal and your goal."

"I did. Some of that came from my mentoring. My dad was a great provider, he just wasn't around a lot because he was climbing the ladder at his work. He wasn't a great influence on my adolescence. Most of my male role models were those guys on that wall at the house. They were a great influence on me. They taught me how to defend myself, in word and action, how to be decisive, how to think, all of this in the absence of an active male role model at home. I know I was not alone in that situation growing up, and I think I turned out okay compared to some of my peers."

"That's interesting. So, who is your all-time favorite TV detective?"

"That can vary from week-to-week. The top five are consistent: David Janssen's 'Harry Orwell', James Garner's 'Jim Rockford', Robert Urich's 'Spenser', and Peter Falk's 'Columbo' are always at the top of the list. Top spot right now, though, has to be Mike

Connors' 'Joe Mannix'." I smiled, "I'm doing the first of the DVD box sets right now. I mean really, how tough was *that* guy?"

"My dad liked him, too. I remember he got beat up a lot."

"Sure, there was no shortage of clichés as time went on. And as Mannix went away after eight years Jim Rockford was waiting in the wings to try to kill those same clichés and bring the genre to a close. James Garner was great at killing those. After six seasons of Rockford there wasn't a lot left to say—most every mystery series on TV turned to big fake explosions and old Chevies doing spiral flips off of pipe ramps instead of good drama and solid writing."

"Any favorites among the recent shows?" She tore an end off a roll, buttered it and bit off a smaller corner.

"Sure. It seems the ones I really like go away really soon. I loved 'High Incident', 'Life' and 'Boomtown' but they all died far too quickly. There's plenty of imaginary heroism to go around. The old shows are favorites for the escapism, but the new material is far more realistic. I ordered a 'Prison Break' DVD set last week. Michael Schofield's tattoo work was certainly more impressive than what I saw on Sutton this afternoon."

"'Monk' was a favorite of mine."

"Brilliantly written show. I have relatives who are like him except for the 'brilliant investigator' part." I lifted my eyebrows for effect.

"Do you still surf?"

"Nope. I tried, but the ocean intimidates me. It's limitless, I'm not. And the bays are not all that clean anymore. An afternoon on the water with a side order of Hep-C has very little appeal." I smiled, resigned to the reality of expensive wall décor. "The boards still look good on the wall in the den."

"Then there's the education thing. Most P.I.s do not possess a Masters' degree."

I put my glass of iced tea back on the table. "Some of the better ones do, and more now have military intelligence or security back-grounds. The degree is something I'm proud of, and it looks great hanging on the wall but the effects of it are of little use in the real

world. The professors taught theory, and that's fine in the class-
room where there is little actual crime. If you want to be a profes-
sor, you can't beat 'theory'. But criminals don't operate on theory
and they don't follow a complicated course of study. They run on
emotion, opportunity and impulse. I was a cop when I was
finishing my Masters'. The 'theories' taught in my classes often got
in the way of the actual methods used by the crooks and criminals.
Eventually I developed sufficient 'instinct' to discern the actions
required. The 'little voice in my head', per Thomas Magnum, has
become more reliable as time has passed."

"Okay, so what does your cast of characters and your education
and your instinct tell you about the matter at hand? Who killed
Ron Connors and his wife?"

"I'm glad you asked. I think it's complicated, far more so than
my client will ever admit. I *think*, but have yet to prove, that there
are people other than Ray Cole responsible for the Connors
murders. Cole is way past flat broke now, and I need to determine
how bad his finances were thirteen years ago. I *think*, but have yet to
ascertain, that there is a connection between the Rick Damarow
murder and the Connors killings. I *suspect* there are common
elements between the two events that will reveal a lot. And it still
bugs me that the pilot of the plane used in the Damarow death is
still MIA. I want that name."

"You suspect that may be the missing link."

"It could be. At very least he is an accomplice to Murder One.
Where is he now? What is he doing? Is Sutton just the fall guy for a
larger operation? Sutton verified that there are other people
involved. Think about it: If they would have Rick Damarow killed
after souring a crummy drug deal, who's to say they wouldn't want
major league revenge against Ron Connors after his testimony put
Arnie Sutton away for 25 years?"

Catherine responded, "That's interesting. I know Bongelli was
beside himself during and after the trial. I can look again, see if
there's anyone I missed."

"Let's double team on that. I'm having a problem with Cole

being a major element in anything substantial. The guy was a world-class cocaine cowboy for the greater portion of his early adult life. He made a lot of money, but a sizable proportion of his disposable income was inhaled off a mirror. He had that role down and he was consistent to type... Borrowed hat, rented saddle, leased horse. All profile, no substance, all talk, no 'do'. I've seen a dozen of 'em over the years. He lucked out hugely when he hooked up with Connors. He was finally making substantial, consistent money. He went a bit nuts with his spending and his coke use for a couple of years and since this wasn't some nine-to-five cubicle gig, he could operate on his own turf. When he needed to have face time with the squares, he'd clean up for a few days, put on a great show, and make the proper impression. Afterwards? Rock on!"

I took a sip of iced tea and continued, "Later on, as he got sloppier and deeper in the hole, he started losing points with Connors. Then here comes the coke truck to the Connors offices and 'BANG!' it's time to settle up. He's three million short on his side of the operation. He lost everything he owned in the settlement, still tap-dancing while he liquidates. Then the hot young wife decides to split, and he's in even deeper. Tell me how, after he's burned everyone in sight, he could have afforded to hire a pair of high-quality shooters. He was beyond bankrupt."

Catherine raised an index finger and interjected, "But lots of people filing bankruptcy have funds that are not included in the legal procedures."

"That's true. And those are the smart folks. Cole was not among them. When Connors teamed up with him Cole was living off his motocross events. Later, with better finances, his funds went up his nose or into glitz of little or no redeemable value. Eventually he was a rimless zero. I think that lets him off the hook for the Connors' murders. Those hits were *very* carefully orchestrated. It was a professional operation start to finish, with advance surveillance, strategy and practice after the initial recruitment of the shooters. It would have cost tens of thousands of dollars to plan it and make it happen correctly. I don't think Cole could have carried it off."

"So, all he really did was threaten the Connors."

"That is all he did. Talk is cheap. His was free. It's all he could afford."

Our food arrived on a big silver tray and conversation took a back seat to savoring a fine dinner. Catherine made quick work of her Chicken Parm and I had a great time with the Crab Cakes. We talked about her work, she made her distaste for divorce work perfectly clear, and we had a grand old time. Neither of us was a drinker so the wine list and full bar suffered a sales slump from our table. The waiters kept the caffeine coming as Catherine and I enjoyed the surroundings and the company.

Catherine observed, "You seem to have some issues with your client."

"I guess I do. Don't get me wrong, I have immense respect for her. There is a lot to admire. She is serious and intensely successful, a truly impressive professional. She knows her stuff and in her own field she is practically invincible. She generously hired me to find her brothers' killer. I appreciate the job and I relish the challenge. I just hope she doesn't expect the same findings from me that she received from her last three operatives. To me, Cole just doesn't fit as the right person to commit those murders in that time frame. My predecessors seem to have just gone through the motions with the intent of fortifying Elizabeth's assumptions. I'll go in a different direction. I hope that doesn't get me fired before I finish the job."

Catherine looked over her loaded fork at me. "I can tell that you're really absorbed in this. Keeping it straight has to be a challenge."

I smiled. "That is where you come in. A separate set of eyes is important in a situation like this. You've already earned your keep by the referrals you've provided, and I have more for you to tackle. Two things about Cole. We need to find his ex-wife and see if her memory of the week of the murders matches up to his. You will be much better at that than I could possibly be. She has re-married a time or two since they split, and I understand she's in Palm Springs now."

"No problem. I can do that."

"Then we need some information on Cole's financials during the time leading up to the murders. I know he was broke, but how broke was he, really? If he had sufficient resources to pull off the hits, I'll have to prove it. I doubt that's the case. Is there a way to search Bankruptcy Court records that far back?"

"That depends. There may be court records available, but bank records, maybe not. Some smaller banks and mortgage companies consolidated during the crash and the recession, so finding 'who bought what from whom' may be a struggle. I'll let you know what I find."

"As I understand it, his only real asset was his very expensive boat, but it was heavily mortgaged and eventually repo'd. If he went through a bank instead of black-market funding, there may be records of amounts owed."

Catherine changed the subject. "I'm curious. You deal with a lot of attorneys and you have an adventurous vantage point on the law. Would you ever take the State Bar exam? With a little study I bet you'd ace it."

I smiled at her. "Thanks, but no thanks. Lawyers live by a strict set of rules and I have far more flexibility when it comes to choosing my clients. Some of the work assigned to attorneys doesn't come out satisfactorily to anyone involved."

"True enough. After a while you learn to detach from letting the results affect you. You have worked with a lot of attorneys though. Any examples from the archives?"

"Sure. My dad's dad was a small-town attorney in Tennessee for about forty years. He was old school. He used his own Christian principals as his guide, and he tried to do right even when it cost him. Sometimes couples from his church would come to him for a divorce and he'd try to get them to reconcile. Of course, most of them would just go down the hall to the next lawyer and get it done, but he thought he was doing the right thing."

"Times have changed. That kind of service would be frowned on now."

"More than likely, and I think that's a little sad. He was a classic liberal of his era, so assisting the poor downtrodden minorities and poor folks was his stock in trade. That didn't always work out. The case that I think finally took him down is an example. He's eighty-one years old, hanging on by a thread physically and financially, and he's assigned a court appointed defense case. A young black guy is accused of offing his wife. There's a mountain of physical evidence but no 'wits.' So, Walt does his thing, makes all the right excuses, finally just asks for leniency, expecting a conviction but pushing for less than a life sentence. Jury comes back after eight hours and damn if it isn't an acquittal."

"That happens. Probably a weak prosecution, or maybe the jury liked your grandfather."

"True. People liked him a lot. He dealt with the victory fine. A couple of weeks later, though, he's in City Hall and the police chief, who grew up with my dad, calls him into his office. Seems this same defendant was back in the slam, asking for his services. One Saturday night soon after his release he's on the front porch of his new girlfriend's house, blind drunk, covered in blood, cradling a nearly empty bottle of 'Jack,' as the cops roll up. He's beaten the new girlfriend to a bloody pulp. She goes to the ICU for four days. The locals hook him and book him, and he's on tape from the back seat of the patrol car, yelling, "You get me that old Street, he'll get me off! I kilt that other bitch, he got me free, he'll do it this time, too!"

I took a sip of iced tea and continued. "Well, this really hurt my grandfather, made him doubt his life's work and maybe put him on the downward slide. He put up a good front, but when he told me about it, I knew it bothered him a lot. He was diagnosed with colon cancer a year later, and he was gone six weeks after the initial diagnosis. I was in college when he passed, and the loss affected me. To this day I am quite fond of seeing that the guilty get their just rewards. All of that to say, I'd make a *really crappy* defense attorney."

"Understandable. So, does your work allow you a social life? Wife? Ex-wife? Girlfriend? Anyone to share that great house with you?"

"I'm single right now. I was engaged when I was in Jersey five years ago. We were on vacation and I won a lot of money at a city-wide slot tournament in A.C. I decided I wanted to move out here like I'd always dreamed of, and I wanted her to come with me and be the biggest part of the dream. She refused to leave her family. I tried my best, I really did, but we finally broke it off and I came out here solo. I've been dating an actress for a while but that's cooled off now. She's filming a pilot episode for a cable soap opera soon so nothing else in the universe matters. We don't see each other a lot anymore." I smiled. "She's still fun to look at though."

She frowned. "Why do I suspect that the political correctness of the Hollywood crowd runs against the grain of the individualistic criminologist? Ever beat up any Key Grips or anything?"

I laughed at that. "You read the situation quite well. Last big episode, a few weeks ago. I was at a party in the Hollywood hills above Sunset, as a guest of the actress. We're at this really cool glass-walled patio ranch house. It's a frequent movie and TV location rental with a huge pool, just a magnificent view of the city. This self-proclaimed 'Producer' who's throwing the party, he's maybe five-foot-three, 125 pounds in a towel, 24 years old. It's like talking to a grade school kid. He's a shiny new USC Film School grad. His dad is cubic money, and the kid is spending part of his trust fund trying to buy a career. I can give him some slack. I'd probably do the same thing in his position. Anyway, he's been trying to look down Cindy's dress all night. So, we're introduced, I'm being 'nice'. It's his turf. I know my proper place. Then he starts talking about his new Prius. 'Prius this, Prius that' and pretty soon he asks what I drive, and gosh, don't I wish I had a Prius just like his? By now it's wearing a little thin, so I ask him one question."

Catherine just smiled and said, "Uh oh, here it comes."

I smiled. "You know me so well... All I ask is, 'Do they come in pairs?' And he lights up. 'Oh! Wouldn't that be cool? Then you'd be 'bi-Prius!'" Then I continue, totally deadpan, 'Well, I'm a big guy. I'd need one for each foot'."

Catherine laughed into her napkin.

"So of course, this sets off the boy producer and it sets off Cindy even though she drives a black Mustang GT convertible, thank you very much, and that's not even *close* to a friggin' Prius. In the meantime, producer boy hops onto the diving board to announce that he has landed funding for his cable soap, and Cindy will star so that he can continue to look down her dress. You get the idea. I was out of my element. I get really tired of the lies, the temporary loyalties, and the subtle deceptions."

"But let me guess...even with all that, you still love L.A."

She had me there. "I gotta say, most of the time I do. There is still a lot of exploring to do. I love that. The texture and variety of the city and its surroundings are always fascinating to me. Sometimes on a weekend I'll pick one road—east-west, or north-south—and follow it, end to end. I love doing that."

Catherine interjected, "I grew up here, and I never looked at it that way."

I drank some iced tea and continued, "It's a really twisty relationship though. I have my limits. I see the negatives of living here, and I know the town I dreamed of does not exist. It never did. There is no 29 Cove Road, there is no 17 Paseo Verde. There never were. In many ways this city can be really painful, and I know I'm lucky to be here with resources. I'd hate to be stuck here if I was broke."

She looked at me over the rim of her coffee cup and asked, "Do you think you'd ever leave?"

"I'll answer that, 'maybe'. If I had a family I'd be gone in a heartbeat. Culturally, educationally, this is not the town for family anymore. I love San Diego, I love Seal Beach, so they'd be at the top of the short list. The current issue is that I have a lot of equity in the house. I will have to wait for the economy to recover. These last three years have been brutal. I'm good for a while unless I want to lose a quarter-million dollars or so."

"That's a common situation now." She took another tiny corner of her roll.

I sipped my iced tea, then said, "New topic: I see you discovered my first name."

She wrinkled her nose and smiled, "I did. It's in your license records. 'Cecil'."

I shrugged. "Yeah, I was named after one of my great grandfathers, it's all historic east-coast family stuff. Not trendy, not cool. That name is really difficult to navigate when you're six and lose your teeth, and it's difficult to make 'Cecil' sound heroic. I've used the initial since I was eight or nine."

"Well, you can handle it. Awkward names build character."

I laughed, "Thanks for that."

"You mentioned you'd won a lot of money at a casino. Do you still gamble?"

"No. I won purely by accident. Two progressive slot jackpots in one weekend? That never happens. After I resigned the police department, I got bored one evening, I went back to the same casino and gave about a hundred bucks back to them. It wasn't fun anymore. Every time I played, I ended up asking 'Could I be more bored?' I saw the losing side and I moved on. That saves me a fortune when I go to Vegas."

"Good for you."

We continued to chat and at the end of a very pleasant second hour I passed my credit card, wrote a good tip, signed my name and we walked out onto the deck overlooking the street and parking lot. As we started down the steps toward the parking lot, I looked across Laurel Canyon Boulevard toward the big Thrifty drug store on the corner. My Lasik surgery paid off again.

There parked at the curb beside the sidewalk news stand was the silver late model Chevy Malibu I'd spotted as we'd left the house almost three hours earlier. A stocky white guy, tallish, wearing a blue satin Dodgers' logo jacket, sat on the passengers' side of the hood reading a USA Today paper, glancing toward the restaurant, trying to look casual. This told me two things. First, it wasn't his car. If the payment book has your own name on it, you don't risk mashing the sheet metal by parking your butt on it. Second, he was on the job, trying for 'incognito'. No one still *reads* *USA Today*.

As we made our way down the stairs he looked across and saw us. None too subtle, he tossed his paper into the sidewalk trash barrel as he made his way to the driver's door.

As we walked across the lot toward the GTO. I kept an eye on him. I opened Catherine's door and walked around to mine as he assumed his driver's seat.

I lit off the GTO, blipped the throttle a time or two for dramatic effect, backed from the space and drove toward the driveway ramp. I checked for traffic then turned left to travel south, uphill, on Laurel Canyon Boulevard. As I accelerated to forty in second gear, I kept an eye on the mirror. The Malibu took a set three cars back in the inside lane.

As I watched in the mirror I reached down and tightened my seat belt. Catherine noticed. "Street, you're quiet all of a sudden." She looked back toward the rear of the car. "Are we being followed?"

I looked across the cabin at her. "Yes, we are. But not very well and not for long," I glanced across the car. "You said you were a Rockford fan?"

She answered, "Sure. Beth Davenport was one of my role models for becoming an attorney. You, too, right?"

I shifted into third as we wound upward toward the Mulholland Drive intersection as I answered, "Sure. And I took notes and practiced a lot."

The response took a split second to 'take', then Catherine tightened her seat belt and put her right hand on the dashboard grab bar. Who knew women paid attention like that? I was impressed.

As the traffic wound uphill through the flowing curves approaching the Mulholland intersection, I signaled left and moved to what would become the thru-lane at the top of the hill. I let the car slow without using the brakes. The cars behind me slowed with me as we approached the light. As planned, I was first in line at the light, which turned yellow as I approached. I kept a steady momentum until the car behind me slowed, then I downshifted to second gear and accelerated, chirping the tires as they caught traction.

The car squirted across the intersection as the light turned red. The suspension stretched to full height then settled without anything scraping. Good. The Malibu, third car back in my lane, had to stop. Mission accomplished.

Traffic management mind games, L.A. style. I love 'em!

Now all I needed was a break, and one appeared as the white glow of the HID headlights swept the landscape past the intersection. A quarter-mile away a shorty diesel cab-over, towing a 'Star Wagon' mobile dressing room trailer was lumbering past the last of the uphill curves on the south slope of the road. You see these trucks all over the Southland, but I'd never appreciated one as much as that one that night.

I let the car coast down to 25 mph as the truck passed, then called out to Catherine, "Hold on!"

There was nothing within sight behind the truck so as it passed, I toed the parking brake and stabbed the gas. As the car broke traction, I cranked the steering wheel full-lock to the left. I released the parking brake as the rear of the car came around, let the steering wheel correct back to center. As we completed a perfect 180-degree turn I slammed the dashboard light switch with the heel of my left hand. The car went dark as I accelerated to hug the rear of the trailer ahead.

Thirty seconds later the Malibu flashed past speeding downhill. I gave a five count, turned the lights back on and followed the rig to the intersection. I took a right after waiting for the light. I looked at Catherine, who seemed really calm.

Deadpan, she asked, "Do you do that often?"

"Hardly ever. It can really tear up the tires. I did it once in Jersey in a police car, it got away from me and I T-boned a parked Jetta. Got on the TV news that night and everything." I checked the mirror again. "Let's get you back to my house and on your way home. I doubt I've seen the last of that guy."

By the time we left that intersection my pulse was back to normal. I took the right onto Mulholland then again onto Woodrow Wilson Drive and took the twisty hillside roads into Nichols Canyon to the flats east of Hollywood proper. We made it back to my house without incident.

Out of caution for Catherine I made a call as I drove out of the foothills. When the party answered, I asked, "You free?"

The other voice responded, "Yeah."

"My house, twenty minutes."

"Done."

14

September 29, 1996

The 'fish'—newcomer inmate—walked up to the older 'wood'—Caucasian—short-timer after the clot of inmates had filed through the chain link fence gate and dispersed to their racially-segregated areas of the yard. It was hot that day and the older inmate didn't extend a welcome of any kind. He just looked at the kid and frowned as he approached. The kid piped up first.

"Unnastan' you gettin' out nex' week."

The older man looked beyond the younger. "Yeah, kid. What's that to you?"

The kid flinched. He'd had a rough week. "Jus' makin' conversation, bro. Whatcha gon' do when ya git out?"

The question irritated the older inmate. He had nothing lined up. "I thought I'd rent a penthouse and write a novel, maybe win a Pulitzer. Whataya think?"

"Naw, man, ain't like that. Ya wanna job? Pays real good. It'd give ya a start, y'know?"

The older con frowned and finally looked at the kid. "What needs doin'?"

"Jus' a job, man. My lawyer said t' ax around, see if someone gittin' out need a job. You know guns, bro?"

Quietly, he answered, "Yeah, I know guns." He looked at the kid's face. First week. Scared to death. "What's the job?"

Quietly, the kid said, "See, doo like put me in here, we gonna 'ice' him."

"Okay. What's it pay?"

The kid was now more animated, genuinely excited about being taken seriously. "The job? Pays real good. Maybe like twenny grand. An' my boy take care of ya. He put ya up till it happens and maybe take ya to Vegas an' shit. That soun' good?"

"I'm listenin'" The man was starting to like what he was hearing. He had nothing else positive coming his way.

Sensing some degree of acceptance, the kid became manic and almost lyrical as he extolled the benefits of becoming a hired killer. "Perfect, man, 'at's perfect! My main bud be waitin' ta pick you up when you fixin' t' roll up outta here. We git a good thing goin', I pass the word an' my boy pick you up! He carry you t' the ranch, feed you some good food, git you some wine, maybe some twinny, gitchoo some strange, too! You up f'dat?"

He stayed calm. Nothing in memory that anyone had promised had ever come through, no reason to believe this clod either. His uppity bitch sister wouldn't care if he dropped dead in the street. Still... "Yeah, fish, I'm up for that."

"Bitchin', man! I pass the word!"

"Great. Done deal, fish. Make it happen." Strings. There were always strings. "Whataya want from me?"

The kid tilted his head and smiled shyly. "Well, y'know, like, you got cred up in here, man. Doo's listen t' you an' shit. Maybe pass the word, say ah'm a good doo', y'know? Maybe git me some breaks up in here since ahmo be here for a while."

The older inmate took a breath, held it for a few seconds, then let it out. "What's that in English, kid?" Receiving no clue of recognition, he said, "Okay, you want to keep the fags and the bro's and the muzzies off your ass, right fish?" He paused and looked at the clear blue sky above. "Tell ya what. You make this happen, you follow through, I'll pass the word around, and I'll talk to the guards about getting you a job so that your brains don't run out your ears. Though in your case it may be too late for that. You're gonna need something to do with your time."

"Cool, man!"

Calmly, the older man said, "You make the call, let me talk to your guy, do it in the next twenty-four, I'll hold up my end. Count on it."

Arnie Sutton, recently convicted murderer, sentenced to twenty-five years-to-life in the California Penal System, practically giggled in response. "I make the call! Ahmo do it! Thanks, homes!" He raised his fists in victory, the older con just gave him a 'Get real' look. A little shaky, he tapped the short timer on the shoulder as varied but great loads lifted from both their shoulders. He walked toward the bank of modified pay phones on the far side of the yard, his knees still weak and trembling from the exchange.

15

Thirty minutes later Catherine was on her way home with my clandestine escort keeping an eye on her, ready to run interference if there were any problems.

After a few quiet minutes at home, I went to the office, checked for emails and looked for something to do. I was surprised to find a message from the Warden at Chino, eight pages including the names of the inmates released in the time between Sutton's arrival and the Connors murders.

There were thirty-eight names on the list, including some that were overkill because of their criminal offenses, but I have always believed that too much information is preferable to not enough, every time. The proper search of the names and their connections would require an all-nighter that took me to the four corners of the nation online. I examined the release dates of each inmate along with their physical description, their original offense and their age at the time of their release. I was searching for a pair of stone-cold killers, one Caucasian, one Latino of specific builds so the overweight third-time embezzler from San Leandro and the black fifth-time car thief out of El Cajon' landed on the floor, destined for the shredder.

The winnowing process went fairly quickly. The tedious, almost mechanical process led me to a final subset that fit the general descriptions and were seemingly difficult to locate. My reward for the tedium was that, thanks to the internet, I was able to read some official crime reports, some of which had remained part of the inmates' prison record. At times those can be entertaining and enlightening, varying between high drama and high comedy but more often just decent human drama. When I was done, the final list of names went on the event board.

The first of my final four was Manuel Luis Vargas, a nineteen-year-old Hispanic gang banger from Lemon Grove, south of San Diego when his term began in 1990. He had been caught driving a stolen '87 Formula Firebird and he had a copious supply of pot along for the ride. He resembled the description of the Latino shooter and tattoos up the sides of his neck were his style statement. He'd been packin' heat at the time of his arrest, so I put him on the short list.

Option two was a bit more adventurous, a trust fund brat gone seriously sideways. Ronald Daniel Faubel was a complicated guy. He had earned a real estate license in California after losing a sizable inherited fortune at the Craps tables in Las Vegas. Increasingly desperate as his financial situation tanked, he used his winning smile and his cordial personality to become a swindler of sorts. His limited emotional range made some of his marks suspicious and he was soon found out. Sensing that the end was near he plotted against both sides of a transaction to help himself to a sizable pile of cash.

His chosen victim was an elderly widow who was in the process of selling a nice, expensive, historic house to a foreign national from the middle east. As intermediary he painted a picture of distrust to both sides. He established to the widow that the buyer shouldn't be trusted. He apologized to the buyer that the widow was such a bigot. After some drama, with the two parties never having met in person, a compromise was reached—the home would be paid for, in substantial part, with cash. He took the widow to the real estate office still keeping the two parties separate, and the cash was exchanged in a nice black leather attaché case. They always use black ones.

He took the widow back to the house for one last walk-through before the new owners took possession, and he soon excused himself to the bathroom. He went outside instead, donned a ski mask as he shed his coat and tie. Moments later he crashed back into the house determined to scare the woman and make off with the attaché full of money.

His invasion of the living room started just as the widow was welcoming her grandson, an L.A. county Sheriff's deputy and his partner, arriving during their lunch hour to accompany the widow to the bank with all that money. Faubel's day went downhill from there, with night stick whacks and handcuffs and *really deep* disappointment expressed by the widow, who had thought him 'such a nice young man'. That's what hurt him most.

Faubel was tried and convicted and served nine years for his crime. He had dropped from sight after his release. He has shown an opportunistic streak and he had gun training from high school, so I put him in the stack.

Former Marine Corp armorer Leonard Lee Stacy had decided to become a bank robber on the wrong day. It had started well. He had stolen a nice bland silver Toyota Corolla from an upscale medical facility parking lot in Newport Beach. He drove to Laguna Niguel where he had scoped out his bank target, a small but busy independent branch in the parking lot of a suburban shopping center. On the chosen day he had waited for the lone bank guard to go to lunch. It was warm that day, so he left the stolen Corolla idling at the curb with the A/C blowing ice cold as he went inside to liberate some cash.

Moments later ol' Leonard left the bank with a big bag full of long green. Happy and relieved, back in the car he paused for a few seconds to open the bag of cash and gaze upon his haul. Suddenly he realized that though the air conditioner was still thrumming away nicely, the Corolla itself had stopped running, having run out of gas while he was inside the bank. As he cranked away at the starter the sequentially timed dye packs inside the bag of cash started exploding. Moments later responding Orange County Sheriffs' Deputies found Leonard and the inside of his stolen Toyota covered with wet runny purple ink blotches. This made for a cool booking photo and a twelve-year stretch at Chino, after which Leonard had dropped from sight completely.

The fourth possibility was a car title conversion scammer from Santa Ana, Ricolito Gomez. He had ripped off his car-dealer owner/brother to the tune of twenty-one grand and his brother had dropped a dime on him. My kinda guy! Six years in prison had seen Gomez become a tough customer within the restrictive, racially segregated boundaries of the penal system. With a little more research, I found that he had been pulled in and questioned three times by the Santa Ana cops regarding suspicion for drive-by shootings prior to his theft arrest. According to prison records he had gravitated toward the violent side of the scale during his tenure at Chino so he earned a place in my 'final four'.

With the research completed I went to sleep for a few hours on the couch in the den. It really is a nice couch, and the housekeeper had left a down comforter draped over the back of it, for whatever reason. I worked out for an hour the next morning, something I tend to ignore when I'm absorbed in a job like this one. Late the next morning I returned to the office and began an online search for relatives of my final four suspects. The results rid me of the need for further study of Faubel and Vargas, whose ends had come in disparate manners, neither pleasant.

The heavily tattooed Vargas, jobless, hostile and alienated, had committed suicide in the bathtub of his mother's house in San Ysidro a year after his release, the event verified by a call to his sister in Chula Vista.

Faubel had been more productive. He had turned his life around. He was making decent money working as an assistant mortgage broker in San Bernardino and had just married one of his associates when he and his new bride were killed in the rollover crash of their Ford Explorer in the median strip of Interstate Fifteen north of Barstow in 1998, verified through California Highway Patrol accident records.

It was an hour I'd never get back, but it provided a reason to narrow my focus to the final remaining suspects. A bit more computer time verified that the final two potentials had dropped from sight immediately after their release from custody. Each had violated the terms of their parole. After I located the surviving relatives for the pair, I made calls to set up visits.

16

The prison yard was abuzz with activity that Monday afternoon as the older inmate muscled his way to the front of the line for the three pay phones with the fish in tow. At the phone bank the fish hit the digits and spoke first to the party at the other end.

"Hey, G! How's it hangin'?"

"Good Arn. You find our guy? You have someone we can put to work?"

"Yeah, 'G'. Good doo', gittin' out tamorra. He's right here wit' me. Name's Stacy."

"Good, Arn. Let me talk to him."

"Kay." Sutton moved aside and gave the handset to the older man.

Into the receiver, he asked, "Hey, I'm Stacy. You 'G'?"

"Yeah, I'm 'G'. There's an audience for these phones, right?"

"Always. What needs doin'?"

"Close quarters technical work, involves the use of personal protection devices. One-day gig, all expenses paid."

"Whatsit pay?"

"Twenty or so."

Stacy looked at the kid standing beside him and said, "Whoa, dude, kid said thirty. Don't be lowballin' me, man!"

'G' exhaled audibly. "Jesus! Okay, thirty! Shit! The extra can come outta his bank. When you ready to bounce?"

"Releases start at noon based on seniority, I'll be on the curb out front by one."

Grant Carty answered, "Okay, bro, look for a Chevy truck, stylin' ride, in the parkin' lot across from the front gate. Oh, and see if you can dial in another helper too. I need a pair of workers. Shorter money though for that one. Got that?"

"I can do that. You be there. Can you get me some cold brew for the trip too? It's been a while, y'know?"

Carty exhaled heavily again. This guy was gonna be a pain in the ass. "Yeah, sure. You gonna need anything else?"

"Nah, man. Just you an' that brew."

"Fine. See you then. Now gimme back to Arnie."

Stacy stepped aside, happy and hopeful for the first time in years, and gave the phone back to Arnie Sutton. Arnie asked, anxiously, "That gonna work, 'G'?"

"Yeah, Arn, that'll work. You need to let me set the budgets for this stuff. Our friend will bonus you next time you see him. Ok?"

"Bongelli? Yeah, bro. that's fine."

"Names, Arn. No names! Fine. Hang up now."

"'Kay, 'G'", he said to a dead line.

17

I spent another sunny, eighty-degree Saturday afternoon on the road. My first stop was the Gomez car dealer in Santa Ana. It would be an eventful day.

A few clicks south of the Disney resort complex and all the fancy hotels in Anaheim, Harbor Boulevard, south of the 22 Freeway overpass, turns into a gaudy ribbon of taco stands, check cashing stores and used car lots, most catering to the area's Hispanic majority. Near the south end of 'Auto Row', the Gomez dealership had grown considerably since the owner's brother had taken a powder. It was now a block long complex displaying dozens of shiny Camrys, Explorers, Grand Ams and Suburbans, many displaying quickie repaints and salvage titles. His advertising and signage indicated that he would finance anyone who could fog a mirror.

I parked the GTO near the rear of the lot diagonally across from the bright blue concrete block building that served as the facility's anchor. As I exited the car a stocky well-dressed, middle aged Hispanic man approached. He had thick black hair and deep-toned skin. He wore a dark brown sport coat over a black shirt with tan slacks and black loafers. He looked like a car salesman.

He approached me and extended his hand. "You must be Mister Street."

"I'm him." We shook hands and exchanged cards.

He looked at the GTO. "I used to sell a lot of these. My dad did as well. He had this dealer for years before I took over. None as nice as this one though. It must have cost you a lot to build it."

I smiled. "You have no idea. This car and I go back a long way." I looked past him at his lot. "Man! This place is huge! How's business?"

"It's just okay so far this year. We work hard at it. It takes a lot of time and effort. The economy sucks right now so we have to work double time just to get these people financed, then we have to deal with the damn repos. We had to go find two just last night." He paused for a moment and looked at me. "None of that is your concern, though. Thank you for coming down. What can I tell you about my brother?"

"I'm just curious when you last saw him. I'm looking for information regarding an old legal matter for a client and his name came up. I'm curious about the time around his release from Chino. Is there anything you can tell me about that?"

Mario looked at me and frowned as he recalled the events regarding his brother. He spoke with a Spanish lilt to his sentences. "Okay. Let's see. That was thirteen, fourteen years ago. When he got out of prison, he took a bus from Chino to Santa Ana, then he stayed here. I gave him the extra room off the shop, starting out at the bottom as a 'lot boy', just like anyone else. I thought he'd be here for a while, getting back on his feet. He did a good job at first. I was impressed. Then a week or so later he got a visit from a friend and he took a Saturday off work."

Mario cleared his throat and continued, "When he came back that Sunday, he told me he had an offer for a better job. I understood that, I was happy for him. He needed a victory, even if he didn't appreciate the value of what I was providing for him here. When I asked him about the job, he wouldn't answer. His friend came for him that Sunday, and that was the last time I saw my brother, ever."

"Tell me about the friend."

Now Mario became more adamant. "Pffft! I'll be blunt, Mister Street. He was trouble. Seedy looking white guy, and I had a bad feeling about him from the first time I saw him. Look, I deal with dozens of people every day, and I've carried my own paper for over two decades. That's *my* money, so you better damn well believe I can read people! I told Rico, 'Be careful! Think about what you're doing', but the die was cast. There was nothing else I could do at that point. I felt sorry for him, I thought maybe I'd been a little rough on him, but...God forgive me for this...I was glad to see him leave that day." He removed his sunglasses and wiped a few beads of sweat from his forehead with a pocket handkerchief.

"I can understand that. It has to have been rough on you."

"I think my brother is dead for many years, Mister Street. If you determine anything about his fate or locate his body, would you please advise me? Our mother passed away three years ago, and she was hurting in her last years, convinced that her youngest son had met his end without his family. If he is dead, we would hope that we could recover his remains so that he could be buried in the family plot in Juarez. I would appreciate your help in that event."

I looked at him. "Mario, you don't even need to ask. If I find anything, you'll be the first to know."

"Thank you for that."

"I know it's been a long time, Mario, but do you have anything that may have belonged to your brother? If we do find any sign of him, we will need to establish identity. DNA is the best method for that. Anything, a hair brush, a toothbrush, even an unwashed t-shirt or socks would help."

"I think there was a footlocker he'd had for many years. It's probably in the garage at home. I'll see if it's still there."

"That would help a lot. Did you see the vehicle that this white guy was driving the day he picked up your brother?"

"Certainly. I remember it like it was yesterday." He paused, "It was a Chevy S-10, midnight blue, extended cab, probably '95 or '96. Grey guts, white letter Goodyears on a good set of custom wheels, and a fancy tape graphics kit on the sides. It looked good. It had a paper plate in a license frame that said, "Sunset Motors' in Jarupa. There was a temp tag on the rear slider window, the number was'10', so October." He looked at me and chuckled. "I'm sorry, Mister Street, cars are my life. I can't help it."

"Mario, I'm glad. Thank you! This is a big help. I'll be in touch if I locate anything at all regarding your brother. I see how busy this place is. I'll let you get back to work." We shook hands again. I saw him walking back toward his office as I drove off the lot onto south-bound Harbor Boulevard.

18

Okay, so far so good. I was one-for-one, gaining an important piece of information that bolstered my developing theory. If only my next visit had been as positive.

I took the I-5 to south coastal Orange County, where the really pricey homes rest atop the foothills west of the I-5 corridor—prime properties hidden behind guard-staffed gates, the better of those having views of both the hazy technicolor landscape to the east and the vast blue Pacific to the west. One such home in one of the more-elite hilltop enclaves was home to the ever-confident Cheryl Ann Hayes the somewhat younger half-sister of the elusive Arnold Lee Stacy. Her Facebook page displayed the visage of an attractive and well-kept forty-year-old wife of a successful import car broker as well as images of her beauty pageant wins from half her life ago. She'd been a major babe back then.

The house was an immense grey brick manse, probably five years or so old, maybe 6000 square feet and five million bucks at the top of the market, way fancier than my place. It was built sixty feet back from the divided street with its string of palm trees in the wide median strip. Eight tall deep-tinted windows with black shutters on each side spread across the front of the house, behind a wide front porch and a black wrought iron perimeter fence. Tall brick stanchions at the corners of the curved fence matched the color balance of the home.

I parked at the curb and walked up the tiled driveway, past the metallic black Lexus convertible, to the wide, dark grey brick walkway then stood on the porch and rang the doorbell. I could hear deep chimes resounding within the house. Momentarily the glass-paned left side of the tall twin front doors swung open and the petite, blonde Ms. Hayes appeared. She was attractive and well dressed with some kind of filmy yellow linen top and a short white skirt. Her jewelry was as color coordinated as the exterior of the house itself. As she looked at me, I introduced myself and offered my business card. She just looked at the card, making no move toward accepting it. I took that as a sign.

"Mister...Street? You're the one who called earlier?"

"Yes ma'am. I'm a private investigator from L.A., I'm looking at a legal situation and your brothers' name came up. Wondering about the last time you saw him. He had been released from the State Prison at Chino a little over thirteen and a half years ago. Did you or your family talk to him or spend any time with him back then?"

She sounded angry and bitter as she answered. "No, we did not. He had been the family pariah for most of his life, and he put my mother in her grave. As far as I'm concerned, he's in Hell where he belongs." I noticed that all her references were 'I' and "Me'. A real charmer, this one.

I smiled. What else could I do? "Well, if I run into him, I'll be sure to pass on your fond regards."

She didn't want to play along. "Don't bother. You'll have to excuse me, Mister Street. I have neither interest in him nor time for you. Please leave the property, now."

'Click'. I try to be nice. I really do, but some people just set me off. Sorry.

"Y'know, you'll never win Miss Congeniality with a crappy attitude like that. Pop a Valium or something and listen up."

She started to respond. I frowned and put my hand up to distract her as I continued.

"Madam. I'm trying to find some information to create a time-line for events around the time your crummy brother was released from prison. A really good man and his wife were brutally murdered back then, and Arnold Lee may have been involved. The victims were great people—the man a living legend. People who never even knew him were impacted by the loss. I'm doing my job to find the killers. I'm sorry to have bothered you. I'll continue without your input. Frankly, having met you I can't imagine you having any interest in anything or anyone beyond the perimeter of your own noontime shadow. You have a nice day, though, okay?"

She seethed through clenched, expensively capped teeth, "You *asshole*. You don't know me!"

Already walking away, I called back, "Lucky me! I wouldn't want to."

I walked back down the driveway to the car as the heavy door slammed behind me, sounding a bit like a distant cannon shot. After I departed the hilltop sanctuary, I drove south on PCH another twenty miles to the seaside village of Laguna Woods to take a look at the residence of the man long accused of the planning and execution of the Connors murders.

From the Coast highway I wound westward a mile to an odd-appearing and truly out-of-place mobile home park. I felt as if I'd driven across a time warp speed bump into 1977. The trailers were mostly very modest pastel-hued single-wides of various shapes and vintages, and most displayed declining conditions.

Space 3-C, to the left on the second aisle from the viewpoint of the beach, the one with the familiar ragged Eldorado parked in the lean-to carport, was home to Ray Cole and his father Quinton, aged 84. The trailer was a chalky oxidized off white twelve-wide with faded pale peach colored trim and weathered, sagging wooden exterior additions. It wasn't the worst of the trailers crammed into the breezy, picturesque six-acre plot but it was no prize. Kudzu vines draped off the top edge of the unit falling onto the open panes of the Jalousie windows. Two green plastic garbage bins, decorated with a sloppy '3-c' in red spray paint, sat in front of the overgrown sidewalk.

I parked in front and rang the doorbell, then stood in the landing as the structure creaked from the movement within. A voice from behind the door called, "Who is it?"

I spoke to the door. "Ray Cole? I'm Street. We talked briefly the other day in Seal Beach."

The splintered wooden door shuffled open and a pale, shirtless, saggy Ray Cole became visible in the space. "Yeah, Street. How're things? You checkin' up on me?"

"Not at all, Ray. I was in the area and wanted to give you a 'heads up'. I'm looking into the Connors' matter a little further, taking a different angle that may lead away from you. I just wanted to let you know. One way or another, I intend to get to the bottom of it, so we may have to talk again. That okay with you?"

"Sure. Anything I can do to help, lemme know. I don't need to carry this shit around wit' me for the rest of my life."

I looked around the area beyond the trailer and asked, "How long have you and your dad lived here?"

"Daddy bought the trailer over twenty years ago after Mama died. He was certain he was gonna seize up and fall over for the final time in a few weeks, then he didn't, y'know? I had money back then. I got him this space in this freakishly beautiful location. The zoning and tenancy here is grandfathered in until 2015. He's on the final glide path, he'll be gone by then. Hell, I may be, too. After that it'll be redeveloped. It'll bring a million dollars or better to anyone with a little slice of it. When you drive out, go one row over and check the beach view past the ravine for the train tracks. It is *perfect*."

"I'll do that. Do you own it outright?"

Cole looked at me, seemingly reading my mind. Wearily, he answered, "Yeah, Street. Free and clear. In my dad's name. No mortgages. It's his only asset. I use his SSI to pay the utilities and buy a little food. There's no ill intent whatsoever. I'm no criminal master-mind, regardless of what you may suspect."

I looked at him. His plight was mostly of his own making but I still felt at least a little sympathy for him. I offered my hand, he shook it. "Understood. Anything comes up, I'll let you know. You do the same?"

"Sure, Street."

Back in the car I drove toward the ledge that overlooked the Pacific. The view, the pearl blue sky and the azure water meeting at the horizon, was stunning. The Pacific always was for me. In the ravine sixty feet below, the Amtrak commuter train whirred past on its way south toward San Diego. I regained the freeway a few minutes later and made my way north with plenty of new refer-ences in my mind.

Despite the second-stop snub I considered the day a great success. I now had important evidence regarding a key element in one of the potential shooters. This was still a speculative investigation but I could sense real progress. The verification of repeated sightings of the same Chevy S-10 truck was the most important aspect yet. It tied Rico Gomez and the truck's driver to the Connors murders. That was an important piece to the puzzle but I still felt as if I was moving sideways at breakneck speed.

Catherine had done some surprising research herself, uncovering another key element in the puzzle. She called me to discuss it. I took the 'wilderness route' toll road from south Orange County toward the 91 to Riverside for a face-to-face.

I entered the small, well-appointed foyer and took a seat as I waited for her last client to exit. My eyes wandered around the room to the various framed landscape photos, recognizing the Nevada desert and the finer points of Cabo San Lucas. Catherine led her client through to the front door and welcomed me into her office. She took her seat behind the desk; I sat in the client chair.

"This is a first-time visit, isn't it?"

"Numero uno. We're even. So who's the picture?"

"That's my fiancé, Tom." She smiled as she looked at the picture. That's a good sign.

"Good looking guy. Congratulations!" I wanted to get to business right away. "Well," I started, "we have some major developments. I have new information on the Connors' shooters." I told her of the phone search for suspects and described my 'final two' of the inmates released from Chino.

She listened, took notes, then looked up at me. "You've been busy. Me, too." She handed me a printout from her side of the desk. "I looked up the car dealer you mentioned. It's gone as of five years ago. The California dealers' license was held by a Nevada holding corporation, so the names are held confidential in casual examinations like ours. State law in Nevada. Resident agent, no shock, Vincent Bongelli, Esquire."

"So another log on that fire?"

Catherine opined, "Yes. It says a lot. We'll have more in a few days. There are many wrong things possible and Bongelli could face serious penalties if he's skating as much as it seems he is. Some of the corporation mills in SoCal have taken some big hits recently. A couple of the noisier proponents have been indicted."

"Yeah, that one based in Anaheim who did all the advertising was a real trip. His middle name should be 'Who, me?'. Do you think Bongelli could be as big a problem?"

She responded after a few seconds. "I doubt it. His specialty is hiding resources for his incarcerated clients. He seems to be quite focused in his dealings. The shadier operators seem to trip over their own words sooner or later. Bongelli's better than that. We'll wait and see." She paused. "One more thing. Do you want to talk to Sutton's father?"

"Absolutely! He's on my 'short list'."

"Well, I found him. He lives in a suburb of San Diego, the same address for forty-one years."

"Great! Let me have the address and phone number. I'll call him and set up a visit for tomorrow. What else have you found?"

"Well we have a new ally. My college roommate works for the

Nevada Secretary of State's office in Carson City. She's in our corner on this. In her spare time at work, she's compiling a complete file for us regarding Bongelli's corporate set-ups. I'll have that by mid-week."

It seemed as if the teamwork was starting to show some results. "Sounds great!"

"The Sheriff's deputy you spoke with called me the other day. You made a good impression on him."

Deputy Wallace? Yeah, he was a great help. He also reminded me of my love of independence. No more cubicles for me, thanks."

"Understood. I don't miss the D.A.'s office, either. I'm curious. Does your criminology training come into play in this type of work?"

"Not really. That's one thing I like about cold cases like this one, there's less squishy stuff and more mystery. In something like this it's more important to find the common elements of various times and places. Today, for instance, I found that one particular dark blue Chevy pickup was seen at multiple sites in the company of one person of interest in the Connors' murders. It doesn't guarantee a slam dunk but it does add weight to the evidence at hand. Add enough weight, give it a little nudge, maybe it'll fall on someone."

"Okay," she smiled, "that sounds like something one of your fictional heroes would say."

"You got me. I crib from the best."

I drove home an hour later and spent a couple of hours poring over Catherine's trial transcripts. It was an illuminating session after an illustrious day and it firmed up my respect for my allies in this effort including the late, great, Ron Connors.

I had intended to take the evening off, but I started studying Catherine's notes on the Sutton prosecution, got 'into it', and finally crashed at 1a.m. That night I took a shower and used the bed and everything.

20

March 6, 1995

Rick Damarow looked in the rear-view mirror of his 'arrest-me-red' IROC-Z Camaro as he traveled west on the Ten freeway toward L.A. He saw the image of the tall copper-color '90s Bronco a half-mile back. He had just left the Morongo Casino, an hour east of the city. He'd traveled east this time to glom onto another 'conquest' sale. He didn't expect to see Carty that far out in 'the sticks', but there he was. Rick Damarow started to sweat as he considered his options when he saw how the truck had gained on his position on the freeway. He decided to try to find a crowded environment as soon as possible so he sped toward the nearest off-ramp.

As he coasted to a stop at the top of the Sierra Avenue off-ramp, waiting for the light to change, he looked back again, seeing the big white letters of the tall off-road tires, three cars back. His pulse quickened. He popped the lid on the center console to access the little pistol he'd started carrying, just in case. As the light changed he took a quick right, then a left across the intersection to the big ARCO AM/PM station on the opposite corner of Valley Boulevard.

He rushed to the middle bank of gas pumps and stopped, again checking the mirror. He hadn't been followed onto the property. Relieved, still shaking, he looked off to the west to see the Bronco travelling west.

21

Sunday morning came early. I had called ahead then I drove south on I-5 past the stadium in downtown San Diego to reach the inland route. Along the north side of Highway 94 past the Home Avenue exit I found a modest older neighborhood, home to Henry Eugene Sutton and his wife Sylvia for the last 41 years. I parked on a mildly sloping street in front of a nicely maintained frame and stucco single story home. A thin elderly Caucasian man wearing a pink and grey vertically striped shirt and grass-stained khakis stood watering his lawn from a pistol grip sprayer at the end of a faded green plastic water hose. As I exited the car, he released the trigger and the water dribbled to a stop.

"Mister Sutton?" I called as I closed the car door.

"Yessir. You the fellow who called?" he approached the sidewalk.

"I'm him. My name's Street." We met on the sidewalk. "Your lawn looks great. I wish I had the time to keep mine this nice." I leaned against the car as we talked.

"Well, thank you, son. It takes a lot of work. Sometimes I wonder if it's all worth it. Hot day like today, a condo starts to sound really good." He wiped his forehead with a checked handkerchief then he looked up at me. "What can I do for you, Mister Street?"

"As I told you on the phone, I'm looking at your son's conviction in connection with another matter and I need some information. I hope you can help.

As he knelt coiling his water hose he asked, "You talk to the boy yet?"

"I did. Last week at Chino."

"Yeah, he's back down here, is he? How's he doin'?"

"I'll be honest with you. I've seen better. His time away has not been kind to him."

He frowned. "No, I didn't expect it would be. I wrote him off years ago." He rose and looked at me as he spoke. "I know that sounds bad, but a man's got to manage his family relationships, regardless how it hurts. All our energy was going to him in those last years. The strain he put me and my wife through that last coupla years he was in high school was ridiculous. I know part of it is my fault, I was so busy with my job, I let a lot of things slip."

"I can understand that sir, but past a certain point, he chose his own path. I know he had a lot of help in his downturn. Do you remember any of the kids he hung out with back then? Maybe his friends from school?"

"More'n I want to, son. You got anyone in mind?"

"Who was around when he started his downward spiral?"

Henry Sutton sniffed his derision. "The only one there is, son, is the one did it all to him, his 'good buddy', that Carty punk, son of the asshole broke up our marriage. They was stepbrothers for five years, during which time he went from being a decent kid—not perfect, I'm sayin', but basically good—to being a thief and a liar and an all-around dirt bag." He looked at me. "Do you know how hard it is for me to say that about my youngest son, Mister Street? Damn near kills me."

"I can appreciate that, Mister Sutton." I had seen the thick gold band on his ring finger. "I'm unclear. Your wife is Arnie's stepmother?"

"No. I remarried her after that asshole died and she came back home. We'd been together since we were twenty, and then all of a sudden both of us were alone. It seemed like a good idea at the time. She's gone to the market now. She'll be back in a few minutes." He looked up the hill from his home, then he looked at me. "You want a beer? Some ice water? Let's go out back." He carried the hose to its place beside the front porch and I followed him around the side of house toward a weathered concrete slab patio at the rear. We sat at a canopied patio set. We had passed his midnight blue Cadillac CTS coupe parked in front of his two-car garage at the back of the property.

It was the first of the coupes I'd seen and it was impressive. I said, "You have good taste in cars, Henry."

He smiled and looked toward the car. "Thank you. I give myself a new ride every couple of years. Maybe it's a reward for surviving. I don't put a lot of miles on 'em anymore. I guess it's just somethin' to have because I like it. That make sense to you?"

I smiled. "More than you know. My obsession is parked at the curb out front." Henry had stuck his hand into an ancient aluminum ice chest and withdrew a cold tall can of Coors Light. I popped the top and took a sip of the cold brew. He took one for himself then he closed the lid on the ice chest. He explained, "He was maybe seventeen, just goin' into his senior year, and he had a buncha friends, some of 'em good-fer-nothins, used to hang out together all the time. Sylvia and I were havin' our problems, an' we just let too much slide by."

"What was he into back then? I didn't get much from him when we talked."

Henry spread his hands. "That doesn't surprise me. There's probably not a lot for him to tell anymore. He was always a follower instead of initiating anything on his own. He had his circle of friends, but he always did *their* thing. I think they call it 'creative energy', and he didn't have any of that. He even adopted their speech patterns. That used to bug the crap out of me."

I was being patient with Henry, but he wasn't giving me

anything of value at this point. I heard a car approach and saw a faded blue-grey mid-90's Hyundai Accent pulled into the space next to the Cadillac. It sounded as if it needed spark plug wires.

"There's Sylvia now. Gimme a minute." He rose from his chair and walked to the driver's side of her car as she opened her door.

He talked to her, a little too loudly, in a stern tone. "Sylvia, this boy wants t'see some pictures of Arnie. You still got some of that crap out here in the garage somewhere, don'cha?"

Sylvia was a tired looking woman in her sixties. She had been attractive when she was younger, but now she just looked worn down. Her back was slightly stooped, and her hair was tinted toward black with grey roots showing. Her long light blue cotton dress looked as tired as she did. She exited her car and walked silently to the side door of the garage as Henry returned to the patio and resumed his seat.

He spoke quietly and restated his tale of marital woe. Watching her, he repeated, "Me and her split up a few weeks before Arnie graduated high school. We divorced and she ran off with Carty senior. They'd met at a Neighborhood Watch meeting. She came back about eight years later, after that asshole died. Here she comes now."

He rose from his chair and walked to her as she cleared the garage. "Whataya got?" He practically snatched the stack of photos from her hand, then said, "You go get your stuff on into the house, let us talk." She hadn't said a single word. Henry was starting to get on my nerves, and I wondered how to deal with it.

He turned back to the table and started sorting through the photos, settling on one in particular. "There's the bastard!" He passed me a snapshot of two teenage boys standing in front of a single-engine Cessna plane sitting in front of a hangar displaying a large Civil Air Patrol sign. One boy displayed a solo-flight certificate and the accompanying FAA Pilot License, the other gazed admiringly at the trophies.

The connection fell into place in my head. I pointed at the

figure holding the license and asked, "Mister Sutton, who is this? Is this Arnie?"

"Him? That's Arnie on the right and that piece o' shit's Grant Carty." His voice carried a note of distaste as he pointed to the figures.

I asked for clarity's sake I asked, "Henry, did Arnie get flight training along with Grant?"

He had taken another slug of his Coors. "No, that was just Grant. Arnie wanted to do that, we told him to get his grades up, but that didn't happen. Grant's ol' man didn't restrict his kid at all. That was part of the problem! He had all the toys, did all the fun stuff, got everything he ever asked for, and he dragged Arnie along most of the time. In the end he was just a dirtbag, and of course Arnie just idolized him."

"Sure. How long were Arnie and Grant tight?"

Henry was more agitated now. "Forever! Like I told ya, bastard's daddy stole my wife. Boys was stepbrothers for about five years, inseparable as Arnie got sucked into every shitty situation imaginable. They ruined my boy, Mister Street. I coulda just killed 'im!" As he finished, he exhaled wearily.

Henry didn't seem to be a guy who wore his heart on his sleeve, so the emotion in his voice and the tear that ran down from his left eye said a lot. Still, this meeting had provided the best evidence I'd found in a week. "I understand that Mister Sutton. When is the last time you saw Grant Carty?"

He looked away trying to recall, then he answered, "I think the last time was at the Sprint Car races up at Irwindale Speedway, one Thanksgiving, had to be seven, eight years ago. And of course he looked like hell."

"Do you know where he was living after he and Arnie left school?"

"Back then he was livin' with his daddy, coupla miles from here. Then after the boys got outta school they did a lot out in Riverside. More recently he had bought some property in Nevada, somewhere up past Vegas. Good place for him, out in the middle of nowhere so he can't hurt people."

"New subject: How long since you've seen your granddaughter?"

Henry lit up. "Lylie? We see her every three or four months. Her grandparents bring 'er down here from Las Vegas and we go to Sea World or Balboa Park or some such. That little girl is a star! She may be the only good thing came outta all this stuff. Her mama's a mess but her folks are great people. We're real proud of her!"

As he spoke, I made another trip through the snap shots, finding nothing substantial. "May I borrow this picture, Mister Sutton? And could I get a number for Lylie's grandparents in Las Vegas?"

"Sure!" He pushed the pictures toward me. "Take the whole pile. I don't care. The number's by the phone." He started to rise from his chair, then paused and asked, "Mister Street, is there some small chance that your work will somehow benefit my boy? Now granted, I think he should pay his debt to society. He has that coming. But do you think he'll get out of prison at some point, even if me and his mama don't live to see it?"

"Mister Sutton, I am working on a matter that may prove that your son is only partly responsible for the murder for which he was convicted. I'm certain that as you described, he was just following orders. It's pretty clear that he wasn't the ringleader. We're looking for the parties responsible for that crime in connection with another matter. If that comes around it may eventually help him. I have to say though, he's not a sympathetic character at this point in time. It'll be a tough sell. I promise that if I find anything that would help, I'll let you know."

Henry frowned, looked back at me and said, "Fair enough. Let me get you that number." He rose from his chair and entered the rear of the house through a wood-frame screen door that slapped as it closed. As he returned a minute later, he carried a torn sheet of typing paper with the number written in pencil. As he settled, he leaned forward and passed me the paper. I folded it over and inserted it into my shirt pocket.

We talked a bit more, about Padres' baseball, the weather and life in San Diego then we rose from the table and walked around to the front of his house. Standing on the sidewalk next to the GTO I took a business card, wrapped it in three hundred-dollar bills and inserted it into his shirt pocket.

"Henry, you have helped me more than you will ever know. Now I need you and your wife to do something for me. It's very important to me that you do this."

"What do you need, Mister Street?"

"I need you to go warm up that Caddy, then I need you and your wife to get dressed up really nice and go have dinner tonight, on me. It *has* to be somewhere nice and fancy, now. No half-measures! Can you do that for me?"

He took the bills out of his pocket, looked at them and looked back at me, as if the idea of an evening out with his wife was some alien concept. "Mister Street, now, that is not necessary at all." He looked at the bills again and back at me and said, "You know, we haven't done that in hell of a long time. That'd be nice for a change." He paused again and started a thin smile. "You're on. We'll do that."

I was relieved at his response. "Good! I'm glad to hear that. Thank you both. I appreciate your time. Have a great day." I shook hands with him again then I regained the car and drove back down the hill.

I had mixed feelings about the Suttons themselves, but I was also aware that with this new evidence, Grant Carty was a key suspect in the Damarow murder and was starting to look good for the Connors killings as well. The kid with the FAA ticket in the picture fit perfectly with my mind's eye image of the driver of the blue truck.

I felt as much sympathy for the Suttons as I did apathy for their largely useless incarcerated son. I could see that their personal histories trapped them in a series of perpetual re-enactments, rendering them unwilling and unable to forget old troubles and move forward. I'd seen it before, closer to home, and I'd hated every minute of it. I hoped that Henry had taken the hint.

As I resumed the I-5, I punched in the speed dial for Catherine's office and left a message. "I found the identity of our pilot, and I have the contact info for Suttons' daughter and her mom. Stuff is startin' to cook!

22

The trial had fallen apart for the defense after the first day. The Prosecution had brought in the kid's uncle as a witness. He was a popular figure, even the defense attorney had known who he was, and dammit he came across like Moses he was so straight. Then after two days the private detective started his testimony and told all he knew, too. Now all Vinnie Bongelli could do was tap dance and hope that it went better than anyone expected.

The kid was completely out of his element and had no clue how to respond or what to say. He leaned toward his expensive counsel at one point late in the trial and asked, "You gonna put me on the stand, man?"

Bongelli looked at his client as if he was a fresh bird dropping on the windshield of his new car. He sniffed his derision and spoke through clenched teeth behind a shielding hand. "Hell no, kid. You just sit there and shut the hell up and let me think."

Bongelli waited for a pause in the proceedings, then he turned to Arnie Sutton and gave him the grim news. He whispered, "Alright, kid, we're sunk here. It looks like you're gonna buy some time. I'm sorry about that, but I can't save all you assholes." He cleared his throat and looked to the front of the courtroom to listen to the judge's order on a procedural matter, then he continued. "I'll try to minimize the damage, get you placed somewhere close where your family can come visit you. You'll get a nice allowance monthly from your business investments, and I'll run appeals as the opportunity allows, same as I do for the others. We'll take care of you, don't worry." He looked at the kid—what a mess. He lowered his shielding hand and whispered through clenched teeth, trying to avoid direct eye contact with this scum, "Now sit back there and shut the fuck up."

23

The information I'd retrieved from my trip to San Diego was a great help to the investigative effort, but as I drove home that afternoon, I started to wonder what was next on the agenda. My newest leads seemed to be pointing me towards Nevada, seemingly the favored location of several parties close to the histories of Grant Carty and Arnie Sutton.

I stopped by the house for a few minutes to check for phone messages and pick up my shoulder rig and pistol. I drove toward the Valley on the raggedy old Hollywood freeway, and made a stop at a friend's business in the flats of Burbank for a little firearms practice, a few new toys, some reloads and some creative input. As I left the house, I noticed a curb-hugging non-descript silver solo-occupied sedan parked down the block. Slow learners.

Ziggy, a tall, thin seventyish 'character', was one of my closest friends. He was a semi-retired actor/stuntman, an ex-L.A. County Sheriff's Deputy, and a longtime gun shop owner. The stories of his exploits were endless, and endlessly entertaining and he was always good for a new perspective on just about any subject. I had learned for instance, of his opinion that Country Music had been vastly improved in the last twenty years. 'Why is that?' I'd asked. 'A new bunch of cosmetic surgeons moved to Nashville', he'd answered. Made sense to me.

I'd met Zig during my first month in L.A. He had become a close friend and an important ally. That afternoon he stood behind the front counter of his glass-fronted Magnolia Boulevard shop space, dust cloth in hand. "Street! How you doin', brother?"

"Hey Zig! Doing well." I reached into my shirt pocket. "Here is your check for your run to Riverside, I really appreciate it." He took the check, looked at it, then folded it and put it under the coin tray in his antique cash register.

"I'm glad to help, Street, any time. Just ask! I'll take any excuse to bring out the Norton." He laid the cloth on the glass cabinet and turned to the shelves behind the counter. He withdrew a light blue box from the top shelf and tilted it open for me to see. "Your camera order came in yesterday, 'C'. It's pretty cool. Solar battery charger, twelve meg, and there's a motion detector built right in. Reaction time, 'on' to full focus is about three seconds. That's not the absolute fastest available, but it should be sufficient for your use. Neat little piece."

"Done. You like it, Zig, that's good enough for me. Let me have a pair of them." I was distracted. I had taken the camera and pointed it across the street at the car that had followed me to the shop.

Zig noted my distraction. "Something up, Street?" He looked out the window now, to the car parked at the curb across Magnolia Boulevard.

"Looks like I have an escort for the day. He picked me up as I left the house. It may be the same guy I saw earlier in the week."

Zig stood beside me and looked out the tinted shop window. "Silver Buick? Idling at the curb with the windows up and the A/C on? He needs to toughen up if he's gonna take you on."

I had long been familiar with the layout of Zig's storefront. Still looking out the window, I asked, "Zig, is your back door unlocked?"

He had already started through the door to the rear storeroom, "It will be in thirty seconds."

We left the showroom, walked through the hallway between the stockroom and the indoor practice range. I exited through the side door and walked across Magnolia toward the silver Buick. The driver, the same stocky white guy with greying temples from the restaurant a few days before, put the car into gear and accelerated from his parking space, cutting off a pickup truck approaching from the corner. I snapped an image of the rear of the car from my cell phone as he squealed away, then I returned to the door of Zig's shop.

"He didn't want to talk," I said, "But I got the plate number and the rental agency." I held up the image on the phone screen.

As we walked back to the showroom, Zig made a face, then asked, "Wanna have some fun with him?" I looked at him as he continued. "Let me call the rental agency and get him in a little hot water."

"Go for it." I handed him the phone. He sent the image to his desktop computer. As it arrived, he tapped the number of the agency, then pressed the button for the speaker. He stepped out of range for feedback as the recorded line gave its spiel.

"Thank you for calling the response desk for Metro Rent-a Car in Riverside California. Please leave your message after the beep, we will respond during business hours."

Zig enabled his 'frightened onlooker voice' as he started, "Oh ma *Gawd*, that *MAN!* He almost hit a *school bus!* He was drivin' one o' yore cars!" He gave the license number and a description of the car, then a name and phone number for their response. He'd play that up later as well. Changing back to his own voice, he asked, "Think that'll work?"

"Z-man, you deserve an Emmy. You said the thermal imager had arrived, too. I probably need one of those." I had talked myself into the purchase of many cool items at Zig's.

He turned and took a foot-long package from the shelf behind him and laid it on the counter in front of me. "It's a thing of beauty. It's best used for what the military would call 'soft incursions'. It won't penetrate structures but it's good for distance and through windows. It's not quite as fancy as the ones the LAPD uses, but they have the older model. This one is almost as good but its smaller and lighter and it costs less. This one should be fine for your use unless you have to fight zombies or ISIS or something. And it attaches with a lanyard so you won't lose it when some pit bull chases you." He grinned at that last.

I smiled at the reference. A year before I had dropped a really good camera into a swimming pool after I jumped a chain link fence to escape a pair of pit bulls who were chasing me up an alley in Canoga Park. Zig had never let me forget it. "Pit *bulls*, Zig, there were two of them. I lost concentration for a few seconds and jumped the fence. Geez! Give it up."

I took the item out of its box, powered it up and tested it through the store window. Orange images of the pedestrians on the sidewalk across the street appeared on the screen and in passing cars. I was impressed. "Cool! I like this. I'll take it." I looked at the invoice and passed my debit card. "Let me have a couple of boxes of ammo as well, the usual plan. And I need some practice time on the range so I can get used to the slides on the new shoulder rig."

As he ran my card Zig answered, "Okay. No charge for the range time if you want to go one for one with your 'pistola'. You beat me last time. I want a rematch. Let's have us a full-on gunfight! You're my last customer for the day. I'll close up here, you can set up the props in back." He turned the ticket toward me and I signed after I looked at the total.

"That'll work." I looked at my copy of the ticket. "I wonder what Joe Mannix's ammo bill was?"

Never a fan of my fictional heroes, he responded, "He used .38s, so not a lot. Certainly smaller than his car insurance premiums and hospital bills. That boy could sure take a beatin'! You need a better class of hero!" He smiled as he made his point, then we went to the back of the shop where he outshot me by a good margin. By the end of the appointed hour, I was more accustomed to the shoulder rig. My firearms performance had long been less than the best, but

I was improving little by little and besides, I had always considered charm and wit to be my most effective weapons. Fewer ricochets with those.

24

After I packed for the three-day trip, I had planned I pulled the GTO into the shade behind the patio and began my ritual clean-up before I garaged it. The process is therapy for me, a period of semi-productive activity that provided some 'think-time'. I had talked myself into many unexpected activities while cleaning that car. That day as I sprayed up into the front wheel well, I noticed a new shape, a small dark grey cylinder, four inches long and an inch in diameter, attached to the front frame rail with a pair of spring-loaded 'u'-clips. I removed the cylinder, looked it over, and set it aside for later examination.

I finished the car, garaged it under its cloth cover, and went to the office to source the alien item's identity and purpose. Turned out it was an import item, a low-power tracker made in Germany. I had seen the items and many similar at a Law Enforcement trade show in Anaheim a couple of months prior. It had the same range and power of a modern Lojack unit. It was a nice piece, far better than those Chinese imports used by finance companies and 'buy-here/pay-here' car dealers. Retail price was $115, now I had one for free. I would probably keep it, have it re-chipped and use it myself in the future. I had concluded that my most-likely current adversary was probably Vinnie Bongelli, well-heeled Counsel to the Incarcerated. The guy with all the rent-a-car miles was probably one of Bongelli operatives, doing legwork to determine the strength of our efforts.

Thinking of the time for the installation of the tracker, I settled on the evening in Studio City at dinner with Catherine. The car had been out in the open in an uncovered parking structure for a couple of hours, and it wasn't unusual for passersby to stop and look closer at it when it was unattended. I would soon take measures to correct those situations. That time frame meant that the trackers had seen my travels for the last few days, but those visits were to 'non-combatants' so I wasn't all that concerned for their safety.

In the office I updated the event board and studied my notes. Now that I had an idea of how serious Bongelli was about checking me out, I knew I had to ramp up my own security measures. I showered and slept a few hours, then rose early and loaded up to leave for Vegas by 7a.m.

I broke out the big guns this time. My GTO had been an element in my life since I was two days old, but I set limits for its' use. Backup ride that year was a new black Chevy Tahoe SS with 1312 miles on the odometer. It had been an impulse purchase a few weeks prior when my old Trailblazer had started acting senile. It was big and black and powerful with a payment book to match but it was also fast and had a great air conditioner. That last item would come in handy on this trip. I'd wanted to snag one of the better high-performance trucks before the wizards of 'no' in Sacramento and DC legislated them out of existence or made them prohibitively expensive. This one fit like a glove.

My journey today had dual purposes. It would take a while. Catherine had prepared a list of Bongelli/Sutton/Carty business holdings. Most were in the Inland Empire of Riverside and San Bernardino counties, so on my way to Vegas that day I did a drive by of the locations on the list. It was informative and also kinda depressing. The business structures were all boarded up and decrepit, with the exception of six coin-operated squirt-it-yourself car washes, themselves sufficiently shabby to repel business.

While I travelled through the lesser areas of the Inland Empire charting obsolete business locations, Catherine's friend in Carson City provided some excellent insight. She theorized that the subject business itself was a ploy to eventually attract government funding for redevelopment. Three boarded-up business locations and one shabby car wash were within blocks of the now-vacant, fenced corner lot that was the former location of Sunset Motors on that wide, dusty road north of Riverside. The whole area begged for renovation. In the distance a large white wooden government-generated sign, itself tagged and weathered, promised government-instituted redevelopment at some point in the murky future.

Halfway through my down-market tour of the I.E. I picked up a tail, a grey Mercury Grand Marquis. I made a few extra turns and stops, and he was always back there lurking. I figured it was the same guy as before, or at least an operative for Bongelli. I hoped he had a full tank of gas, because I hit the northbound Fifteen toward Vegas and kept my foot firmly planted on the loud pedal, hitting 85 or so up the Cajon Pass. He followed. Rental companies just hate that. I stopped at the Jack-in-the-Box drive thru in Barstow and he parked right across the street in clear view though I doubt he thought I was onto him. I played along as we approached Las Vegas but past the south end of the valley I laid a plan that would get rid of him for a while.

After you come into view of Las Vegas across the desert floor you still have quite a hike, over twenty miles, before you actually 'hit town'. Over the past decade a thriving business community had sprung up south of the city on the west side of the freeway, but with the current crappy economy—2009/2010 was not a good year for growth in southern Nevada—there had been collapses of businesses and the banks that fed off them. I was familiar with one of them with which I'd had dealings and I figured they deserved a return visit.

I let up on the speed a bit as I approached the city, down to 70 through the heavy Interstate 15 enforcement corridor approaching the airport exit. Approaching the last exit south of McCarren Airport, I took the outside lane and signaled an exit. My little friend did likewise. At the top of the ramp, I kept to the left to cross over the freeway toward the west side business district. As we drove from the freeway, I kept a brisk pace, switching lanes a time or two then making the appropriate left turn onto a four-lane southbound bordered with tilt-up business parks and commercial complexes.

Across another intersection I finally reached the bank parking lot I was seeking. The grey Mercury was an easy half-block behind as I turned into the driveway and drove over the parking lot spikes with the Tahoe's tall, deeply-treaded tires. As I drove toward the vacant building I watched as the big sedan took the same path, but the driver hit the brakes too late and crashed across the spikes, causing the car to slither to a smoky stop a few car lengths into the lot. Four blown tires. Let's see ya explain *that* to Hertz. Heh, heh, heh.

I drove past him again and resisted the urge to wave and stick out my tongue. One must have standards.

25

October 7, 1996

After the job that morning the driver and his two passengers
traveled straight through Vegas to the desert ranch without saying a
word. They had stopped in Baker to take a break at the big Arco gas
station for a few minutes while the driver filled the tank. Then they
had jumped back in the truck and pressed on. At the ranch Carty
had rushed right into the house to get a fast noseful. As he left the
truck he said, "You guys stay out here. I'll leave the truck running
with the a/c on, and I'll be back in a few."

Wordlessly the two shooters looked at one another. They had
already decided that they didn't like or trust this bastard. Each of
them expected him to attempt to short them or cheat them entirely.
They'd be ready. Stacy, the senior of the three, had a plan in case
there was a problem. He'd scarfed one of the pistols they had used
for practice sessions. Carty's 'few minutes' in the house stretched to
over an hour, a sure sign of a dedicated coke freak. Both men also
knew that dedicated cocaine users could be mean as hell when they
got amped.

Eventually Carty came out of the house and walked toward the barn. As he passed the truck he pointed at the Mexican kid and called out, "You! Gomez! Come with me!" and pointed at the barn. Gomez left his seat in the truck as Carty smiled at him and said, "Stace, you stay there. I'll be done in a minute, I want to talk to you about something else,". The two men went into the barn and Carty closed the door. Stacy turned up the volume on the radio, tuned to a classic rock FM station from Vegas. The Stones... He'd loved that music before he went inside, and he'd missed it.

He'd looked forward to catching up on the things he'd missed, but he genuinely regretted agreeing to this method of getting his stake. He'd promised before he left prison that he'd 'get' and 'stay' straight, never to replay the loss and humiliation of that first-ever dumbass bank robbery arrest, a lifetime ago. He'd held out for thirty grand as a start of a solid life, but he knew that amount wouldn't compensate him for the nightmares from the actions of that morning. He'd deal with those as they came, just as he'd dealt with other nightmares daily during his prison term.

Sitting in the idling pickup with the door open, the A/C blowing cool air and the music turned up, Stacy didn't hear the 'chuff' sound that made it past the weathered, sun-parched walls of the barn. As Gomez stood smiling, counting his cash, Grant Carty, standing a foot behind, shot him at the base of his neck. Gomez died within seconds, collapsing forward, face down into the wide bucket of the old Pettibone skip loader, unaware that he gashed his cheek on the edge of the rough metal. Carty put a guarantee round into the young man's back, and lifted his feet into the bucket. He then fired up the tractor, engaged the PTO and raised the bucket to its highest level, tilted it toward the rear. Then he cut the ignition and climbed down.

He stood, took a breath, then looked to see if the kid had dropped any money. He picked up three fifties, put them with the stack he had retrieved from the body, and laid the stack on the table. He retraced his steps toward the door, stopped to sniff the air, then sidestepped to turn on the old pole-mounted industrial fan that sat toward the center of the room. It took a couple of minutes to rid the 'aromatic' barn of the cordite odor from the pistol shots.

Carty opened the side door and called out, "Stacy! Get on in here, boy!"

Still suspicious, the older man turned off the ignition and pocketed the truck key. He stood from his sideways perch, stretched for a few seconds, and walked toward the barn. He could see Carty standing inside the door, smiling, looking calm considering the nose-load he'd taken a half-hour before.

"It's payday, brother! Git on in here!" Carty entered the barn behind Stacy, who sidestepped so that they stood side by side. Still fresh from prison, he didn't willingly turn his back on anyone. Carty had a big stupid grin on his face as he stood next to a workbench topped with a stack of large denomination bills. "So what'd we decide for your part, Stace? Twenty?"

"I heard you say thirty." Stacy was a little nervous as he stood with his host in front of a stack of cash. "Where'd the kid go?"

"I sent him on his way. He's doin' me a favor, droppin' off a car in town for me. He said t'tell you 'bye'." Before Stacy could think about the comment, Carty picked up two stacks of banded cash and turned to face him. "Here ya go, bro, thirty thousand dollars, cash American." He handed Stacy the money. "You did a good job." He smiled, then said, "Look, I'm goin' into town a little later, get some well-cooked dead cow, drink some vino, maybe do th' strip club in North Vegas, ya wanna go with me? I'm a regular there, an' those ol' girls're easy pickins' on weeknights if you're so inclined."

This came as a surprise. "Umm... Sure, Carty. Can I go clean up first?"

"Yeah, bro. Go on in the house, take a shower, maybe get a little sleep. Already been a long day, right?"

"Sure, it ain't even noon yet. When you wanna leave?"

Carty thought for a second, then, "Take your time, buddy. We'll leave about five, get an early start."

Later, as he stepped into the shower, Stacy looked out the bathroom window and saw Carty driving that big tractor thing, bucket high in the air, out of the barn toward the field to the north.

26

The Tahoe's OnStar system led me to the Silverton Resort, away from the Strip in Vegas. I checked in, cleaned up, and changed clothes. An hour later, back out in the harsh glare of the desert sun, I found the gated driveway that led into an upscale mobile home park in Henderson. A couple of turns later I found the home of Roy Johnson, his wife Dale, and their granddaughter Lylie. Roy was washing the debris from the stiff desert breeze off the deck of the charcoal late-model Chrysler 300 in his driveway as I parked on the street opposite his space. He wore tan Bermuda shorts and a red UNLV t-shirt.

He turned off the nozzle and stood to meet me as I approached. Probably sixtyish, his arms were thick and his hands fleshy as he reached toward me. "You are Mister Street?"

"I'm him." I passed him a business card.

"Just call me 'Coach', Mister Street. Everyone else does. C'mon to the patio. There's some shade. It's cooler there." I followed him to the patio. There was some shade. It was cooler there.

We sat at an aluminum patio table and he passed me a tall cold can of Arizona Iced Tea. I popped the tab and started the conversation. "As I mentioned on the phone, I'm looking into a matter that may peripherally involve your daughter. She is not a person of interest in any criminal activity, but some of her old friends are, and I am attempting to establish a timeline for certain events. I need to talk to her directly, if you know how I can contact her."

"Right now, Mister Street, I'm not exactly sure where she is. Over by Pahrump, I think. All my wife and I have here is her daughter, Lylie."

"Yes, sir. I had been told that Lylie lives with you."

"That's right. A child needs a good home, and we were in a position to provide her with one. Reanna's still not equipped for parenthood. We didn't do all that great a job with her, we consider this our make-up test."

As if on cue at that moment the sliding glass door to the patio opened and Lylie, a willowy natural beauty at almost thirteen, with a sharp smile and bright green eyes, stepped onto the patio. She smiled at me then spoke to her grandfather. "Pops, I finished the paper, you said you wanted to check it over."

Roy smiled as he spoke to her, "Thank you, sweetie. I'll look at it in a few minutes, okay?"

"Kay. Thanks." She smiled again, showing braces and walked back inside.

I smiled at her proud grandfather. "She's a beautiful girl. How long has she been here with you and your wife?"

Roy put his can on the table and looked back at me. "We've had her since she was almost two. You wouldn't believe how they were living, Mister Street."

"She's lucky to have you. You and your wife home-school her?"

"We do indeed. She'll start at a private high school soon. We want her to get a good start on life. She wants to be a biochemist when she grows up. That'll probably change a time or two, but at least she's aiming high." He looked toward the glass door. "It's worked well so far. She's an Honor student."

"I'm impressed. I'm hoping you can help me fill in a few blanks, perhaps from a non-sympathetic vantage point, and clue me in on the connection that Reanna and Arnie Sutton had when she was in high school. Do you remember the people he hung with back when he and your daughter were dating?"

He sniffed his derision. "Too well! The only one you need to be concerned with though is *Grant Carty*. He was pallin' around with Sutton back when the trouble was starting, and they ended up as stepbrothers for a while. Carty led that poor kid around by the nose."

"You were around when things started to go south for Sutton?"

"You better believe it. Late in the process you could smell that kid going sour from a mile away. Look, my wife was a teacher and a Principal, I was a coach, so kids were our business. Sutton and Reanna had been high school sweethearts. We liked him at first. We thought he was a good kid, so we tried to make him a part of our family like Reanna wanted us to. 'Course she was way out of his league, but that's not unusual. We knew his parents were splitting up but that's not his fault either."

He cleared his throat and squinted a bit as he continued. "The two of them spent a lot of time together and my wife thought they were a 'cute couple'. Then as Arnie started hangin' with Carty, Reanna started sneaking out and stayin' out all night. They were bangin' like bunnies and she started lying to our faces about everything. Eventually she's knocked up and she chooses them over us. It's not the first time that's happened to adoptive parents but it hurt just the same."

I interjected, "I'm looking at Grant Carty for possible involvement with Arnie in the Rick Damarow murder from thirteen years ago. How well did you know Carty?"

"Damarow. He's the kid that Sutton dropped from the plane, wasn't he? I remember reading about it."

"Yes, he was."

"All of the teachers knew Carty, and we all had to deal with him at various times. He shouldn't have even been in that school. He was older, he would've graduated at age twenty, and he used his age and influence to intimidate younger kids, especially the girls. He had no respect for anyone but himself, and precious little for himself."

"So if they were involved in something like killing a rival..."

"Mister Street, if there was anything crooked going down, Carty would have been the instigator. I guaran-damn-tee you."

"Do you know where they operated from after Carty moved to Nevada? That happened a couple of years before Sutton was sent to prison. I heard there was property near Las Vegas, somewhere in the desert."

"Yes sir. Out north of the city, way out past the Speedway and all the business parks maybe twenty miles or so there's a little place, not really a 'town', called Caraway—like the seed—east of the freeway. There's a little store, some government offices and a sheriff's substation, between the interstate and the north end of Lake Mead. We drove out there a coupla years ago, we just looked around, the ranch looked pretty shaky. Property's probably worth a lot at the top of the market, if we ever see *that* again."

"When did Reanna break off contact with that crowd?"

"I don't know for certain. I think it was quite a while ago, at least five or six years. She's chosen her own path, Mister Street. We don't really talk to her all that much." He looked at the sliding glass door off the patio. "Ree is convinced that her daughter would benefit from a far grittier approach to parenting, though to what end I can only imagine. God only knows where that child would end up if we let her go. We have nothing to apologize for with regard to Lylie. She's a bright, poised, popular, confident, beautiful young girl. She'll grow out of her innocence with time. She doesn't need her mama's assistance or acceleration in that respect."

Ray seemed to have jumped to a single track, and my need for information was now secondary to him. "I understand. Could I get Reanna's number from you? I need to talk to her about her pals Carty and Sutton. There's a possibility we can help her situation a bit down the road. And could you give me directions to the Carty ranch? I'd like to take a look for myself."

"Sure thing, son. I have that inside. Stay right there." He smiled as he rose to walk to the patio doors, slid them open, and disappeared inside while I drained my iced tea. He returned moments later with a page from a loose-leaf notebook with block-printed cell phone numbers and a rudimentary map drawn in pencil. We talked for a while, about college football mostly—I was a lifelong SEC fan —and I left within the hour.

Roy had unknowingly provided the day's itinerary for me. I left Henderson, spent an hour on the I-15 north past the speedway complex to the desolate-looking Caraway exit. I drove east on the sun-parched, high-crowned two-lane road. There are plenty of small 'towns' in the desert, most often wide spots in narrow roads featuring a general store, a gas pump or two, maybe a post office. If you felt stranded by the emptiness of the area you'd gravitate toward those places, but they also saw plenty of local traffic and they often knew everyone in the area.

A half-dozen miles east of the Interstate I found one such establishment, a sad looking wooden building fronted by two Shell pumps under a large hand-lettered sign proclaiming, PAINTED DESERT FOOD GAS and SUNDRIES. The building been there for decades. A sun-bleached Jeep Comanche pickup would be my only neighbor in the parking lot. I wheeled to the pumps, committed the nozzle to the Tahoe and walked across the lot to the front door. The interior fit the exterior perfectly, dark and dusty though it did look 'clean'...no caked dirt or dust bunnies in evidence. I walked to one of the coolers just past the cashier's cage, snagged a Sprite and a bag of peanuts, and paid for twenty bucks worth of unleaded. The clerk, an Indian gentleman in his fifties, seemed friendly enough so I quizzed him for a moment.

I asked 'Ted', "Are you the owner here?"

"I am. Fifteen years and counting, first stop after the plane from Bangladesh. I inherited the business from an aunt."

"Perhaps you can help me. I'm looking for an old friend, a guy named 'Grant'. Fortyish, white, thin, maybe a little sloppy from time to time? Probably drives nice cars. Do you know anyone looks like that?" I showed him Grant's CAP picture.

He looked at the picture. "Hmmm... Not really anyone recently. There was a 'Grant' used to come in a few years ago, lived a few miles closer to the Lake. To be perfectly honest, he looked like a drug addict." He looked at me and shrugged.

"Nervous, suspicious?" I asked. He nodded. I said, "That sounds like our boy."

He scratched his chin. "I haven't seen him in a long time, though. Sorry."

"Do you have any idea where he lived? I heard it was a decent place, a couple hundred acres, house and a barn, near the top of the Lake. I think he was working on cars at his place."

"Sorry. There are ranches out here that you'd never find if you didn't know exactly where to look. I spend all my time here in this place." He looked at me and smiled, "You a city man?"

I smiled. "Most of the time. Is it that obvious?" The clerk just lifted his eyebrows in response. "This is my first time out here. I owe the guy a visit. I'd heard there was an accident out there a while ago, he or some of his relatives might've gotten torqued pretty good."

The clerk responded, "I don't know anything about that. The desert is not a forgiving place. My vantage here lets me see traffic passing by but not much else. I wish I could help."

"Thanks anyway. I appreciate your help. Have a good day." I left the store and went to the pumps, and watched the scenery as I gassed the Tahoe. As I stood there a tall late-model Dodge van passed on the road. It was solid grey with red lettering telling of 'PRENTISS MEDICAL SUPPLY' with an 800 number in smaller letters beneath the logos.

I gave it some thought and quickly decided to follow the truck at a respectful distance. It travelled east on the frontage road for a mile, made a left turn to a side road for another mile, then north into a driveway. I drove past the driveway, turned around a quarter mile away, and parked on the shoulder to see what happened next. Fifteen minutes later the truck returned to the road and drove out. Using the field glasses, I looked at the entrance to the driveway.

There was a metal grate covering the shallow ditch that ran along the road. I'd learned in an earlier job that these are called cattle guards, used to keep livestock from struggling with ditches and steep elevation changes. Farm tech. Part of the gig. Who knew?

I decamped, drove toward the Interstate and saw a sign for a Sheriff's department substation. I found it, then found a place in its parking lot from which I was able to leech a few minutes of internet service for my laptop. Google Maps cross-referenced with Catherine's property list showed me the plot for the Carty ranch. I cued satellite mapping and studied the terrain a bit, then made a decision.

Returning to the area of the ranch I looked at the driveway entrance itself. Beyond the cattle guard about twenty feet stood a metal apparatus that held a large, galvanized metal mailbox. There was also another element, though, light-gauge wiring that connected the structure to a nearby power pole, from which the power lines to the house ran. There were three more poles visible alongside the gravel driveway running presumably to the property structures, which were hidden past the richly sculpted landscape.

To the west, technically on a neighboring property, a set of rocky foothills, between 200 and 300 feet tall, jutted up from the desert floor. I drove past the driveway to the property line. Just the other side of the vestigial property line post lay a faint path onto the property. I looked around, finding no hostile observers besides cows, then crept across a shallow area of the ditch onto the property. The Tahoe, though it had knobby, somewhat taller tires, was still a two-wheel drive so I kept the speed low and chose the path carefully.

A half-mile onto the desert turf I found what looked like a decent spot from which to climb the foothills. I parked the truck in a shallow depression behind a thick clump of desert Mesquite and went to the cargo area to dress for the occasion and 'gear up'. I changed to a set of desert camouflage and a pair of climbing boots, collected the two new cameras and my field glasses along with operating components for the cameras. Looking at the range I didn't expect there would be need for rope, but I did add my side arm and backup piece in case desert critters were packin' heat.

After a ten-minute jaunt I topped the foothill, getting a full view of the Carty property. There was a long, tall barn, grey and weathered, a collection of blockhouses of concrete block construction and what looked to be a sixties-style tract house with a newer addition built onto the rear. There were a variety of derelict cars between the barn and the tract house. More pertinent were the cars near the house. There was a dark blue late-model Mercedes E-class sedan, a white GM compact—indeterminate brand and vintage—and nearer the barn an older model charcoal GMC suburban SUV on older Jackman style steel wheels and tall off-road tires. Each of the vehicles was parked at such an angle that the license plates weren't visible. That would eventually change.

Convinced of my find, I found a solid rock outcropping and unpacked the camera gear. I constructed a base from a pair of fist-sized sandbags and positioned one of the new cameras to cover the property below. I turned it on and tested the reaction time by waving my hand in front of the lens. It whirred convincingly and the images seemed satisfactory. I adjusted the angle of view a bit and sat and watched for a half-hour. Not much happened.

The ranch was at that point in time the largest, most valuable, and most active of the Sutton corporate holdings. It was an interesting find, considering that its title holder had been incarcerated for over a decade. It was a decent-sized, well-sculpted slice of valuable land. Its most prominent features were a mile-long driveway, a collection of run-down buildings, and for some reason, daytime occupancy and activity. The medical supply truck had been but a hint. I would learn more soon.

The site would at some point require an entry and search. That would come later. I sprinted down from the hill, returned to the truck, changed out of the desert camo, repacked the supplies and headed toward the highway, southbound.

27

I spent the next hour on the I-15 south through Las Vegas along with about four million semi-trucks. The traffic back then was made worse by freeway construction. Vegas is a betting town, so I privately bet the renovation would be obsolete by the time it was completed. Eventually after passing the bulk of the freeway redevelopments I turned onto the smooth, freshly paved state Highway that led west to the little burg of Pahrump.

The town had spent the better part of a century as a railroad stopover between California and Las Vegas before becoming known as a mecca for the more adventurous aspects of the state's legal prostitution industry. While the trade is illegal in Henderson County and LV proper, a short drive to various outposts would enable all the bimbo-cizing one could afford.

Pahrump had more recently become a bedroom community for the booming Las Vegas area, but the deep and ongoing late-decade recession had dealt a blow to the economy here as well. Many strip center storefronts were boarded up and there were even a couple of shuttered 'quickie casinos' alongside the highway. I had fun with the possible double entendres' that the terms invited.

Traffic was moderate into the town. I had a great time driving the new Tahoe along the wide, shaded highway. Soon enough the OnStar lady directed me to make a left turn onto a road that would lead to the last of the corporate-owned entities on our list. Approaching the appointed address, I pulled into an empty parking lot at the side of the road and put the field glasses to use. An eighth of a mile away sat a cluster of mobile homes surrounded by a parking lot that hoped for prosperous times. A subtle hand painted wooden sign behind a chain link fence stated that this was 'Desert Fantasy—members only'. A flashing red arrow indicated the entrance.

I had called to set an appointment with Reanna Johnson, Arnie Sutton's long-ago paramour. She had suggested a local diner that I had passed on the way in. As the appointed time approached, I started the truck and backed from my space. A red late model Dodge pickup passed by my position on the dusty road, so I gave it a half-mile lead, hoping to avoid a fresh layer of dust on the new black truck. Fat chance.

I followed the Ram into the parking lot of the appointed diner and parked a few spaces away. An attractive blonde woman with a striking resemblance to Roy's grand-daughter Lylie walked toward the diner. I followed. As I entered the foyer of the diner a minute later, she was standing by the cash register.

"Reanna Johnson?" I asked as I let the smudged glass door hiss itself shut behind me.

She looked at me and answered, "Yes. You're Mister Street?"

"I'm him." We shook hands and followed the waiter to our booth, something with a view of the door and our trucks in the parking lot. Reanna was a very attractive woman but up close she looked a little older than her 32 years. Her long light blonde hair was tied back into a ponytail worthy of a high school girl. She wore a filmy yellow sun dress over a slender and well-proportioned body. Her sunglasses were huge and almost completely covered an aging greenish bruise under her right eye.

I passed a card across the table and introduced myself as we waited for our beverages to arrive. "I'm looking into the Rick

Damarow murder, trying to clarify a couple of aspects. Your name has come up a few times because of your prior relationship with Arnie Sutton. I appreciate you meeting me like this."

She said, "That's okay. That's all water under the bridge for me, but I hope I can help." Her voice was small and feminine, but I got the impression that she could adjust that as needed. Some professions foster acting skills.

"How long have you been out here?"

"A few years. Too long, really. I help manage the house sometimes. I'm too old to be a feature girl. I do have a few regulars."

I looked for some hint that she was displeased with her station in life, but hers was just a pretty face with little expression and less introspection. "Surprising career choice."

"Yeah, I get that sometimes. A girl's got to capitalize on her skills I guess. When I started I was desperate. It wasn't easy. An offer was made, and it seemed to be the most lucrative of the immediate possibilities, so I gave it a shot. It's not as bad as most people think, really. Once the emotional bond to physical activity is broken it becomes an acting job more than anything else."

The waitress arrived with two iced teas and took out orders. Reanna asked for a tossed salad, I ordered a grilled cheese with a pickle spear on the side.

Resuming, I answered, "Okay." It sounded like self-justification, a company line perhaps used in recruitment programs. Did these people recruit? I smiled at her and frowned. "I'm not really sure how to respond to that."

"That's okay, Mister Street. I doubt that you'd partake under current conditions, though the offer is certainly open. We'd have fun. I guarantee it." She smiled.

I grinned in response. "We probably would. Thanks for that." Okay, how do I broach the subject? Just fall right in? "I met your dad and your daughter earlier today. I take it Roy doesn't know."

She seemed resigned. "No, they don't, though I'm certain that Roy has his suspicions. I think he tries to cope with what he considers the sad outcome of my wayward life, like I'm already dead or something. I can appreciate that." She looked at me as our food arrived. "You didn't drive out here to try to save me from my awful fate, did you Mister Street?"

"Absolutely not. You're of legal age and you know which road leads back to the real world."

"I do. And I'll be gone before long. I've saved some money. I have plans." She had a distant look in her eyes as if imagining a different place and time.

"Good luck with those."

Now she placed her sunglasses on the table and I could see her bright green eyes and the faint greenish outline of a bruise under her eye. I asked, "So when is the last time you had contact with or talked to Arnie Sutton?"

"Years ago." Question answered, she was left with a distinct look of distaste on her face. "We're so over I can't even remember his face. He's indescribably bad, just insufferable. About ten years ago I wanted to take Lylie to see her daddy, so I drove all the way up north of Bakersfield, where he was back then. I got lost on the way up there, it took us half a day to get there and finally get into the prison. After all that, the moron just assumed it was going to be a conjugal! I wanted him to meet his daughter, y'know? He couldn't have cared less about her. We stayed about ten minutes, and I turned around and left. That was the last time I even tried. I send him a card at Christmas, and a picture of Lylie. She's still his daughter and all but we're just 'done'. Even I have standards and he will never make the cut."

"Good call. Trust me, he hasn't fared well in captivity. You're not missing a thing. And actually, you might rethink sending the picture. Those have a high exchange value in prison." I changed the subject. "Your daughter is a beautiful girl. I see where she gets her looks." Reanna smiled, swept a lock of her hair back from her face and mouthed 'Thanks'. "Do you see her often?"

"Just once in a while. She won't talk to me. Dale, my mom, has pretty much poisoned her against me. That's not Lylie's fault, of course, I was pretty edgy for a long time. I do hope we'll get back to some kind of relationship before long. When she was younger I used to drive to San Diego and park down the street and watch for her from a distance." She gave me a weary smile and looked at me. "Hard as it may be to believe, Mister Street, I do have a soul, and it aches for some of the things I've had to do to survive. And I do love and miss that child."

She seemed sincere and perhaps authentically bothered by her plight. I kept my usual method of subject hopping to keep her off guard. "Back in time again. You attended Arnie's trial in Riverside. Do you remember Ron Connors?"

She sipped her tea, then, "Yes. Certainly. He was the witness who turned the tide. Bongelli was useless against him. After he was done testifying, Arnie just gave up. He lost all hope."

I stepped it up a bit, introduced fact to gauge her reaction. "Grant Carty was overseeing the drug trafficking operation that Arnie worked with. Grant piloted the plane from which the Damarow kid was dropped. Arnie was just following along but he took the fall for the murder. He is the only one paying any penalty. Did you know what was happening at the time?"

"It was sad, Mister Street. Bongelli and his staff told Arnie to just keep his mouth shut, that he'd be taken care of. He was taken care of, all right. By the time Arnie caught on, it was all over and done with."

I speculated, "Seems like Arnie was a little slow on the uptake. That cost him a lot over time. Didn't he have anyone in his corner directing him, other than Grant?"

"I tried. I really did. When I found out I was pregnant I begged him to leave all the crooked crap behind. We had wanted to get married, we wanted to go to college together. He begged me to stay with him. He loved me. I could tell. As soon as he let the word out, Bongelli and Grant double-teamed him, talked him out of it. Soon it was back to 'all Grant, all the time' and I had no say at all. Then Arnie was arrested, and it was all tossed away. No one else had a word of influence." She paused then nearly spat, "Bongelli and Grant, the dynamic duo." She shook her head sadly.

"You knew Grant. Do you think that, after Arnie was sent to prison, he would have had the presence of mind to plot the murder Ron Connors, out of revenge for Connors having sealed Arnie's fate?"

She didn't hesitate. "Sure! He's one ruthless bastard. He would stop at nothing to take out someone who opposed his goals. He was incredibly self-centered. The only person Grant Carty ever served was Grant Carty. Everyone else was expendable. I think it got a lot worse as time went on, too."

"So even though Bongelli more-or-less sacrificed Arnie to cover for Carty, that conviction set Carty off onto Connors. You definitely think Carty set up the hit."

Reanna was adamant. "Yes. He wouldn't have given it a second thought."

I asked, "How well do you know Bongelli?"

She smirked, "Too well. Talk about useless! Arnie would have done better with a public defender."

I concurred. "That's probably true. Did you ever see Bongelli and Carty together?"

"No. I know Bongelli set up the businesses that laundered the cash, and he handles a lot of financial affairs for his clients who have been convicted. He has lost a *lot* of trials. Carty and Bongelli always claimed that Arnie was actually the legal owner of all of the businesses. Bongelli kept all the numbers straight and handled all the paperwork. I didn't get into it any further, I just heard bits of phone conversations."

I was still curious. "Tell me more about Carty." I took a bite of my grilled cheese sandwich.

"Spawn of Satan, Grant Carty?" She exhaled heavily. "He's the root of all evil. Even when he and Arnie were in school, he would instigate all the little adventures they went on. If it all blew sky high, good ol' Arnie was always there to take the blame. Grant would stand back and laugh his ass off. It used to make me so mad..."

"What kind of stuff?"

"Well, let's see..." She took a sip of iced tea, then raised her index finger to make her point. "Okay, one of our Physics teachers, a really sweet old guy, had a massive baseball card collection going back to the 1920s, some of the cards worth thousands of dollars to collectors. They were his one passion besides his teaching, and he loved to show it off to his male students. Grant and Arnie and a dozen other guys had been invited to his house on a Saturday afternoon, as he'd done for decades. The teacher proudly shows these guys the card collection, as he has for probably a dozen times before. Grant palms a couple of them then he stuffs them into Arnie's back pocket. The teacher had a hunch, and he sees the corner of the card envelope peeking out of Arnie's pocket. He grabs Arnie and threatens to call the police."

"Ouch!"

"Yeah, ouch. Poor Arnie had to talk his ass off to keep the teacher from calling the cops. Grant took his time, but he finally spoke up for Arnie and the teacher took *his* word for it! Needless to say, word soon got out to the rest of the faculty. Arnie's senior year was pure hell for him. None of the other teachers trusted him or took his word for anything so they were five times harder on him they were on anyone else. Good old Grant Carty, 'elder statesman' of the class, even with his D-minus grade average, came out smelling like a rose."

Trying to mine this vault of information on Carty, I pressed her. "When they started expanding their business, Grant started making a lot of money. Did he have a lot of 'flash'? Did he show off? How did he express his new wealth?"

She took a sip of iced tea, as I did, as she considered her answer. "You have to understand something first. Grant was two and a half years older than Arnie, and Arnie was a senior when I was a sophomore. Grant used that age and experience as a leverage every chance he got. He was a real operator. Flash? Maybe not as much as you'd expect. In school he had a blue Mustang fastback, a '68 I think. Nice wheels, loud exhaust, stuff like that. After he had money, he didn't show off much more. I remember seeing a big

Bronco that he used to run around the desert in, but that was later. He probably had someone else work on it for him."

"Girlfriends?"

"A few, but never for very long. He played with some of the 'easy' girls, but he just used them. He never took them anywhere or spent any money on them, it was always just physical. He was really pushy and I suspect he rushed the 'three-date' rule by one or two dates. He tried for me once, but I turned him down flat. He was an oaf."

Liking the progress here, I pressed for more. "I have heard from other sources that he had a temper when he didn't get his way. He was vindictive. Did you ever see a hint of that in the high school years?"

"I think he trashed a guy's new Firebird one night. The guy had dissed him after he refused to buy pot from him. The Firebird was beautiful, it was an early graduation present for the class valedictorian, whose dad had died from cancer a few weeks before. The kid was just crushed. Grant laughed his ass off. Again. If he targeted you, he was ruthless. I was afraid of him. I stayed away as much as I could."

I smiled. "Good call. How early did Carty team up with Bongelli?"

She thought for a moment, then answered, "Let's see. Bongelli had defended a couple of Grant's friends who'd been busted, so of course they had been convicted. Some of the equipment the guys had been using reverted to Bongelli as well as the property for the car dealer. Grant cut a deal with Bongelli and the rest was history. Within a year or two Grant went bigtime trafficking up and down the I-15 corridor, Vegas to San Diego, with sources and contacts as far as South America. I know Bongelli made some key introductions."

"And Arnie hung around, regardless how he was treated."

"Yeah. It was sad. Arnie just followed Grant's orders. When things got ugly, he was always there to take the rap, pay the tab, take the beatings or make the excuses. Eventually Grant established a complex network of distribution, with really clever methods of transportation"

"That's where Sunset Motors down in Riverside came in, right? I know Bongelli set it up to launder money from the drug operation and provide the base of the transportation methods of the drugs manufactured and packaged at the ranch. How else was it involved?"

"Bongelli had taken the property as a fee for legal work that he'd screwed up, as always. He turned it over to Grant and Arnie so that they could have a 'clean' southern delivery point for the cars coming from the ranch. Do you know how it all worked?"

"Some of it. You know more." I smiled conspiratorially. "Tell me."

"Okay. A licensed car dealer, in this case Grant, would go to the big car auction out near the Speedway north of Las Vegas, and buy a car—something really nice, like a big Acura or a 7-series BMW. The car would be taken to the 'detail shop' at the ranch to be loaded up. Then it would be sent to Riverside to the car lot with one of us driving. The drugs were distributed from there. The car would be unloaded there and either put in the inventory or sent to another auction. The cars were just the tools of transport. They often sold at a loss."

"How were you involved?" I asked as I put my tea back on the table.

"I was a transport driver. Grant usually had three or four of us, all of us young women, some of us rather 'hot', making two or three trips per week. If there was high volume of traffic on a certain day, we'd drive in early, they'd take us to Ontario Airport for a quick trip back to Las Vegas, and we'd make another trip the same day. I really liked those days." She smiled.

"How much did you carry each trip? Was it meth? Coke?"

"I have no idea. I never saw the stuff. They were at least good about that. Grant said the less the drivers knew, the better he liked it. He told us how to act if we were stopped for speeding, and he gave us numbers to call if we were ever arrested. We were prepared regardless what happened."

"Did it pay well?"

"We got $500 for each trip, cash, half in front. I averaged three trips a week for over two years. It was easy money."

I had lots of experience with the route, so I asked, "The Fifteen is a heavy enforcement corridor for the CHP. Were you ever stopped for speeding?"

She smiled. "Sure, a time or two when I first started, just for speeding, but you know cops. Hey, I was a hot young blonde in a really nice car, dealer transfer tag in place. I could unbutton a bit and get away with anything, even when I was preggers out to here." She cupped her hands six inches in front of her stomach. "And after Lylie was born I could pinch her foot and I suddenly had the advantage of a screaming baby in a car seat as a prop. After I started using cruise control, I was golden." She smiled again. "I got a few cops phone numbers back then, too." Now she looked at me and squinted her eyes a bit. "Have you found Grant's ranch property yet?"

"Desert parcel? Out by Caraway?"

"That's the one. Grant was always really paranoid about its location. The one time someone drove me there to pick up a car, they drove around in circles for a half hour trying to confuse the direction. When I left, I drove straight out to the Interstate, three or four turns. No mystery there at all."

"Did you ever see the operations there?"

"No. I only know it was the location of the drug labs and center point of the distribution system as it grew. Grant would usually have one of his guys meet us at a predetermined location in Las Vegas, often the parking lot of one of the resorts on the Strip. The car would be there, with a full tank of gas and half our pay on the sun visor. I'm sure the cars were watched by someone on the crew until they were picked up. It was an efficient system. I felt secure when I was working with them when it started."

"When did you last see Grant? Where is he now?"

"It was about six years or so ago. He called me and asked that I meet him at some crappy restaurant in North Las Vegas. He wanted to cut our pay and he was getting worse about paying at all. And he was using by then, too. No way am I gonna risk getting busted for trafficking because he got high and sloppy. He wasn't going to keep up his end of the deal, so I was gone."

"Understandable." Out of the blue, I asked, "Where did you get the shiner?"

She touched her cheek with her fingers. "This? That was a couple of weeks ago. We'd been busy and I had finally taken a break, drove to a liquor store. As I walked back to the truck I was blindsided. I found myself in the gravel on the ground. I have no idea who did it, but it gave me a few days off work. Maybe it's a hazard of the trade."

I left the topic at that point. I was about ready to close the interview, and our allotted hour was almost up. I had wondered whether she was aware of the ownership of the brothel where she worked. I asked, "Do you know who owns the place where you work?"

"I honestly don't know who's at the top. The service industries in Nevada are all corporate now. No pimps, just accountants." She looked at her cell phone. "I do need to get back. Thanks for this. It's good to talk to an outsider sometimes."

"So Reanna, you agreed to talk to me because...?"

"I got an e-mail from my dad earlier today. We talk that way sometimes. He said he'd met you and he liked you and maybe you could do some good. And I don't know, sometimes it's just good to cleanse." She looked past me, perhaps envisioning a distant future, and continued. "I'm starting my transition out of here. If you can help, that'd be great. If not," she smiled, "I got a nice lunch."

"Last few questions. After Arnie was convicted, what were you promised, financially? Arnie is still getting paid from the business interests that Bongelli set up for him. I know promises were made regarding financials for you and your daughter. Were any of the promises ever kept?"

She looked at me as if I was a fool. "Mister Street, if I were being paid any support by anyone, do you honestly think I'd be where I am? They told me I'd be overpaid for driving so that I could be paid from Arnie's share. Then later Bongelli called me and said that Arnie's money was gone, that those accounts were in the red. I got 'zip' from then on, just as I had suspected."

I answered, "Tell you what...Give me a little time, let me work on a few suspicions I have. I may be able to change that situation for you and your daughter. If you think of anything else, please give me a call." I passed a business card toward her, clipped to two hundred-dollar bills. It may have been a cut in her day rate, but she didn't complain.

Quietly she rose, murmured her thanks and walked out of the restaurant. I watched her get into her truck and drive away. I finished my sandwich and iced tea, paid the ticket and left to drive back to the hotel in Las Vegas. After meeting with Roy and Reanna and taking a look at the ranch I took the evening off to decompress. That evening I took in the excellent house band in the lounge and had a great dinner; a big salad, sautéed shrimp and a unique 'broiled' baked potato and a carafe of wine before I went to bed at midnight and slept like a fallen log. Good stuff all.

The next morning, I hit the ground running, starting with a spot at the breakfast Buffet at 7:30. I was checked out of the Silverton by 9. I drove north to Caraway and retraced my steps up the to the peak of the foothills. I took a different path this time, one that gave me a better vantage of the property, though I could only see the plates on the white compact. The derelict cars and the line of outbuildings was clearer from that viewpoint but again a half dozen dead, dusty beaters in a cluster was nothing special in this rural area.

I crossed to my former position to check the cameras, which had worked as intended. The time code for the pertinent action sequences were the 9:40 arrival and 3:25 p.m. departure of the blue Mercedes, driven by a well-dressed female. The white compact arrived at 8:05a.m. and left about 5:35p.m. The SUV I'd seen yesterday hadn't visited that day. I figured the Merc carried the majordomo, and the white compact the wage worker. What was happening within those walls? I went back across the peak to the preferable position, repositioned the spare camera on the sandbags and sat and watched for a while. No drama this time at all.

After that I backtracked to the truck, again hidden in the depression behind the desert shrubbery. I de-camo'd and hit the highway south. This desert session had been instructive and had of course raised more questions. The more I knew about Grant Carty, the more certain I was that he was the force behind all the villainy. It bothered me that he'd been MIA for five years or so. His hit list of walking wounded, now including Reanna and her daughter as well as Arnie Sutton, probably the Connors and who knows, maybe their hit men as well. Lotsa possibilities afoot. I just needed to find him.

The sun was high and hot as I hit the southbound Fifteen that morning. I left the freeway at the Speedway and took Las Vegas Boulevard south to the eastern set of the loop freeway to bypass the maddening construction-clotted I-15—Vegas wants to be L.A. now —saving a little aggravation but no time to speak of. By the time I hit the slope south of the Las Vegas valley and passed the recent landmark of the 'M' Resort I was tooling along as designed, with the cruise set at 85. I put some music on, the Beach Boys late sixties 'Smile' album with its classic cuts that predated my birth by a handful of years. The Boys and I do pretty well when no one is listening, and it works wonders for passing the time on the road. I offed at Barstow for lunch, hitting a literal hole-in-the-wall Barbecue spot in downtown for a quick sandwich and a bag of chips. Then I took old 66 south through town to the next return route to the freeway.

Barstow was a sad place, bereft of significant modern growth or progress since the seventies when the completion of the intersection of Interstates 40 east/west and 15 north/south bypassed the town completely. Route 66 through the desert oasis had died soon thereafter, replaced by six fast lanes just over the next hill. Zig and explained it, calling Barstow 'a wide spot in the road, then they moved the road.' The sight of the recently-deceased Pontiac dealer was particularly depressing for me, for other reasons.

After the tasty and filling 'cue and an eventual return to the freeway, I took the most direct route home and made great time except for a stretch of the I-15 south past Barstow where a slick-roof CHP Crownie paced me from a half-mile back. Eyes like a hawk...

Catherine was spending a few days with her fiancée so there was no need for a side trip to Riverside. I got a little jealous at times realizing that friends and colleagues had strong relationships that were headed in positive directions. It had been a while for me, and I missed it, though the most recent prominent ending had not been my idea.

Maybe it was a natural event that day when I turned into the driveway at home and spied a familiar black Mustang GT convertible parked in the shade behind the patio. The car belonged to a certain up-and-coming blonde actress who also had a house key.

Cindy and I had met three years before when she had backed into my old Trailblazer in the parking lot at Gelson's Market on Ventura Boulevard. The apology extended to dinner at a great restaurant and a week later, more. It had been a great off-and-on relationship in the interim until the party at the house above Sunset eight weeks prior. Since then, she had signed on to work for the Prius-addicted wunderkind producer wannabee. We had talked on the phone a few times, but I could read the tea leaves and predict what was approaching.

She was perched on a lounge chair, glistening in the sun as I walked from the Tahoe going to the office door. Ever sensitive, I chirped, "Hiya cutie! How's tricks?"

She turned toward me, looking all pouty, her exquisite lower lip displaying just the right amount of 'puff', the way it did when she was sad or in a bad mood. As always, she was smokin' hot. She was wearing one of my old light blue Shelby t-shirts, cut to strategically-placed and somewhat distracting ribbons, and a pair of microscopic cut-off denim jeans. In her small voice, Memphis accent fully intact, the one she used when she wanted something, she said, "Street, honey, we need to talk."

My approach to manipulative soon-to-be-former girlfriends was carefully-crafted. I knew what she wanted, I knew what she was going to say, and I knew what my response would be. My turf, my rules.

"My thoughts exactly, Cin. Let's go inside." I led the way to the door then held it open for her, getting a whiff of her perfume as she passed under my arm.

She started as she stood by my desk, I sat on the corner and listened. "Where have you been? I called a few times, left messages." She talked as if we'd had an understanding, something I'd wanted for a while but probably not anymore.

"Yeah, I know. Sorry I didn't get back to you. I'm on a big, complicated job right now and I'm hammered. I was in Vegas for two days, just got back. This thing is ramping up now and I probably won't be great company for a while."

She spoke quietly. "That's okay, I can't stay long. Um, Jacob has asked me to move in with him, and since you and I don't seem to be an item anymore I just wanted to let you know."

I kinda figured that Jacob was one of the tribe working on her latest project. I recalled meeting a group of young entertainment industry wannabees at the party in the hills. The party and the company had given me a headache, so I brought a bit of attitude to the exchange. What's she gonna do, *leave* me?

"Which one is 'Jacob'? They all looked alike to me and I don't recall the name."

"You met him. He's the Director of Photography for the Pilot episode of the series and he's been a great help to me."

Do tell. "Cin, who wouldn't be? I would think he'd thank you. Gazing upon your fine white body for a few hours a day is not tough duty. Did they ever get a real wardrobe for you?"

Cindy smiled and the room brightened. Excitedly she explained, "Oh, yeah! They've done a lot of development on the character. She's a strong-willed young professional woman trying to get ahead in a man's world."

We'd had this discussion before. "Oh, yeah. She's maybe a twenty-seven on a ten scale and never wears a lot of clothes and she'll bang anyone who doesn't move out of the way fast enough. Cin! Please! I read the screenplay, remember? They've been hustling this crap for two years. It's a schoolboy's wet dream! You showed me the script when you took the first cattle call. How much has it changed since then?"

She looked hurt now, and she was defensive. "They've rewritten it, Street, specifically around me. And they have funding now. It's a solid deal, 'C', really."

"Does that mean they've *paid* you? Do you have a SAG-quality contract?" I could feel my anger and suspicion rising.

"Yes, 'C', they did."

I looked at her for a few long seconds, resigned to the reality, ready to move on, and regretting it already. There was twelve years in our ages, and right now I felt like a dad or a big brother—except for the 'two years of great sex' part. I took her hand. "Okay, girlie girl. Here's the thing. I loved you for a *long* time, I can get over that if that is your wish, and you can go do whatever you want to do with whomever you want to do it. What *I* won't do is stop caring what happens to you. *Do not* fall into the traps that too many women fall into out here. You know what I'm referring to." She had received numerous offers for porn work when she first arrived from Memphis. A couple of them had eventually become a problem that I had dealt with personally.

Quietly she said, "Sure, 'C'."

"And if they hurt you or lie to you or abuse you or cheat you, you know that you come talk to me. They need to be really afraid of me if they do any of that to you, don't they?" I added, "Especially that friggin' pansy with the Prius." She laughed, finally.

Tears. I'd expected tears. Cindy was a drama queen of epic talent. This time she played it straight. She smiled, touched my forearm, and softly said, "Thank you, 'C'. I need to get my stuff, and I'll give you the key. That okay?"

Quietly, I said, "Yeah, go for it. You know where everything is?"

"Sure. There are just a few things. Seems we never needed many clothes when I was here, huh?" She smiled that smile.

Do tell. I watched as she strode down the hall then returned thirty seconds later carrying a beige valise she'd bought during a weekend in San Diego a year ago. She put the key in my shirt pocket then tilted toward me and kissed me lightly. "'C', honey, I..."

"Go do your thing, girlie girl. Make yourself famous...after you make yourself proud. You know where I'm at." I stood and kissed her lightly on the forehead. There really wasn't a lot there anymore.

In her little girl voice she said, "I know, 'C'." I followed her to the door, then watched as she strode to her car. As she opened the door and tossed her valise into the back seat, she looked back over her shoulder at me and smiled. Ever the actress.

29

With Cindy's departure came the return of solitude, but I was also tired. A renewed sense of urgency would have to wait until the next morning. I took a shower and changed clothes and had a sandwich before I went to the office to check messages and prep for the next push. I made a few calls and updated the event board, but I was still tired and buzzing from the long drive. I knocked off early and sat on the couch for a while.

Wanting a distraction and some noise in the house I selected a Mannix ep from two years before my birth and snagged a trio of Sam Adams Oktoberfest, the remnants of a case I'd found on closeout at Gelson's market a few months before, as I vegged on a recliner section of the sofa. Joe was again instructive, busting a youngish William Shatner even after getting whacked over the back of the head for about the hundredth time. As the addictive Schifrin theme music subsided, I went to cable for an ep of *CSI Miami* so I could continue my exhaustive character study of that truly fine LaRue lady. Good Lord. How come the lab techs and assistants I hired never looked like her?

Sometime around the second commercial break I fell asleep. I had an odd dream; I was helping Joe Mannix find Grant Carty. Joe wore Horatio Caine's 25-pound sunglasses, the back of his head was bandaged over his hair and Cindy was a topless lab tech. Too much beer.

It bothered me later. Old TV, a nap, and ice-cold beer were not my preferred remedy after ending a relationship with a young woman who was about a twenty-seven on a ten scale. I told myself that I was tired from the trip and had a lot on my mind. Thirty-five isn't *that* old, is it?

The next morning, I fired up early and went right to work, watching the DVD developed from the desert camera footage. It was an important bit of information because it verified that there was significant traffic in and out of the ranch property. With the small camera's limited field of vision, I couldn't ascertain the specifics of each vehicle, just the color, size and style. My obsessive collection of mostly useless automotive information did put me at an advantage here.

There were definitely commercial deliveries of linens and medical supplies to the ranch house, but the quantities of each were not large, most often small boxes or bags and one-man, one-trip deliveries. The grey Dodge high-top van from Prentiss was a regular visitor and the blue Mercedes was always present when the drop-offs were made. That woman was probably the one paying the tab and managing the facility. If someone was being 'kept' there, why was there no caretaker after hours? My curiosity was sky high and rising. I also found that ground squirrels are curious buggers, brave enough to stand their ground when the faint operational clicks and whirs started from the camera. No need to run, little dudes, it's your turf.

After a couple of hours, I was glad to see the 949 area code on the phone screen at 10a.m. sharp. Lawyer hours. "Yes, Catherine."

She sounded perky. "So, Street...how was Nevada?"

"Great. It was a long hot trip."

Curious, as always, "What did you find there?"

"Lots. Some weird critters live there, and victims and some good people too. Anything new on your end?"

"Plenty! I received Bongelli's motion to commute Sutton's sentence. He has a lot of pull at that courthouse. I plan to be there in force, but I'll need your assistance. We have a little while but I'm sure he'll be pulling out all the stops this time."

I smiled, "Whatever I can do to help, you know that."

"Thanks. I also heard from Carson City about those corporations we talked about. When my friend there did a series of key word searches in state data banks, tons of information appeared. Bongelli now apparently represents 31 incarcerated parties with corporate holdings, all over the state. Most of their names can be found in business structures similar to what we found with Sutton. That is impressive if only for the consistency required. I can't get over the amount of paperwork needed to keep everything straight."

I was curious. "Question on that. If all these clients of his are in the can, how does he profit from it? He doesn't look underfed, and he stays busy. Do the inmates pay his fees? Is his brand of prisoner maintenance a lucrative pursuit?"

Catherine was in a conversant mood, and of course also on the clock. "It could be if it was worked correctly, but there are always ways for attorneys to make money. I'm sure he's wired to the hilt. He sets their corporate entities up and provides them with cover businesses in their usual area of interest or expertise, partially for support of their families but also to launder drug money. You've seen from his material, there are car parts vendors, car stereo shops and video stores through the years, more tobacco stores and sex shops now. If and when pot is legalized in California, they'll go to that, and I'd say by 2015 most of the businesses will be online instead of brick and mortar. The businesses will fit the style of the day, as always. He, or 'they' or whomever will be able to turn on a dime."

I asked, "So does he select his clients by their business acumen or by the likelihood that they'll end up in prison? If they get sent up for whatever reason, he wins either way, right?"

"Perhaps the latter. If they are arrested, he represents them and provides a weak defense. If they go away, he manages their affairs, on the clock, still using their assumed name for day-to-day business operations. Any real estate or property holdings are mortgaged back to another Bongelli entity. Consider it the true definition of 'power of attorney'. *He* was the attorney. and he had *all* the power. After their conviction he'll run their businesses for a while, build up credit, skimming in the name of legal fees at regular intervals. Some of their funds go to give them a stipend while they're behind bars, in an annuity of sorts. He can do as he wishes with their resources while they're in the slammer. If they get out or change counsel, he has to settle up. *That* doesn't happen that often."

I thought about it for a few seconds. "So, for the most part, it's in his best interest that they stay in prison. He takes his fee and part of their gains for himself from the business entities. The sloppier his work, the more charges they face, the longer they're out of his hair. Geez! Pass the Motrin!" I scratched my chin and asked another question. "Have you seen any indication that Grant Carty is still above the sod?"

"I looked. There's no death record, no tax filings for a half-decade, no current operators' licenses Nevada or California. He may be completely below the radar and off the grid but from what you've said of him I would doubt that. I did find a couple of old bank accounts, each under fifteen thousand with no in-and-out activity. If he's alive he's doing a great job of keeping an incredibly low profile. I'll keep digging and keep you posted."

"You do that. I will, too. He's been invisible for five years... a long time underground." I paused, "and I think I might know exactly where to dig. Can you do a check on Bongelli? I'd like to know more about him. And, can you call your friend the Warden? I want to talk to Sutton again. I think I know where to twist him."

30

That morning after I talked to Catherine, I looked at the 'to do' list on the event board and saw 'Harass the adversary's detective.' I played a hunch and called the Bongelli law office. A bit of subterfuge provided me with the name of the driver of the Mercury I'd trashed in Las Vegas.

Vance Boyd was, according to my research, a veteran P.I. working out of Riverside with offices and licenses in California and Las Vegas. Vinnie Bongelli was his biggest client. He was a former officer with the Covina P.D., bounced after fifteen years for undisclosed reasons. As an Investigator he actually had a decent rep, considering that he was usually toiling on behalf of a well-known reptile.

I limbered up my southern accent and used one of my burner phones for the contact. Working from notes, I tried to sound desperate and angry at the same time, but my biggest challenge was to keep from laughing.

He answered on the third ring. "You Mister Boyd? You a private detective like on th' teevee?"

"Yessir I am. Not exactly like the tv characters but I have done investigative work for over twenty years. What can I do for you?"

"Good. Mister Boyd ah'm Rick Simon. Ah'm out here from Tulsa this summer fer some awl field work an' I brought ma wife with me. An' dammit, Mister Boyd, ma wife is cheatin' own me. She's taken up with her boss. He's a country singer at a kicker bar an' a friggin' life coach durin' the day. Bastard's tryin' t' steal ma woman and dammit I want proof! How much you cost?"

"I get seven hundred a day and expenses for divorce work and I get a five-day deposit. Can you afford that?"

"Oh, hell yeah. I got that. That ain't no big deal."

"Okay, Mister Simon, can we meet this afternoon? I'll be in the area for a few days as I wrap up another job in the next few days so I'll have time. I like the sound of this one."

"Why don't we meet fer lunch? I'll buy ya a sandwich. You know West Covina?"

"Sure. I live near there. Where do you have in mind?"

"They's a real good place there. You like Pastrami? You know 'The Hat'?"

"I do. How about two-thirty this afternoon?"

"Fine. Tha's fine. See ya thinn..." I did paperwork and returned calls until noon, then I left for Burbank. When I do something like this I often swap cars with Zig. He has a cool red mid-nineties Pontiac Grand Am GT coupe that I like a lot. It's great for tight maneuvering and it is common enough to be nearly invisible in traffic. I drove from Burbank to West Covina, arriving at twenty after two. I parked at the eastern edge of the parking lot. The grey Mercury arrived five minutes later and parked beside the building. I called him, in character, and begged forgiveness for a delay in arriving. He was fine with it. Another call a few minutes later had him sounding annoyed. I made another call to cancel, citing a work conflict and he stomped from the restaurant to see me standing beside the Mercury sedan.

He looked at my extended hand and did not meet it. He had dressed for his client, a pair of stylishly ragged jeans, a pearl-buttoned off-white shirt under a decent denim jacket over tooled boots. "So, Vance, I wanted to say hello, since you followed me a few hundred miles in the last week. I feel like we should at least say 'hi'. You're working for Bongelli, right?"

"Man? Don't even ask. You know better than that. I mighta figured that was you on the phone. Where did you come up with that stunt in the bank lot?"

"Oh, one of my mentors showed me that. You're lucky I didn't use the high-speed dumpster." I looked past him to the car. "Where'd you get the tires?"

"The rental company sent a flatbed tow, they swapped 'em out. I owe you payback for that, Street." He was not smiling.

"I'm cool with that. Look... you're a pro. You need to keep your distance from Bongelli. A lot of bad stuff is getting set to fall on him, really soon. You don't want to be there when it happens." I considered it professional courtesy. He just glared at me. "Okay, Vance. Your choice of response. Have a nice day." I started to walk to a taxi that had just pulled up. "Oh, and it looks like you have another flat." I pointed at the passenger's side front tire, wearing a broken X-Acto knife blade in the sidewall. He looked down at the tire as I closed the door and the taxi drove away.

Street's the name, minor vandalism's the game. As the taxi rounded the corner of the parking lot, I asked the driver to stop. I flipped him a twenty for his time, left the taxi and regained the Grand Am. As Vance Boyd did the guy thing and changed his own tire, I did the drive-through, got a pastrami sandwich, parked at the back of the lot and watched him. He worked diligently as I ate. Eventually he slammed his trunk, wiped his hands and resumed the driver's seat. I followed him at a respectful distance as he went about his business. All things considered, his workday was a little boring.

Just after four he stopped at the business park that included Bongelli's law office. Attorney Bongelli was taking delivery of a new car, a new bright silver Mercedes S-series AMG coupe—low six figures. Nice piece. Seeing the array of vehicles in the lot I had a sense of familiarity that I couldn't quite put a finger on. I broke off the surveillance, went to Catherine's office and did busy work while we planned the next strategy.

31

Vinnie Bongelli was walking across the courtyard toward his office after taking delivery of his new Mercedes when he heard a car door close behind him. He saw his man Vance walking from his rental, called to him, and motioned for him to come to the office. Moments later the detective walked in and took a seat on the client side of the desk. Boyd wiped his brow with a handkerchief and commented, "Hot out there. I'm not used to this humidity."

Bongelli looked over his glasses and responded, "We're in a desert, near the ocean. It gets that way. How is your project going?"

Boyd chose to avoid mentioning the latest 'issues' with his surveillance. "It's a little slow right now. That guy's pretty good. I'll get it done." He stuffed the handkerchief back into his pocket.

Bongelli looked at Vance Boyd as he worked his key ring. "Tell you what, if you're going back to Vegas in the next day or so, take my black car with you. She says she wants to take it off my hands. Take her blue one and put it on eBay, or Craigslist or somewhere, get rid of it. Get it detailed first though, her cars are always filthy." He lifted an envelope and dropped the keys inside, then slid the envelope toward Boyd.

Vance offered, "I remember when you closed the dealer in Jarupa. Too bad. You could've sold it there."

Bongelli sniffed his derision. "That's the only advantage to that place. That was way more trouble than it was worth. You just leave your rental here, we'll call the agency and they'll come get it." He stood up and added, "And Vance...please...keep an eye on that guy and keep him outta my hair!"

"Whatever it takes, Vin."

32

Catherine asked about the camera equipment I had used. "This is neat. How do you get it to do all the starting and stopping?" She lifted her coffee cup, took a sip, then held the cup by the rim as she put it back on the saucer as she watched the monitor.

"It's something my gadget guy rigged up for me. It's a motion detector operated digital camera. Solar charger, fast reflex auto-focus, and it's small. I can mount it almost anywhere. Works well most of the time, but in this case the critters were curious. I never knew that ground squirrels have such big eyes, did you? Looking past them, there was some traffic to and from the house, but I can't tell who or why at this point. I have another camera working there now, I'll know more when I look at that."

She sipped her coffee and asked, "When will that be?"

"Soon. Couple of days probably. I want to do some more background research first. I'll start here in Riverside. Tell me more about Bongelli. What's he into?"

She grinned, "Himself, mostly. That's not unusual for really successful practices, and he's done quite well."

"Solely from his niche of dealing with prisoners?" I offered.

"And managing their absentee business holdings. Bigtime drug dealers and traffickers love to diversify their holdings, but they usually have a short attention span. Without guidance they'd hop from business to business and from shiny object to shiny object. Bongelli covers their butts using hourly billings or retainers until they get busted, and his real profits start after that. He can build up credit and debt in their name; all he has to do is keep up with the payments, and no one's the wiser. What do you know about Nevada corporations?"

I answered, "Lower bureaucracy than California, lower taxes, and the names of corporate officers are held confidential. More non-profits and entertainment entities are based there than anywhere else. I have one as a trust holder for my house."

"Good. All you mention is true, Nevada is a great place to hide cash, as is common with the Mob. Bongelli has free reign on the resources of all those corporate entities, so the sky's the limit for him. The Feds might want to look at the co-mingling of resources from one corporation to another." Seizing on that idea, she wrote herself a note to look at same.

I asked, "Do you really think he'd be that easy to trip up? Something that basic would bring his empire down? I would think he has ways to cover his ass on all that. And if he has his bases covered would there be a chance that he could come after you for uncovering it all? Would the State Bar get all upset and cause *you* problems? I'd imagine he has a lot of pull there like he does with the Prison system. I don't want to put you at risk."

"Funny thing about that, Street. I didn't initiate all of this, the office of the Nevada Secretary of State did. It's all in their hands. All he's done so far is use his machinations to create lots of billable hours. Nothing wrong with that. If they find other issues, he could have a few problems."

I thought about that. "Good answer. How many employees does his office have?"

"The figures I have say there are six attorneys in Riverside, split between different disciplines; Criminal, Bankruptcy, Civil, and Litigation. Fifteen non-practicing employees, including one or two who he's mentored from high school. There is another similar operation in Las Vegas. They take very little work other than their specialty. He actually has an excellent rating though the score is tabulated using really questionable means. Some of my contemporaries actually respect him, though they are often also the same ones who have beaten him soundly in court."

"What is the valuation of the practice as a whole?"

"That is unpublished. It could be in the tens of millions, on up. It's hard to get a handle on numbers now that the economy is down. No one wants to make their troubles public. Bongelli has no such problems, but he'll keep everything close to the vest anyway."

"Mmmm. It still seems like tons of work, keeping all the balls in the air. If there were issues, could he just turn his back on everything and bail out?"

"I don't doubt that there is a fail-safe somewhere that would provide quite well for him. Skate to a small non-extradition country, live on the beach, not a worry in the world. *You* have to keep that from happening." She lifted her eyebrows.

"I do. And *we* have to watch for him making that kind of move. He's not there yet, but he doesn't know what we know about him. I think we have the advantage at this point and probably into the near future.

"One can hope."

"Let's try this. Search what records you can find on him, let's try to find former clients, including survivors of prisoners who died behind bars. Let's see if there are any who were disgruntled or left penniless from their involvement. We may even be able to get statements from prisoners whose cases he screwed up. I can handle those referrals if you can get the names."

"That'll work. What's your next move?"

"I just have to do some more legwork. It's pointing me back toward Las Vegas. I want to see what's going on at that ranch."

33

Driving back from Catherine's office I made a side trip through the Jarupa area north of Riverside, where most of Sutton's businesses had been located. I parked in front of one of the car washes down the street from the former home of Carty's used car lot, waiting for some sign of what I needed to bring this thing to an end. Nothing came other than a renewed sense of purpose.

I drove home and realized how hungry I was, so I took some time off and got all ambitious and prepared a rather impressive dinner. I broiled some Alaskan King Salmon on the kitchen grille, and did a 'broiled' baked potato like I'd seen in Las Vegas. I added some garlic butter and cracked pepper and made it my own. It was a great combination that I would repeat from time to time. Taking a cooking class with my former fiancée in New Jersey had shown me the charm of the creative process. I had liked it, and I tried to stay in the game as much as time allowed. The only downside was the necessary cleanup, but I've always felt that if the food was good enough that didn't matter. The dishwasher was my favorite kitchen appliance.

Around seven I received a fax, seven pages from Catherine, whose efforts had paid off with an extensive list of Bongelli's former clients. Several of the parolees and a few of the surviving family members of deceased prisoners were in the L.A. area so I made six calls that evening. I needn't've bothered. The most receptive of the six was only moderately surly and two of the others were downright threatening. I tried to point out that I was only trying to get Bongelli to make things right with his clients, but the very mention of his name brought extreme vitriol. Hey, ya can't win 'em all.

I woke early the next morning and started updating the event board. At 9:30 the phone rang. I had expected to hear from my client at some point, so the call was welcome.

She sounded friendly when she started, "Good morning, Mister Street. Are you in Los Angeles today?"

"I am. I've been hoping to talk to you. I've wanted to update you on our progress on your behalf. I have significant news for you."

"Excellent, Mister Street. I have a luncheon appointment at noon. Can we do eleven-thirty?"

"I'm open. Where can we meet?"

"Do you know Michael's in West Pasadena?"

I'd been there a couple of times with Cindy on her 'be seen there' evenings and had found the place pleasant if overpriced...not unusual for L.A. "Certainly. At the east end of the Arroyo Bridge. Great place. I'll see you there."

After initiating a printout of the pertinent information of the ongoing investigation I prepared for the main event. I dressed the part of a highly-paid executive for the pre-lunch meeting, wearing my overpriced three-piece dark grey suit with a dark blue silk tie and a really pricey silver-pinstriped white shirt. I had complimented former client, a Dubai businessman for whom I had worked briefly the prior year, on his shirt and he'd gifted me three of them a month later. Tailor made, and from halfway around the world impressed me, even though I wasn't the wear-it-once and toss it kinda guy. I now had a lifetime supply.

Well dressed, with hair and complexion pummeled into submission, I went to the garage and uncovered the GTO. It's my favorite 'make friends and influence people' tool. At eleven twenty-five I rolled onto the ever-so-classy cobblestone paved driveway of the upscale West Pasadena eatery and gave the Goat to the stick-proficient actor-slash-valet working the gate. He left a foot-long patch of rubber on the pavement when he popped the clutch, but he did park it up front.

Elizabeth had arrived in her own elegant pearl white Bentley Continental coupe. I met her at the portico approaching the front door. "That is a beautiful car, Mister Street. I always liked them. My husband had a '70 GTO convertible. It was Sunset Gold with a Parchment interior. I loved that car."

As we approached the door I offered, "Those were great cars from a great era. I would have loved living out here back then. Being on the cusp of society at that time had to be an amazing experience." I held the door for her as we entered the foyer of the restaurant.

"Oh, it was. My children were young and curious. My husband was building houses, Ron was at the top of his game, it was just...invigorating." The Maître d' greeted her warmly and looked at me with a bit of suspicion. "I'm with her," I whispered as I passed.

Elizabeth was wearing an off-white business ensemble that morning. Her nails were painted to match, and she wore delicate diamond jewelry that accented quite beautifully. We were led to our table. After we took our seats and she ordered coffee Elizabeth started the drill. "So Mister Street, how is the investigation into Ron's murder coming along?"

"I've found a great amount of new evidence. It's complex and much of what we've found points us in new directions. There are numerous previously undiscovered players in the mix. I need your input before I continue."

"Very well, Mister Street. Continue."

"From One: Early nineties, your son Rick finds some success in the shallow end of the drug trade. After a while he decides to step it up a bit; he makes contact with people who are far more serious, more aggressive and far meaner than Rick would ever be. He says or does something that offends them. They take great offense. He is abducted and killed."

Elizabeth's facial expression said, "I already know that, moron," but I continued.

"Arnold Lee Sutton is located by Wayne King, the detective hired by Ron. He is arrested and brought to trial in Riverside County where the crime is alleged to have occurred. Ron and Detective King testified at the trial, and their testimonies were described as 'brilliant'. Arnie Sutton is convicted of murder and sentenced to 25-to-Life, dealt down from a straight life sentence."

I watched her expression. It didn't tell me a lot. I continued.

"Unapprehended, unmentioned, and completely absent from the trial and the other proceedings is one Grant Carty, who at the time was Sutton's stepbrother. He was the energy and intellect behind their narcotics trafficking operation." I laid the picture on the table, pushed it toward her, and put my index finger on Carty's image. "Grant Carty is also a CAP trained pilot. I needn't tell you that the pilot of the plane used in your son's murder was never identified. I am developing evidence that indicates that the pilot of that plane is the instigator of Ron and Annie's murders. There are witnesses whose testimony will tie that pilot to the pickup truck that delivered the killers to Ron's house that morning."

Elizabeth had listened intently. She looked at me, frowned a bit, and asked, "Mister Street, why have none of my other investigators brought me any of this information?" She lifted her delicate porcelain coffee cup as she waited for my answer.

As she sipped her coffee I answered, "I looked at their reports. I read every word. They did well for the effort they expended. If I were immodest I'd just say I'm better at my work than they were at theirs." I tried not to grin. "I am better than most, and our work at this point is more comprehensive than theirs ever would be. In this instance there was another element at work."

Elizabeth's eyes narrowed a bit. "And that is?"

"Your intent on putting Ray Cole in his place. Everything I have found indicates that you refused to look in any direction other than his. Every word in your volumes of publicity for over thirteen years pointed to the single conclusion that he was the engineer and instigator of those killings. People who never *heard* of your brother know of your efforts on his behalf. I'm sorry but our evidence at this point indicates that you're just mistaken." I hated to exorcize my client but her presumptuous attitude was getting on my nerves.

Her defense was more pointed now. She retorted, speaking slowly and quietly through not-quite-clenched teeth, "But Cole threatened Ron repeatedly. Everyone heard him! He was the most obvious suspect!"

I raised my index finger to signal agreement. "My thoughts exactly! Talk is cheap, Elizabeth, and his, near as I can tell, was practically worthless. I met with him. We talked. I wasn't impressed. I have looked at his financial condition at the time of the murders and he always comes up short. Look, I agree, he was a clod. He may have inhaled his own body weight in cocaine over the years, and he still displays some of the signs of a heavy user. It's inside his head. I imagine he was a total pain when even he was at the top of his game. I wouldn't trust him as far as I could throw him, then or now. But I have to tell you, it's a long transition from being 'insufferable' to becoming a double murderer."

Elizabeth was still insistent. "He made death threats, in public, and we have witnesses who say they saw him watching Ron's house. He was very public about it."

I tried to be calm in my response. "Yes, he did. Multiple times. He *wanted* to do the deed, in the worst way. He planned to act, and he may have tried to hire people to do the deed. From our information at this point I firmly believe that someone else, someone with more resources and a clearer head, did the job first." I again put my finger on Carty's picture and tapped.

She put her coffee cup back on the saucer but kept her fingers around the handle as the waiter refilled her cup. She didn't look happy, and she sounded a little impatient as she said, "If you insist. What is your next move, Mister Street?"

Finally, it was time for a conclusion. "My time is already paid for, so I am going to Nevada to find Grant Carty."

Her coffee cup back on the table, she put her hands together, exhaled, raised her eyebrows and looked at me over the tops of her delicately framed glasses and spoke quietly, sternly. "Mister Street, I have hired hundreds of people for many different jobs over the years I've been in business. I have a long and consistent history of finishing any task I start, and I insist that my operatives and employees do the same. I appreciate your passion for our cause. I am unconvinced of your theory at this point in time, but I do hope that you are correct in your suspicions. I want answers, but this time I want the *right* answers. I will support your work, per our agreement, but be aware, Mister Street, that my patience does have its limits. Proceed carefully."

"Fair enough." I smiled. So *there*, Street.

34

May 11, 2002

Wayne King was built like a really tall fire plug. His head was shaved to end the struggle against a receding hairline. He looked, in the words of his daughter, 'tough', and she had teased him, more than once, of scaring away her potential suitors. "Only the really grimy ones." He'd said, smiling.

He had been a private investigator for five years, since the year after his Marine stint had ended with an E-7 rank at an even twenty years. His Base Police supervisor work in the Corp had come in handy and had provided credibility for his new work. He'd put in for retirement after he'd taken offense to the words of a sitting president, prompting him to declare, "That pinhead is not gonna get me killed."

He's been proud of his capture a few years earlier of the little creep who'd dropped the Damarow kid from the airplane, and that job had helped make his professional reputation. Sutton had been rewarded a 25-to-life term in the State slam back then, but the solution had never felt 'complete' to him. Now here he was, back in the same neighborhood north of Riverside. This time he was onto something even bigger.

The lady DA had told him that if he brought the office evidence of a huge drug ring, there would be a substantial reward. Wayne needed as much as he could get his hands on now, with a college age daughter and a wife starting chemotherapy for cancer treatment. Work was slow, the nest-egg was getting low, and money was a precious commodity.

But Wayne was a self-starter, and a hustler. It had been a busy two days for him. He had watched the scraggly guy at the car dealer welcome the hot little blonde in a black 7-series BMW to the car business that morning. She had taken a cab directly to Ontario Airport for a quick trip back to Vegas. Wayne had followed. At McCarren in Vegas the girl had been picked up as Wayne rented a car. She had been taken to the parking lot of the Sahara Casino/Resort where she picked up a pewter-colored Lexus Coupe.

King had followed the Lexus back to the car dealer in Jarupa, arriving close to dusk. He'd taken the rental back to the airport, regained his pickup, and resumed surveillance of the car lot. Minutes after the girl's arrival the scraggly guy turned off the lights, locked up the store, and left with the girl. Wayne watched from the cab of his F-150, parked in a vacant stall of the tacky coin-op car wash across the street.

Wayne gave it an extra half-hour before he walked across the street to casually check out the dealer's inventory. He looked at the units on the second row then ducked around the side of the building to find the Acura coupe parked between the office and the shop, in front of the pole building fifteen feet behind. His dark blue jacket and cap rendered him almost invisible against the dark corrugated siding of the building.

The Lexus was an easy one. He used his trusty repo tool, a thin slim flexible metal ribbon Slim Jim, that slipped between the glass and the rubber weather stripping of the drivers' door. The lock gave up in fifteen seconds, giving Wayne access to the interior. He gave it a cursory inspection, finding the carpeting in front of the seats raised slightly. He pulled the rugs away from the floor to find a layer of flat zip-loc bags containing white powder that he recognized as cocaine.

He avoided the media cliché of tasting the stuff, settling for snapping a series of images on his digital camera. Then he pressed the carpets back into place, looked out the deeply tinted windows to check for movement, opened and re-locked the door and skulked away from the car. He checked the knob of the walk-in door, finding no movement at all. Knowing a repeat visit would occur soon, he returned to the front of the lot and calmly returned to his truck. He would return the next evening, better equipped and with access to DEA and local law enforcement backup.

In his truck he called his wife, telling her that their problems may be close to the end. Then he started the truck and drove away, unaware of the observer parked across the street beside the chiropractor's office.

35

Now that I had tacit approval from my client, I wanted to make a quick return to Nevada to get a look at the ranch. I drove home, changed into more casual 'guy clothes'—tan khakis, a black polo shirt and a pair of New Balance walking shoes. I swapped cars, covered the Goat in the garage, then I checked and repacked the Tahoe and hit the road. Traffic was predictable, the Fifteen was bearable, and the trip took a decent four hours twenty minutes. My only stop other than the freeway reconstruction area was the drive-thru in Baker for my staple fried Zucchini and a coke. Guys gotta eat.

In Vegas I drove the loop freeway to the Boulder Highway exit then east for a few miles to the East Side Cannery, a recently completed neon-rimmed resort tower, casino and buffet on the edge of Henderson. After I checked in, I drove out Nellis Boulevard to the Air Force base, past the industrial park at the Speedway then north to the Caraway exit. I parked the truck and changed clothes as before then climbed to the camera perch where I just sat in the moonlight for an hour and watched. There was some faint light through the window of the room addition of the house but there were no cars on site, there was no movement and there were no real signs of life.

Checking the images on the camera I saw that there had been the usual daily traffic with the same cars and the same nameless, formless people. The moonlight was sufficiently bright that I could use binoculars to check out the physical features of the house and the grounds.

It had started as a three-bedroom, one bath semi pre-fab 'Kingsberry' cookie-cutter tract house, common coast-to-coast for decades during the frequent domestic 'boomtown' periods into the seventies. Copies of property documents I'd accessed online showed that it had been the replacement for a previous dwelling that burned to the ground after a lightning strike. The ranch had been acquired from an estate in the early eighties and had been deeded to Bongelli in the late eighties after the previous owner was sent to prison. In 1994 Bongelli had stuck it into Sutton's corporate holdings where it remained after Arnie went away himself. I sensed a trend.

At some point, sans permits, a maybe 600 square feet addition was built, probably a bedroom/bath suite on a concrete slab. The roofing material of the addition was far darker than that of the original house. Looking at each of the rooftop appointments I determined the use of contemporary dish antennas and phone terminals. None of the telephone poles or visible exterior surfaces on the property showed any sign of surveillance equipment of cameras. Good.

After an hour onsite with no surprises, I dismounted from my hilltop perch, returned to the Tahoe, changed clothes and drove back to the hotel. I hit a drive through on Nellis for a sandwich and some onion rings which I scarfed down in the room with a Sam Adams from the cooler in the Tahoe. After that I took a shower, and crashed. The annoyance of a really bad Van Damme flick and too many too-loud 1-900 dating-line spots was solved by a poke at the remote. I slept like a stone. The next morning, I hit the breakfast buffet and was paying the tab when my cell rang. Nine sharp. Catherine.

"Lady Lawyer! How things be?"

"Just making some early calls, Street. I have some news. Ray Cole's ex-wife returned my call last evening. She verified his story of their being together on his boat offshore at the time of the Connors murders. She says she'd testify on his behalf, even though they haven't spoken in several years. We talked for a while. She says he was insane about his vendetta against the Connors but he was out of money and no one else wanted to play along. That was part of her reason for divorcing him. He talked much more than he worked. She was supporting them from her family's estate, they were dodging his debtors, and she was tired of his bullshit. On the day of the murders, they got the news of the shootings when they returned to port that afternoon. She sounds 'real' to me, C."

"Thank you for that. It saves me a lot of time and legwork."

"You're welcome. Also, the P.I. that Ron Connors hired to catch Sutton was killed in a hit-and-run pedestrian accident in Jarupa, a half-block north of the former location of Sunset Motors. This occurred eight years ago. I faxed you a copy of the accident report."

"You're kidding."

"'Fraid not. We're on the right track, Street, I can feel it. Anything we find just verifies something else we already know. That means we're heading in the proper direction, right?"

"Works for me." Now I was stoked. I had hoped to talk to Wayne King, and his death was yet another addition to the growing list of startling coincidences attached to this matter. "Catherine, let's see if there are any surviving family members for him. If they still have his business records, or if his business was acquired by another entity, we may still be able to learn something from him. I'll take a look at the accident report when I get back home. Thank you for that. Anything else?"

"No. That's all I have right now."

"Well, that's plenty. I think the ranch is the most important element at this point. There are specific tasks being performed there, the same traffic every day. Other than Pahrump and a few tacky-looking car washes it's the most active of the corporate properties. I'm going back tonight for a peek inside. I'm shopping for assistance with that this afternoon. Thank you for your effort. Call if you find anything else, and stay in touch."

"Shall do. You, too."

I spent the rest of the morning running errands and continuing my research on the corporate holdings of the Bongelli and Associates Empire. Boring stuff, but I was learning my way around Las Vegas east from the Strip, a rhythm completely different from what I was used to in L.A. Mid-afternoon I drove to a small feeder airport off Boulder Highway near the older part of Henderson. Tanner Aviation was based in a long, tall tan steel metal hangar with a silver corrugated roof at the west end of the small airfield. There were helicopters displaying the call letters of local radio and TV stations parked at the open end of the hangar. I found a parking spot marked 'visitor' then braved the oppressive heat and made my way to the spartan lobby at the front of the structure.

The walls were ringed with aerial photos of the Las Vegas area dotted with photos of local and national celebrities, usually standing in front of a Tanner copter. Drafty wafts of cooled air wandered around the large room. The waist-high windows looked out into the shop where numerous technicians labored on a variety of aircraft. One of the techs looked toward the windows, called to another who stood, looked my way and started walking toward the office.

"You must be Mister Street," he said as he came through the door. He extended his hand. We shook and I passed a card.

"I'm him. You're the owner here?"

He smiled. "Me and the bank. I'm Danny Tanner." He was about my height, a little thinner, with the square, symmetrical face of a matinee idol. His coal black hair had a natural wave that led to the little curl dropping to his forehead, like Clark Kent or Joe Mannix.

"Like I said on the phone I'm a P.I., up from L.A., here looking for a link to an old unsolved double murder. I need to get subtle, low-impact entry into a ranch facility in the desert about thirty miles north from here."

"Okay. Is this a simple fact-finding mission or blatant trespassing?" He grinned conspiratorially, eyebrows lifted.

I answered, "It'll be a little of both, leaning toward the latter. Depends on what I find."

He chuckled in response. "Cool! So do you like helicopters?"

"They're cool unless you're Davey Allison. Don't ask me how they work though."

"Ah. Now *there's* the mystery." He smiled a wide bright smile and motioned for me to follow him as he walked to the shop door, which he held for me. "I have just what you need. Follow me." As I walked through the door he asked, "When would you like to perpetrate this little adventure?"

"Later tonight if possible."

"Great! I love flying over Las Vegas at night. Nothing like it anywhere on the planet." He led me across the hangar, turning to talk as he walked. "We rent out to the local media and cable nets to cover news and traffic and special events. That gives us some spare time in the evenings and a little extra budget to play with. Let's go for a ride in my new toy." He handed me a helmet as we reached a snarky-looking low slung craft that had been towed outside as I arrived.

Five minutes later we were airborne in an alloy-and-carbon fiber capsule with a big round bubble window that left us completely open to a stunning view of the glittery Las Vegas valley. Minutes after take-off, Danny made a pass at the Stratosphere Tower where he paused to hover and wave at the spectators at the top of the glass enclosure. It felt as if we were floating. I never really *liked* floating, and I was starting to have issues with the sense of uncontrolled motion.

Tony was smiling as he waved at the tourists. He asked, "Is this great or what?"

Oooookay, you asked. "Would you be offended if I answered that, 'What'?

Tony looked at me and realized the intent of my comment. "Oh, geez, Street. I'm sorry! I get carried away when I start chasing clouds. I guess I just still miss all the yumpy stuff. I'll back it off a notch or six."

Tony relaxed his grip on the control stick and the ship's path levelled. My stomach gave a sigh of relief, my sphincter took a rest and my pulse evened out as well.

He smiled wide as he said, "I love this thing! It's like an airborne Ferrari!"

"How long have you flown?" He was obviously a talented, enthusiastic, well-travelled pilot.

He looked at me as he started a gentle arc to the north. "Altogether, about twenty years. I started with the CAP in high school, went into the Air Guard during college, got my commission then lucked out and did a nickel with the Thunderbirds here at Nellis. I got hurt in a traffic accident, got a medical discharge and a buyout, then I went into debt doing this. It's fun, and I have some great partners."

"Sounds like a hell of a life. Glad to have you on board."

"Thanks. I've been thinking about that area you mentioned. I remember the Metro cops had a thing about a drug operation somewhere out there a few years ago. The State did a cursory check of some remote places, didn't say if they found anything so they probably didn't. They'd have bragged about it if they had. A State trooper friend told me about it. Maybe you can find what they were looking for."

"I hope so. It's a long twisty road that has led me here. I hope it's worth the trip." We were flying over the Red Rock National Monument and, the view was stunning.

"Anything I might've heard of?"

"The initial assignment is the Ron Connors murder from thirteen years ago. Long unsolved, and the client only wants to look at one suspect. I've proven him a non-player but I need a credible replacement, as soon as possible. I have found connections to other crimes and at least one other murder, now all I need is the correct warm body so I can redirect the attention."

"Sounds like a nice piece of work. Let's make a high altitude run out that way so we can find our way around after dark." We leveled at 9000 feet. Danny flew parallel to the Fifteen freeway until we reached the Caraway exit then he banked east following the proper route toward the ranch. For the return trip to town, pending Nellis Flight Path approval, he would fly a straight line back to his shop.

We finally spotted the ranch property. From our altitude I was again surprised at the dramatic sculpture of the desert landscape. The late afternoon sun was low and bright. Danny's ten-mile oval flight path afforded me an excellent reference for the coming trip. At one point, he pointed to a dark patch of earth a few hundred yards from the ranch house, and called over, "I wonder what that is? Looks as if that area has been worked a lot more than the rest of the ranch. That doesn't make a lot of sense, does it?"

He passed his binoculars to me and I looked for myself. There were two grooves leading away from the cleared area near the house and barn to the overgrown patch That area was irregular in shape, pretty much just a random spot on the desert floor. Still, it was curious. As I returned his binoculars I answered, "No idea. Might be worth a look later. Good eye! Thanks!"

Looking back at the ranch I surveyed the vehicles in attendance. The white compact, now verified to be a Chevy Cavalier, was there, as were the blue Mercedes nearest the house and the dark grey Suburban parked near the barn. There were open drapes at the rear of the main house. My camera surveillance indicated that the truck usually departed at 5p.m. or so and the Merc soon after. The white Chevy usually pulled out about 7 in the evening. It seemed I'd have no problem making an appearance after ten that night. We made another loop then I signaled to Danny, and he headed toward Henderson and his home base.

After we touched down Danny went to his office and wrote an invoice for the upcoming mission. The math was correct and because I knew less than nothing of the costs for such an endeavor

I could only assume we were on solid ground. I was just glad this expense wasn't a frequent occurrence. I looked at it one last time and passed my VISA card. He processed the order, I signed the invoice, and he returned the receipt. Then he said, "Gimme an hour, let me close up here, and we'll go to dinner. I'll buy, because you just did."

36

We drove in Danny's blue 2005 Corvette to a low-slung single story casino on Boulder Highway, an utterly unglamorous structure trimmed in pastel Stucco and neon tubes. It looked awful in the sunset light. Inside, we threaded our way past a few dozen geriatric slot players, making our way to the restaurant. Danny claimed the food was excellent, and well worth the trip. Fortunately, their dinner menu featured a hubcap-sized steak that, when it arrived, removed all doubt to the spot's value. Lesson learned: When in Vegas trust the locals.

After we ordered I explained the CAP pilot's connection with the Damarow murders and asked Danny's opinion. He explained in some detail. "The training and instruction we received was top notch, limited mostly by the small, low-power aircraft we had at our disposal. If you could pay for the fuel and the seat time you could get an excellent education on keeping the plane in the air. For the specific situation you describe, the murder, you'd need to know how to maintain the plane's balance and keep it under control. That small plane would be borderline overloaded with three guys inside. With one of them 'inert', I have to say one guy piloting, one guy tossing the body."

"So with Carty on the stick, Sutton would have done the deed."
I offered.

"True enough, but if he was dead when the plane took off, you
have to know who did *that* deed. Maybe your boy Sutton was just
guilty of 'high altitude littering'." He smiled at his point.

After our food arrived we talked about anything and everything
other than Bongelli, Sutton, Carty and company. It was a welcome
respite for me. Women, cars, Las Vegas weather, politics, and the
future of small business in the current difficult economy were all
situations discussed and solved during that session. Danny Tanner,
Utah native, USAF veteran, boffo pilot...I forged a friendship that
evening that would last long into the future.

We finished dinner and returned to Tanner Aviation after ten
that evening. I changed clothes, transferred my gear bag from the
Tahoe to the copter, and prepared for the late-night recon venture.
Danny approached me as I arranged my backpack, offering an
addition. "You have desert camo, let me loan you a jacket. It's wired
for our electronics package that feeds to the bird. I'll have eyes and
ears for you if needed. The temperature drop can really sneak up
on you out there so the jacket part is of value, too."

"Thanks! That sounds good. I have everything else—boots, suit,
climbing tools, night vision goggles, thermal imager, sidearm and
backup piece. I'm ready. We can go anytime you want."

As he plugged the tiny camera and mic into the battery pack at
the bottom rear of the tricked-out jacket, he explained, "Guy who
developed this works for one of the TV stations we fly for. We trade
out services. He'd think this job was cool." He handed me the jacket
as he finished the installation, then we walked to the copter and
plugged in the helmet mics. Danny lifted off two minutes later.

The cloudless, dark suburban sky was filled with stars that
looked as if they were painted on the outside surface of the canopy.
The air temperature was still eighty degrees after the 106-degree
afternoon. We approached Caraway from the south. Within a
dozen miles of the ranch, Danny killed the lower lights on the ship
and opted for more silent running by directing the exhaust ducting

upward, before he made a shallow loop over the adjoining property to touch down on the back side of the foothills adjoining the ranch property. I hopped off the skid and crouched beside the copter as he lifted off again.

I got my bearings and started the climb toward the perch where I'd stationed the camera. I dismounted it and checked the images, finding nothing new, then I used the field glasses to check the view of the ranch property. Again, nothing out of the ordinary. As I descended the hill, Danny lit my earpiece with, "Street, I'm at altitude. Stay in touch."

"Gotcha. Five by five." What does that even mean? I stopped at the base of the hill to get my bearings again. I took the end caps off the thermal imager, turned it on and made a 180-degree arc from my location. There were a few 'dots', desert critters probably, but no threatening figures. So far so good.

Danny lit up my earpiece. "Hey Street, let's set your camera focus. Point it toward that light at the back of the ranch house." I did so. "Okay, turn the outer ring of the lens till you feel it click." I did so, and felt the stop at the detent. Pointing it again at the house, I heard, "Perfect."

Past the base of the hill at a point maybe 400 feet from the driveway I stopped at a single strand of barbed wire held up by weathered wooden posts, the property boundary. I stepped over it and walked toward the fresh-looking gravel of the driveway, another hint of active management of the location. A hundred yards further I reached the clearing around the barn, then went to the north side of the tall structure, shadowed in the bright moonlight. Fifteen feet further along the side of the barn was a wooden double door. Trying the knob, I found it unlocked and easily opened. As I entered I unsnapped my sidearm holster and clicked on the larger of my two LED flashlights.

The interior of the barn was more complete than I'd expected. The floor was dirt-strewn concrete, the surface a bit rough. suggesting a rushed pour. Working from the top end of the barn I saw a compressor and numerous hoses strewn on the floor, some shop lights, and a gas-powered generator. Near the entrance door to the right was an offset wash basin and toilet, both dust-covered from non-use, and a cheap, plastic-rimmed mirror, about four feet tall, hanging crookedly from a nail in the wall next to the casement window.

The far wall of the barn looked more like a mechanics' shop than an animal barn. A couple of tall red Craftsman tool chests stood in front of low wooden cabinets with ceramic countertops, most layered with a coating of dust indicating long periods of disuse.

More interesting further down the side of the barn was a tall, bronze-colored 1990s Ford Bronco. It was lifted on tall off-road tires and alloy wheels, festooned with numerous period-correct billet aluminum accessories. It leaned to the left, due to two flat tires. I remembered reference to the truck in my earlier interview with Reanna.

More interesting, further toward the end of the barn was a newer, mid-decade GMC Denali SUV with no license plate. Its' lighter front window tint suggested California as its home. Other than the surface dust the truck looked pristine. I wondered if it had been stolen or if it had been stock for the Jarupa car dealer, though it didn't really fit the mold of the drug transport cars. Its hood stood open by about a foot, so I looked in and saw the detached cable for the side-terminal battery. I moved toward the cab a few steps, wiped some dust from the corner of the windshield and snapped an image of the VIN plate just behind the glass. I looked in the driver's door window and saw the OnStar fixture above the rear-view mirror, so I went back, raised the hood further and looked for the attachment bolt for the battery cable. It lay atop the radiator shroud. I inserted it into the cable and finger-tightened the bolt into the appropriate opening. This brought a faint staticky click indicating some faint battery power that, ideally, would power the OnStar locator. We would learn a lot from that soon.

I lowered the hood to its original position then turned my attention to the rest of the barn. Toward the other end of the interior sat an antique Pettibone skip-loader, well-preserved, dusty, and perhaps lightly used. Its bucket sat at ground level, surface rust around the edges of the raw steel but spotted at the edge with thick brown crust—blood? I took an image then a scraping on clear tape and slid it into a small zip-loc bag. An old tractor and assorted farm implements were scattered at the other end of the barn.

I opened one of the cabinets on the wall opposite the entry door, finding an assortment of 'deal folders' for Sunset Motors, nothing of any real value. I replaced the files and slid the doors closed, looking around to make certain that I left the area looking untouched. On the inner wall of the hay loft a glint of chrome caught my eye. A pair of Huffy ten-speed bikes hung from the wall by the rims of their back wheels... the assassins' bikes? I took an image and shot close-ups of the tire tread, intent on comparing layer with the crime scene pics.

Turning toward the door again, I saw a wood-and-glass curio cabinet and the trend continued. On one of the shelves lay a variety of handguns, two revolvers and two semi-automatics. I jimmied the lock of the cabinet and took the pistols, putting them into a large ziploc bag from my backpack. When I left the barn I laid the bag near the edge of the door jamb to retrieve on my way out.

Danny asked in my earpiece, "Find anything, Street?"

"Danny, you wouldn't believe it. I'm, going to the house." I was a little tense now, and the faint hum of the copter far above was a comfort to me amidst the stark silence of the desert.

"Got eyes on ya, man."

I tapped the mic twice in response as I started across the yard toward the ranch house. As I walked past the derelict cars, I turned my attention to the block houses to my right. They too had been out of service or function for some time. Splintered wooden doors stood partly open, loose windows hung at a slight angle from their openings. The first three of the five shacks were similarly shabby but the fourth of the five showed considerable damage. There were dark burn stains around the blown-out door and window openings. I used the feed cam to record the images.

Danny asked over the com system, "Street, point the camera up toward the ceiling." I did so. "Dude, that's a meth lab explosion, sure as hell. See the dark scorch marks inside? They go from counter-level up. When they build these things, they make the roof the weak point. See the openings at the roof joists? That was blown off. We had DEA training at Nellis, they showed us a lot of examples of those explosions. They build them from concrete block so that there's something left in case the thing pops off. I'm bettin' nobody came out of there less than medium well."

"Copy that. Thanks for the info, Danny. The only place I've seen a meth lab explosion is on TV. Hang in, I'm going to the house." I jogged across the forty feet between the last of the derelict cars and the house and stood by the weathered aluminum siding. The electric meter mounted next to the kitchen window hummed softly and its internal disc rotated once every ninety seconds, indicating little internal usage, certainly nothing exorbitant. I had used a similar reading years before in New Jersey to verify and locate a well-concealed and elaborate marijuana 'grow house' and the evidence had held up in court.

I moved a foot to my left, flattened myself against the side of the house and looked into the first window. It looked in on a sparsely furnished living room or den, nothing special but apparently clean and decently maintained. Kitchen, then a Living room or den, standard furnishings, NBD."

"Copy that," came the reply.

I went to the next opening a pair of sliding glass doors, then the next, a bedroom. Neither window was open and the blinds were drawn inside. The addition to the house started a few feet from that window. A windowed wall was built perpendicular to the original structure. The dark screen kept me from seeing in, so I lifted the thermal imager and pressed its control button as I pointed it toward the window from three feet away. The screen lit with an orange image of a reclining figure. Paydirt.

Now I was stoked. "Danny! There's someone in there! I'm going in."

"Careful, bro."

I returned to the sliding glass doors to the patio and examined them. The doors had probably been there for the life of the house but I knew its' weak point. An old B&E artist in Jersey had shared one of his methods with me. I lifted the outer door as far as possible then let it drop. The sudden motion dislodged the simple 'hook' latch in the door from the metal frame and enabled me to slide it open. I stamped my feet on the patio to dislodge most of the loose dirt from my boots then cautiously entered and slid the door closed.

Inside the den I stood silently and listened for seconds to the silence. A stereo-speaker sized ionizer hummed away in the corner of the room, giving the room a clean but slightly staticky aroma. I looked around the ceiling for indications of a camera or some surveillance apparatus, finding nothing. I ticked on the smaller of my LED flashlights and surveyed the room. A two-person sofa with a floor lamp at each end and a spindly coffee table sat opposite the glass doors, a small flat screen TV and a DVD player on the wall to the right.

The hallway opened to the left and I followed it. The first door to the left toward the rear of the house, was ajar, the room stacked with boxes for medical equipment according to the outer brand labels. Opposite that doorway was the bathroom, obviously remodeled at some point in time. It was clean and small, a decent glass shower stall at the far end accompanying home-store sink and toilet fixtures. I reached toward the towel rack and felt the thick dry towel hanging on the rack across from the sink. So far so good.

To the left and four steps further, probably the original master bedroom on the front of the house, was now an office of sorts. An Ikea-style desk with a brass lamp and a desk pad, a rolling office chair on a plastic base, and a phone sat against the far wall, a single bed with a spread and pillow stood next to a pre-fab nightstand against the wall opposite the doorway. I backed out of the room and returned the door to its former position.

So far this little adventure had been easy and eventful. Time to hit for the fences, Street. I ticked off the flashlight and opened the final door across the hall, accessing an original second bedroom plus the room addition and the orange shape.

The door opened slowly into a dark room. I ticked the smaller flashlight and clipped it to a hook on my belt to shine onto the floor with a wide beam ahead of my path. The room was wide and long, spacious probably by design. Along the far west-facing wall a complex hospital suite was arrayed as well as any I'd ever seen. Another ionizer hummed away in the corner next to a pre-fab-looking desk, chair and desk lamp. The desk held a phone, an answering machine and a desk pad. An open folder on the desk pad held signed receipts for several medical supply businesses including Prentiss Medical Supply in Las Vegas. At first glance the medicines mentioned were pain killers and sedatives.

A single male lay under a thin thermal blanket. Out of caution I checked the perimeter of the ceiling, finding only a single camera attached to the upper frame of the bed itself, enabling an image of the...what was he, a patient? That would indicate a medical professional in attendance at least to some extent. A small table stood at the foot of the bed held a notebook-sized folder open to a white page opposite the cover. I lit it up and read the entries. The page labeled CARTY at the top had four-hour listings of pulse and respiration rates. A wire-bound notebook offered notes in two hands regarding periods of lucidity, scale 1-10 scores usually not exceeding four, and the dosage of what I knew to be a fairly stout sedative, perhaps from one of the IV bags?

There were various medical apparatuses attached to the bed, including an IV feed and a series of catheters leading under the blanket. One of the lines led to a half-filled gallon bottle of urine visible under the bed. White circular adhesive contact pads were visible through his thin pajama shirt, lead wires connected to a monitoring apparatus in turn attached to a larger system a few feet away. Three six-inch screens read blood pressure, pulse and respiration. While the machines were clean and shiny, they were not all that contemporary-looking. Then again, what did I know? I took images of the apparatus, the machines and their model numbers if visible, for a future internet search.

Looking at his features I could see half of an older grant Carty from the CAP photo. The left side of his face had been severely burned and now, however much later, thick brown scar tissue covered that side of his face. The mouth, eyes and nose were intact but the ear was damaged and most of the hairline was covered with the same scar tissue. I speculated that this was a product of the meth lab fire less than a hundred feet away. There had to be a story there.

If I was to formally verify the identity of the wounded subject, I would need a DNA sample. I took a small zip loc bag from my shirt pocket and looked for an available site, settling on the right foot that peeked from under the thin blanket. There was a plastic cup on the shelf of the desk provided a clean pair of toenail-appropriate nail clippers that suited the job quite well. I knelt at the foot of the bed and gently grasped his right great toe and did the deed with a hearty 'click', holding the zip-loc below to catch the clipping. I shot an image of the bag and the toe, returned the clippers to their cup, and put the bag in my upper jacket pocket. So far so good, Street.

From the lower vantage point I found a weathered plastic clipboard hanging from the footrail. From what I could decipher, the notes there verified the text in the notebook. Perhaps since this was a private care facility—if not just a warehouse for the victim—there were no signatures apparent. I rose silently.

Standing at the foot of the bed I surveyed the scene and considered the situation. I was looking at the benefactor of untold pain and death and the proof of my own theories. My fictional heroes would be required to say something witty, profound, or at least smug at this significant point in the story. Suddenly tired and stressed, my mind almost a blank, all I could think to say was, quietly, "Grant Carty, at last we meet."

As soon as those words left my lips Grant Carty's eyes popped open. Without moving his head his eyes searched the room, perhaps finding focus, until they settled on me, the big stranger standing in the soft light at the foot of his bed. I watched as he stared, my heart pounding, as I tried to minimize, or perhaps rationalize, my presence. His arms were lying at his side and a cord attached to some kind of button on a coned handle lay a foot away from his left hand. Who knew what that was attached to or whether he could even operate it? I put my index finger in front of my lips to suggest quiet, hoping that he was muted by his injuries. He gurgled for a few seconds then he seemed to lose focus and fade, taking with him the five years that my life had just been shortened. I finally exhaled, remembering to get images of this room and its occupant.

As I snapped away, and just as my pulse started to return to normal, my earpiece lit again. Danny's stolid tone was as efficient and detached as a weather report. I could hear the hum of his copter behind his voice. "Street. There's a car turning off the road onto the driveway. Late-model dark Mercedes coupe, occupied once, in your *lap* in about forty-five seconds. Get the hell out of there."

I keyed the mic and muttered, "Check. Thanks!"

At that same time a monitor on the desk flared to life showing a dark car crossing the cattle guard at the end of the driveway. That explained the apparatus attached to the mailbox and made me glad I had taken another path onto the property that first day.

I took one more look around the bedroom, set its door to its original position, then made my way quickly down the hall and across the sparsely furnished living room to the front door. All of the images I'd taken had shown traffic and parking at the rear of the house so I opened the front door and stepped out onto the slab front porch as the headlights started to shine through the sliding glass doors at the rear. The landing sat a few inches above the surrounding yard and the layer of grit indicated that it hadn't been used in a while. I had locked the door as I passed through so now all I could do is stand there at the edge of the porch, frozen in place for a few minutes.

It struck me as I stood there that there were no shrubs, no flow-

ers, no 'trim', no acquiescence whatsoever to residential 'friendli-
ness' anywhere near this house. Utilitarianism was the rule here,
like at some stark mental hospital or warehouse. This house was
Grant Carty's storage facility.

I secreted myself as much as I could, being a big guy dressed in
desert camo, standing in the shadows against a stark beige frame
house, dead center in the middle of nowhere. I heard the car park
at the rear of the house near the patio. Its lights stayed on as the
door opened and shut, sounds that were distinct in the desert
stillness.

37

After the kitchen and den lights came on inside the house, I made my way around the side of the structure, past the black Mercedes and toward the barn and the line of derelict cars. I looked back at the Mercedes after I passed it, noting that it wore a Nevada temporary paper tag. That made me curious. I'd figure it out soon enough but now I had other issues to address. I knew I'd seen it before, though.

I crouched as I ran across the space then I leaned against a wrecked Lincoln next to a dirty pickup draped with a tattered beige car cover. More lights had come on inside the house and the sole occupant of the car had stayed inside. I crouched undetected at the line of cars, shielded from view from the house by the cinder-block shacks. As I knelt there, low, still and silent, I finally took a look at the pickup that I faced a mere five feet away.

It was a badly weathered dark blue '90s Chevy S-10 extended cab, partly covered with a tan flannel car cover that lay over the right side of the cab and drooped into the pickup bed. Desert turf piled up around the tires told of an extended rest. The wind, sun and heat exposure that had killed the clear coat had also turned the once stylish and colorful vinyl graphics into a gnarled mass of burned brown plastic ribbons stuck to the side of the body. Pocked and tarnished directional-style billet aluminum rims carried cracked and dry-rotted Goodyear Eagle ST tires with near-new tread depth. The rear tire on my side was deflated and separated from the bead of the rim.

Whoa! This was the one!

I crouched and moved through the sand to the drivers' side of the truck, where the window of the drivers' door was open. I reached inside, moved some grit from the face of the gauge panel, seeing 2239.8 miles on the odometer. The back seat was piled with clothes and old newspaper, and the whole cab had a dry but misty aroma, fittingly, of paper and moldy cloth. The cloth and vinyl upholstery had also succumbed to the elemental beating and GM's powdery tan foam rubber backing peeked through at the tops of the door panels and seats. I made a mental note to clean the Tahoe when I got home.

The drivers' side front fender had been smashed almost flat, with the impact damage extending inward to the hood and back to the sheet metal of the door. That front wheel hung at a twisted angle, the upper control arm broken in whatever crash had happened. The plastic grille and headlight on that side were also past-tense.

I gazed into the cab again, looking toward the rear window. There, hanging by a wisp of dirty scotch tape, hung a five-inch square temp tag paper, the original registration slip for the title transfer. Barely visible when I risked using the smaller of the flashlights, a faint digit '10' surrounded by a blotchy faint pink field. I remained crouched as I walked to the rear of the truck and pulled the tarp from the tailgate. There above the tailgate latch handle was a quarter-size dent, the paint chipped to the bare metal as referenced in my first interview with Jorge'.

Amazed at my discovery, I pulled out the little Sony digital camera, adjusted the settings for low light, and started taking images of the elements of the truck and some of the surrounding cars. You never know what might turn up from the pics, and too much information is always preferable to not enough.

Mission gleefully completed I retraced my steps past the barn, retrieved the bagged firearms by the barn door. I stuck that bag inside my jacket, rezipped and made my way to the end of the barn. There I stopped, made another 180-degree pass of my intended return route with the thermal imager. Finding nothing of value, I hit the comm button to raise Danny. "Danny! Crank it, I'm on my way back to 'One'."

"Copy," came the response. I heard the faint distant sound of the copter change pitch as he began his descent to the rendezvous point. As I topped the hill I saw the copter touch down at the base. Ninety seconds later I ducked beneath the idled blades and resumed the passenger seat. I plugged the comm cable into the receptacle as I donned my helmet and gave thumbs up as Danny revved for takeoff.

Danny looked across as we lifted off and asked, "Find anything?"

"Ohhhh, yeah," I smiled in response. "More than you can imagine."

As we reached altitude for the return trip south, I could see the sky start to lighten over the range of, fittingly, Sunrise Mountain. A half-hour after touchdown at Tanner Aviation, in the harsh glare of the chilly desert dawn, I texted Catherine with a few pictures and a message relating my finds. It was now Saturday, and Catherine had mentioned that she would be away for the weekend with her fiancé.

Within an hour I'd returned to the Hotel, showered and attempted to lie down and rest, but I was too wired to accomplish that. Instead, I out-loaded my stuff from the room to the truck, went to the buffet for breakfast, then checked out. I threaded my way up Boulder to the 515 freeway, looped back to the Fifteen southbound. Taking the uphill curve past the 'M' resort I set the Tahoe's cruise control to eighty for the duration of the trip.

The extended drive gave me time to ponder the situation I'd uncovered. The discovery of Grant Carty, 'alive' but not all that 'well', asked as many questions as it answered. My main concern now was that someone *not* Grant Carty, probably the female in the Mercedes, was pulling the strings, paying the bills, keeping the lights turned on, and running the show at the ranch. Had I been allowed a few more minutes in the house I may have uncovered that identity.

Grant's physical challenges made it obvious that he was being maintained in at least marginal condition by some variety of medical professional. I considered the camera above his bed, the 'cattle grate sentry' video feed, and the electronic apparatus on the roof of the house and figured that there was some arrangement for a video feed to an outside destination, probably someone's laptop.

The furnishings in the house, modest but functional and complete, suggested that there was or had been a resident caretaker at least part of the time, perhaps the owner of the white Chevy compact, likely a day-care worker tending to Carty. The bedroom suggested around-the clock care in the past. I wanted to determine the identity of those people as soon as possible. Catherine would help with that.

Lest we forget, the hanging bicycles, the Chevy S-10 and probably the guns lent credibility to my theory that Carty being the kingpin for the Connors murders *and* the pilot of the plane from which the Damarow kid had been dropped—maybe not 'slam dunk' but pretty close. Elizabeth might be surprised when shown the evidence. I had reason to appreciate the desert ranch, and I was equally relieved that Carty hadn't bought the farm.

And what was the story behind that Denali?

After weathering the southbound traffic down the Cajon Pass on the Fifteen, I drove west on the 210 toward home, hoping to decompress for a while. I went to the kitchen and made lunch, a ham and cheese sandwich—Honey Baked and baby swiss on oatmeal bread with brown mustard and kosher dill pickle on the side to be specific. Later I did 'domestic' stuff, writing checks to pay bills and tending to the trivial matters facing any homeowner. I fixed a broken sprinkler head out by the front sidewalk and changed out a couple of light bulbs, nothing all that interesting or challenging. Homes in L.A. are intensely expensive compared to elsewhere and even marginally 'nice' homes border on 'stupid money' for purchase and upkeep. The recent and ongoing deep recession coupled with the housing crash had put me in a net-loss position with the house value, and I was fortunate to have savings and stable earnings. The house had gained and lost value in my five years in L.A's uneven economy but it was still 'home.'

I tend to get attacked by insecurities when I'm tired and stressed, and that afternoon I was as tired and stressed as I'd ever been. Given that, though, there was work to do, and a pity party would just be a waste of time, so I locked up the house, went to the garage, took the cover off the GTO. I gassed up in the valley at my friend Walt's station in Nan Nuys, and went for a short road trip, one of my favorite routes. That car on those roads had always done wonders to put my head straight, just as my dad had said it did for him when it was new.

After the non-ethanol fill-up, I hit the 405 north to the 118 west. Past Simi Valley toward Moorpark I cut north through the foothills, taking the sparsely-trafficked curves at 50% above the speed limit onto the agricultural flatlands to State Highway 126 toward Ventura. I stopped at a produce stand alongside the highway for some fresh orange juice and noted that their bagged oranges were nowhere near as good as those Jorge had passed to me. Count your blessings Street.

As the 126 met the Pacific Coast highway in Ventura, I hung a left and drove south along the coast, always a steadying event for me. The day was clear, and the Pacific was an epic tone of azure, almost matching the color I'd chosen for the GTO when I had it painted.

As I passed the entrance to Paradise Cove, home to my fictional heroes of yore, I gave a two-finger salute. "Harry, Jim, I promise that I'll see this job through to the end credits." I pulled into the driveway at home an hour later feeling stronger and more confident than I'd been in a while. Guy's gotta take a break sometimes, right?

38

May 22, 2002

Wayne King had told his wife Adrienne at the hospital that afternoon that he was finally on to that big break they'd been looking for and that things were about to get a lot better. He swapped his truck for her old Taurus and drove the 60 miles from Santa Clarita to Carty's car dealer in Jarupa north of Riverside. He parked in an empty stall at the car wash across the street and down the block and waited. A little after 7p.m. the last remaining staff vehicle, a white Chevy pickup, pulled away from the darkened business. Anxious to continue his discovery he waited a few minutes then, seeing no signs of life he locked the car and walked to the crosswalk.

Wayne wanted to get into the pole building this time. There was far more traffic to it than to the car dealer itself, and he thought he knew why. He needed to verify the drug operation and call the Riverside Sheriff's office to initiate the raid, then try to participate in it himself, solidifying his witness status and guaranteeing his eligibility for the reward. He had brought his lock pick set this time so the door to the pole building wouldn't be a hindrance.

He went there first, gained entry and found in a side room a bench and metal table used for packaging the drugs hauled in from the ranch north of Las Vegas. He shot images of the plastic baggies, the measuring tools and the gallon containers under the table holding more, probably cocaine. He snagged two of the packed baggies to take for examination by the Sheriff's Department.

Wayne King looked out the side window of the building for a moment to check for movement. Sensing none he left the barn and quickly started back across the street to his car. As he stepped off the curb he opened his flip phone to call the Sheriff's then his wife. He was halfway across in the crosswalk as the first call started ringing. He may have sensed an approaching shape as he crossed the center point of the road.

––––––––

After Grant Carty closed the lot that day, he had driven past the car wash and absently noticed a car parked unattended in one of the stalls. He drove another block, made a left and stopped at the 7-11. Walking back out with his cigarettes he had second thoughts. Maybe he should check.

He drove back to the car wash, parked at the back of the lot and walked to the old Taurus—what, a '92 or so? It was locked so he found a rock near the back fence and used it to smash the front passenger's side window. He sat in the driver's seat and looked around the interior. In the console ash tray, he found a grey business card for Wayne King, Confidential Investigations with an LA county phone number. Where had he heard that name before? Then it came to him—this was the PI who caught Arnie and testified against him at the trial. Oh shit. This is trouble.

Carty looked around the interior of the Taurus and found the spare ignition key beneath the driver's side floor mat. The car started first try. He drove off the car wash lot and down one block, waiting on the shoulder for the intruder to leave the lot. That happened after about ten minutes. As the fat guy who'd come out of the pole barn started across the street Carty put the Taurus in gear and gunned it, lights out. As the detective passed the center point of the street with his cell phone to his ear, he started to turn his head toward the approaching shape.

The car caught King just above the right knee at a shade less than 52 miles per hour. King's upper body smashed into the hood then flew, less the right leg, fifteen feet above the Taurus, coming to rest in the unmown grass alongside the street. Carty slammed on the brakes and the car skewed to a sideways stop. He backed to the body, left the idling car and went to the warm, twitching body. He checked the pockets, retrieved the zip loc bags of dope and some cash, then he kicked the side of the ruined skull and walked back to the car.

Carty drove the blood-spattered Taurus with the broken plastic nose to the dumpster at the back of the 7-11, then another mile to a stalled housing tract that he was invested in. He found one of the unlit paved side roads and stopped in the middle of the street. He let the car in idle in neutral as he lit a wad of newspapers and strewn them around the interior. He opened the drivers' door then reached in, pulled the shifter into 'Drive' and stepped aside as the Taurus rolled on its own down the street. By the time the car rolled into the ditch at the end of the street Carty was halfway across the field that separated the housing tract from his own house when the Taurus loped into the drainage ditch at the end of the street, its interior now started burning in earnest.

Carty, sour-sweaty from his snorting and smoking, but energized from the adrenaline rush, slept well that night knowing that one potential crisis had been averted. That didn't happen very often anymore.

39

I slept quite well that night and rose early Monday morning, continuing the computer searches including later property transfers and sales from Arnie's holding corporation. I will admit that I didn't know what I was seeing half the time, but I wanted the information catalogued. Mostly there was a stillborn residential development about nine years ago that raised questions in my mind. I certainly didn't see Arnie Sutton taking the persona of a real estate developer. The face tatts would kill that vibe in a heartbeat.

The hit-and-run death of Wayne King within a block of the location of Sunset Motors bothered me far more than anything about Sutton. I looked at the accident report that Catherine had faxed—high speed contact, dismemberment, all made it smell like a targeted hit. I'd seen a few of those among the gang types in Jersey. Couple that with the discovery of his wife's burned out Taurus, two days later, three miles away near a Sutton property? No contest. I looked for pictures of the car with no luck.

King's widow, undergoing cancer therapy at a hospital in Santa Clarita at the time, had passed three months later. They were survived by a college age daughter and an older son living in Salem,

Oregon. I looked up the daughter, found a Canyon Country address but a Burbank number. I called and left a message for her.

I worked at the details of that until 10:15 when Catherine called. We set a noon appointment at her office. I'd bring lunch, she asked for 'good Mexican' if I could find some. Oh, but to ask.

I had almost forgotten the pistols I'd purloined from the barn. I stopped at a for-hire forensics lab in Pasadena on the way out and dropped them off for analysis, with an expedite order since they were 'backed up' with work. Seems they were always 'backed up' when I called. I smelled a racket, but their work was top notch, so I let it slide. I arrived at Catherine's office loaded for bear, research materials, photos and a seriously aromatic lunch in hand. She ushered me in, and we spread the meal out on the conference table in the room adjoining her office. She broke out a bottle of red wine. "This is where divorcing couples come to confer, yell at one another and curse one another's very existence, C. Beware of evil spirits lurking about."

I smiled and responded, "That's okay. Pepe's hot sauce will kill anything." A half hour later, sated, we cleaned the table and resumed our positions at the office desk.

The 40-inch monitor on the wall behind her, enlarged the pictures as I moved the mouse. I started with the barn then the house then the derelict pickup. I returned to the first of each group after the first run through of each collection. She asked pertinent questions at each stage, and it was an interesting session.

"What's the significance of the Denali?"

"I ran the numbers, it comes back as a San Bernardino stolen from six and a half years ago. That is in turn attached to an active Missing Persons case, same locale. The parents are big into used cars for decades, and very successful. They have five lots within a twenty-mile radius including one just a mile from the former Sunset Motors. And, there is a one hundred-thousand-dollar reward for the identity and capture of his murderer and the return of his remains."

"Sounds as if they're serious about the conclusion of the mystery. And you think..."

I answered, "I think Carty offed him and buried him at that ranch. Tell ya what...If we find that to be the case, I'll split the reward with you. Call it an extraordinary performance bonus or an early wedding present."

She smiled. "Aw, thanks, 'C'. Okay, moving on, guns, bikes hanging..."

"And the tread patterns match the impressions made in the mud outside the Connors' front gate."

She lifted her eyebrows. "Good." She moved to the file with the pics from inside the house.

I continued, "There's the boy wonder, right there. Not a lot to work with at this point. I got DNA samples, dropped them at the lab on the way out. He's monitored somewhere offsite, that will be the key to the 'who' of this. The 'why' will be much more complicated, I'm sure."

She pointed a laser pen at one of the machines tending to Carty. "I don't pretend to know a lot about hospitals, Street, but I know there is a huge market for recent-model, used medical equipment. Do you think that could be the source of what they're using to monitor him?"

"I wouldn't doubt it. It's like they're biding their time taking care of him for some reason, perhaps until they think they don't need him anymore. They're not over-spending on this place. The equipment they use is clean and working but not state-of-the-art. There's no extravagance in the house itself but it is very clean. I have to give them that. He did come awake for a few seconds when I disturbed him, so his senses are not 'gone' at all. He is seriously scorched though, and I want to research that if we don't have a direct source for the information."

Sarah nodded. "I'll send you what references I can find, and you do the same. This is interesting."

She moved through the house file to the end with minimal questions and moved to the derelict cars. I was excited by the S-10. I pointed out all the similarities to the descriptions I'd heard in my travels, all the way down to the little dent in the tailgate. Catherine was less than impressed. "This is all fine, Street, but it's a big zero in court. It would almost be a waste of time to even bring it up. Your witnesses say a new, or almost new truck what, thirteen years ago? This one's junk. The jury wouldn't buy it."

"I'm sorry to hear that. Oooookay. Moving on..."

The next image was of the dark blue late 70s Mark V Cartier Edition Lincoln Continental. There was dirt covering every surface and the rest of the car looked great but for smashed upper front sheet metal. Whitewall tires wound around factory alloy finned wheels, tires long flat and the beads separated. Mr. Cartier would not be pleased.

I looked at Catherine, she had a stunned expression on her face. "Street. That car! Oh my God!"

I looked at her then back at the screen. "What? What is it?"

She sat silently for a moment, and drained her half-full wine glass in one gulp. "Okay, you remember I told you that my husband died in a car wreck?"

"Yes. You didn't elaborate."

"Well, we were returning from a weekend at the Del Coronado. We were celebrating our third anniversary and we had finally decided to start a family. We were *really* happy. We were almost home, and it was almost dark. We'd turned onto Van Buren from the freeway when we were hit from behind by a car—*that* car, Street! It hit us again from the rear then from the side and he finally forced Brian to jump the curb and run down the depression beside the road. The truck flipped. I was out because I'd hit my head on the back glass as we were hit from behind the second time. When I came to, Brian was already gone. I crawled out and a passerby who'd seen the wreck came to help me. I was lucky, just a concussion, but I lost my husband and later the pregnancy. "She sat and exhaled. She just looked sad in the indirect light. I didn't know what to say or do so I let her call the shots. I let it lie for about a half hour as she sat, the truth of her great loss finally explained. I had questions that could wait.

After a half hour she looked up at me and quietly said, "I'm sorry, 'C'. you've been so good about all of this. I don't mean to add to your hassles."

"Don't give it a second thought, Cath. This took us both by surprise. May I ask you a few questions?"

"Sure."

"What color was your husband's truck?"

She smiled. "It was a pea soup green Ford Ranger. I *hated* that truck. Brian didn't." She took a deep breath after saying that. "I have some pictures at home in an album.

"Okay, let me guess. It was a 4 by 4? Lifted? Tall tires?"

"Yes. How did you know that?"

"Look at the damage on the Lincoln. The grille, the corner lights, the header panel in front of the hood, all mashed up. The bumper, lower than the bottom of your truck, was not damaged. That truck was also a single cab, with no space behind the seat. Am I right?"

"Yes."

"See? Hitting that back window accounts for your concussion. Had this been an extended cab your injuries could have been much worse. There are also tire marks and damaged or missing chrome trim on the passenger's side of that car, where he attacked you from the side. I'm surprised that car made it back to the ranch. They may have had to use a flatbed to move it. Any cop who saw it on the road would have lit him up to check it out. It just looks suspicious."

Catherine looked at the screen, then at me. "I really don't feel all that lucky. Sorry."

"Don't worry about that. Look, you are incredibly strong to have come through all that you did. And I could not be more pleased and honored to be working with you." She smiled. I paused. "Now, are we ready to get back to chasin' our bad guy?"

"Sure." She looked at me and asked, "So where do we go from here? Time is running out for that hearing on Sutton's sentence, and I need to at least get a delay on that if we're still looking at this. Is there anything we're missing?"

I paused. "I keep going back to Bongelli. He's running this show. Trip him up and the whole deal could implode."

"Well, I knew you'd be asking, so I built a file on him."

"As I knew you would." I smiled, "He's in this up to his chubby little ears, and I'm wondering if he is in over his head or has lost control of the ongoing operation. Just read the high points to me; audible sometimes shakes things loose for me."

She hit the keys that brought the text to the screen, and read, "Vincent Adam Bongelli, via Facebook, the California Bar Association and his own practice's website. Age 51, Chicago native, U.S. Air Force three years and change advanced to E-4, early-out with an Honorable discharge. JD degree from Cal State Northridge on the GI Bill, Cal State Bar exam top fifty percent. Associate at a large West L.A. law for six years before he started his own firm, Briggs, Bongelli and Associates at age thirty-two. Partnership dissolved two years later. Riverside and Las Vegas offices; six associates in California at the last filing; specialty, corporate formation and narcotics defense. California Firm's stated gross forty-two million last year reported. Yikes! Must be nice!"

I asked, "Is that a lot for a seven-attorney firm? They have what, maybe twenty employees total?"

"Probably that or more. Lots of corporations doing his bidding, lots of state filings, tons of paperwork."

"But," I said, "I know word gets around in the legal world, some of the attorneys I've known gossip among themselves like a minivan full of eighth-grade cheerleaders. What's his reputation around town?"

"He gets a modicum of respect and he has a select clientele that the rest of us won't touch with a ten-foot pole. He was considered a joke when I was with the D.A. He was an easy 'get' for a conviction. The people I talked to regarding him are marginally civil in their responses."

"And the ones in prison are kept quiet because they still think he'll help them." I pondered the theory.

Catherine resumed her description. "Okay back to Mister Wonderful. Uh oh! Separated, his wife resumed her maiden name, Shirley Parris, Las Vegas residence, one of the condo towers off east from the old Desert Inn property, and it's a 'P' for 'Penthouse'." She looked at me. "I know this address. My parents have one as a time share. They're a really nice walled-community surrounded by golf courses."

"Oh, the struggles we face..."

"Car..." She paused for effect and looked over her reading glasses at me. "New transfer, black Mercedes S550 coupe."

I looked at her, a smile growing on my face.

"Occupation, oh, Street, this is good." Her eyebrows raised. "Registered nurse."

By the time she spoke the second syllable I had opened my phone and was speed-dialing Elizabeth Damarow's number. "Cathy, that's it! It's the ex! She's the caretaker!" into the phone I spoke, "Elizabeth Damarow, please. Tell her it's Street." Then to Catherine, "What else do you have on her?"

"Okay, professional profile via LinkedIn, Nurse practitioner at a big hospital in Riverside, specialty? Recuperative Therapy."

Over the phone I heard, "Yes Mister Street. It's good to hear from you. Are we making progress in the investigation?"

"Yes ma'am, we are, and we just caught a huge break that is time sensitive. Question: Didn't you tell me your corporate planes were based at Ontario Airport?"

She sounded excited herself now. "Yes, they are. Where do you need to go?"

"Henderson Airport, east of Las Vegas, the sooner the better."

"Very well, Mister Street. Our pilot will be waiting. How soon can you be there?"

I tapped my wrist, Catherine lifted her index finger and mouthed, "One."

As I looked at her, I said, "We can be there in an hour, Elizabeth."

"Our pilot and plane will be waiting. Good luck, Mister Street."

"Thank you, ma'am." As I disconnected, Catherine was gathering her briefcase and digital recorder and approaching the door, preparing to turn out the lights.

40

June 14, 2004

The tall young man left his silver-blue GMC Yukon parked near the barn and started looking for Grant Carty. One of the moon-suited Hispanics returning from the portable toilet to one of the mixing shacks pointed to the field to the north where a yellow skip loader was moving dirt.

Donny Priess was amazed at what he'd seen and smelled there in the last few minutes. His home territory of San Bernardino County was a hotbed of drug activity, and he'd tasted his share at parties, but this was huge! He shook his head in disbelief as he assembled the factors of what he thought he knew about Grant Carty. To himself he marveled, 'Ho-lee shit. They are not gonna believe THIS!'

It made him smile as he approached the clearing a hundred yards away. He saw the idling skip loader but almost didn't recognize the gaunt, shirtless Carty as he sat at the steering wheel maneuvering the machine. He approached out of the bright afternoon sun. "Yo! Carty! Donny Priess! How you doin', brother?"

Carty looked at the kid, recognized him from Jarupa and the

dealer auctions. He didn't have time for this, and he was not in the mood. He answered, "Not worth a shit, Priess! Car business really sucks!"

"How can you say that?" He stopped in front of and off to one side from the skip loader next to the rough-hewn ditch. "We're having a record year. We're looking to expand again. You shouldn't complain. You don't work your lot anymore. Place looks like crap! A business doesn't run itself, y'know? That's why I came out here after the sale at the Vegas auction today. Do you want to sell your place?" He smiled. "I see you have other interests now. I have cash, man!"

Buzzed, sweaty, Carty looked at the kid and laughed. "You stupid fuck! That dump is just a means to an end. I don't give a flyin' purple shit about the car business. I hate it and every asshole in it! Bunch o' backstabbin' pricks!" He took a pistol from the back of his belt and pointed it at the kid, who stepped back in shock.

"Whoa! What's that for? What the fuck's wrong with you?"

Carty smiled and answered, "Y'know, there's a reason we have this place out here in the middle o' nowhere, Priess. It's supposed to be a secret. Then here you come, all shiny and new, pokin' around in shit that's not your business. Bad move, junior. You ain't leavin' here vertical, buddy."

Now the young Priess was sweating through his $40 tee shirt, thinking, 'This guy's nuts!'. "Naw, man, don't take it like that. Look! I don't care about any of the drug shit! That's your thing, do it in good health! I just want to buy your store! I have cash! We can work that out, right?"

Carty looked at the kid. "In a word, no." He pointed the gun toward the ditch. "Move over there,"

The kid stood his ground. That had worked with the rougher crowd all through school, it'd work here too. He straightened and asked, "Why?"

Carty wasn't playing. "Um, 'cause I have the gun? Yeah, that's it." He aimed toward the kid's leg and fired once, the round hitting three inches in front of his foot. He jumped back, lost his balance and fell onto his back in the ditch. As he landed he felt something below him move. He looked as he tried to regain his footing to see a foot in a shoe, attached to a leg that was peeking out from the pile of dirt beside the ditch. He looked up at Carty, now standing beside the idling machine.

Young Priess, his eyes now saucers, wasn't done trying to avoid a desolate death. "Carty! Listen to me! I'm wired in at Cal State! I can move product for you, lots of it! Give me a rate and a quantity! I have connections!"

Carty, toying, played along for a second. "Really? You'd do that for me?" He sneered at the desperate kid standing below him.

Desperately, Priess played his hand. "Sure, bro! I have friends! We can set up a network! We can make it happen! Let's give it a shot!"

Carty pursed his lips. "See? That was my first thought when I saw you walkin' out here. I gotta do just that! I gotta give you a shot." With that he raised the pistol and fired, hitting the man dead center in the chest. The blast spun him around and threw him back two feet where he landed flat on his face at the bottom of the ditch. Carty put a second round in the twitching body, top of the neck.

Donny Priess never heard the shot. You never hear the one that kills you.

Grant Carty stepped into the ditch and rifled through the man's pockets, finding a money clip holding $1,200 in large bills, a large ring of keys to who knows what, a billfold with more cash and gas receipts inside, and a fancy cell phone, one of those pricey deals. He tossed the billfold sans currency, pocketed the cash and keys. He checked the cell phone screen, no coverage, then popped the back off, tapped out the battery onto the dirt and tossed the phone further up the ditch. He climbed back up to the seat of the tractor and within ten minutes had filled the ditch and leveled the sandy soil atop it. He was getting good at this, but it really didn't matter. Dead center middle of nowhere, killing a guy didn't make any difference.

He took the 'loader back to the barn, then brought the kid's

Yukon in and parked it at the far end by the big door. He popped the hood, used a closed-end 5/8" wrench to pull the battery cable, cutting the OnStar feed. He stood back and looked at the truck. It'd be a good parts source sometime maybe. After he cut the shack crews loose early, he went back in the house, sat at the round Formica kitchen table and did a phat line of coke, good stuff this time. Funds from Donny Priess' pockets funded a healthy round of blackjack at a tacky North Las Vegas casino and a visit to a North Las Vegas strip club later that night. He lost at the tables, as usual.

Catherine had transferred all of her files to her laptop as I spoke to Elizabeth and was ready to leave the office when I disconnected. My kinda woman! I followed her red Blazer from downtown into the foothills to the south to a well-kept residential development and her house, a nice ranch on a small lot. I waited in the driveway in the Tahoe with the air on high. She reappeared three minutes later carrying a valise and a small garment bag, enough stuff to equip any guy I knew for maybe a week. Be prepared, right? It took us about twenty minutes to reach the Damarow hangar at Ontario Airport.

When we arrived, I was directed to park the Tahoe beside the hangar inside a chain link fence, and I was given the gate code in case I needed to retrieve the vehicle during off-hours. Good call. The plane was a bright beige custom painted Citation Sovereign, a totally luxe twelve-passenger thing with high-end furnishings and appointments, as I would expect, knowing Elizabeth's style in everything. The woman does not half-step. We were in Las Vegas airspace within thirty minutes, sans the aerobatics that Danny had provided last time I was aloft. I could get used to this private jet thing.

The pilot requested and was granted clearance to land at the airport that encompassed Tanner Aviation. We taxied to the Tanner hangar two minutes after touchdown and deplaned to Danny's welcome. He was standing next to a new Arrest-me-red Corvette Z06, looking like a latter-day Robert Urich. We were, after all, in 'Vegas'. I made the introductions and stood aside as he and Catherine got acquainted. Each seemed 'taken' with the other. Who am I to interfere?

I carried Catherine's bags and my laptop to the 'Vette. Danny asked, "So Street, what do you think?"

"Impressive! You didn't tell me about this one."

He smiled, "I had one ordered, this one came in first and I liked it better so I got it instead. I'm swamped, so you and Catherine get to check it out first. My courtesy cars are all out with other clients. Do you think you can handle it?"

No sweat. "I did the Bondurant Advanced course four years ago. Is that good enough?"

"That'll work." He tossed me the key fob/control module. "Please bring it back clean and full of gas and don't break it."

"Of course!" I looked at Catherine, who was ready to go. She entered her side and belted in as I plugged myself in and got a feel for the car and its controls. Momentarily, after I blipped the throttle twice for dramatic effect, we hit Boulder Highway traffic and made our way toward the walled fortress that housed Shirley Parris.

We found the address easily enough and BS'd our way past the gate sentry easily enough. Finding the tower itself, Catherine tried the number she had for the Parris condo with no luck, so we parked nose-out in the shade next to the front portico to wait for her return. It was 'only' 91 degrees in the Vegas valley that afternoon, so I let the Corvette idle with the A/C on medium. Understand that this vehicle grossly violated my standards for a proper stakeout mount. I was the kid that sneered at the Mannix roadster when I discovered the reruns, and I'd thought the Starsky and Hutch Torino was a cartoony bad joke. This thing still stuck out like a sore thumb but at least it was a clean, well-manicured digit.

I was pleased to have a few minutes to sit and talk to Catherine after just a couple of hours ago she'd been broadsided with the cause for her years-ago heartbreak and injury. I looked across at her and asked the most pertinent question. "So Cath, how are you doing with all of this? You seem to be holding up well after having found out about Brian's death."

She was introspective, as I'd come to expect from her. "Street, I'm still trying to process it all. If anything, I feel blessed. Look, I am still standing and in good shape personally and professionally. I have a great fiancée, I love him and he loves me, and he would marry me this afternoon if he was here with us. I may be the only one not killed off after being targeted in this shitstorm that started with Bongelli and Carty and Sutton." She paused for a second then continued. "If anything I'm in better shape than I've been in a long time. Thank you for that."

I answered, "That's great, Cath. I'm glad."

My cell phone rang then, displaying the number I'd sourced for Wayne King's surviving daughter, Dierdre. Since her father's murder and her mom's death she had graduated from the University of Spoiled Children, taking a job as an Assistant News Director at one of the big L.A. TV stations.

"Miss King. Thank you for returning my call. I appreciate it."

"Oh, anytime, Mister Street. I have been wondering when or if anyone would ever re-open an investigation regarding my father's murder. I'm glad that someone is finally interested in finding the 'who' and 'why' of his death." She spoke with the clear precise voice perfect for someone in her profession. "I took the liberty of gathering some information on you. You get good reviews from the legal community and the police seem to like you well enough. Checking references is a big part of my job here. I hope you don't mind. I hope we can work together to find the truth and get some traction on Dad's death after all this time."

Sounded about right. "I hope so, too. I know that we have accumulated considerable information during this investigation and there is circumstantial evidence that points toward our prime suspect in another major case was also responsible for your dad's death. Did your dad leave any files or material regarding the case he was working on when he was killed? His death occurred in close proximity to elements of this other matter I'm involved with, and I have this thing about connecting and complicating these situations."

"He did indeed, Mister Street. I have his files and records at home in my office. When can we meet? Are you available later this week?"

"I should be. I'm in Las Vegas right now, chasing evidence, and I know it would be really valuable to look at what he was doing when he died. I should be back in L.A. in the next 36 hours. Let me catch up with you when I get back to town."

"Fine with me. I just got a promotion, I'm producing the Nightly News at Ten for the station now. My schedule is flexible until I get adjusted to the shift change. I'll send you my contact info. I know I have some things you need to see." She gave me the pertinent e-mail and phone contacts for home and work and verified mine.

"I'll be in touch. Thank you again for returning my call." I rang off and looked at Catherine. I smiled.

She said, "That sounded promising."

"I hope so. This thing is getting tedious."

Just then another bit of good luck arrived, the e-mail from the private forensics lab in Pasadena, verifying that the test rounds from the pistols I had left for testing did indeed match, metallurgically and surface-wise, within acceptable variances the identifiable material taken at the site of the Connors murders thirteen years ago. I showed Catherine the e-mail. "Y'know, we are on your basic roll here. It feels pretty damn good."

"Yes it does." She looked forward as a car passed a dozen feet in front of Danny's 'Vette. "And here we are sitting in this silly-ass car as the elusive black Mercedes arrives home."

42

Now it made sense.

The familiar, now dust-streaked pearl black AMG Mercedes coupe—the same car I'd first seen at the Prison at Chino, the car that I'd seen outside Bongelli's office a few days before—rolled to a stop under the portico next to the ceremonial stairway that led to the front door of the tower. Shirley and a somewhat younger male companion dismounted at the behest of the resident valet. Shirley was in her mid-forties, visually an odd mix of middle age professional woman in her carriage and an early-twenties club hopper in her hair and makeup. Think Chris Jenner a couple of decades ago. Her companion was a relaxed-looking, confident twenty-something with carefully tousled hair, an expensive smile and the casual demeanor of a kept man.

After their departure from the car they walked hand-in-hand up the wide, mild slope of the marble stairway, through the massive front doors and across the spacious lobby toward the bank of elevators. Catherine and I, each toting attaché' cases, had departed the Corvette and were a dozen paces behind as the elevator doors opened. They stepped in and Shirley looked at us dismissively, then spoke. She stood in front of the bank of buttons and looked at us. "We're going to the Penthouse. Which is your floor?"

We each passed our business cards to her. Catherine said, "We're going there too. We need to talk."

Shirley looked at each of the business cards separately then exhaled. "There's a buzzkill." She gestured to her companion. "This is my friend Chad. If we can make it brief, I can talk with you, but we have dinner reservations. Perhaps we could make an appointment?"

Catherine was on a roll. I stepped aside to give her room. "No, I don't think so. Ms. Parris, we have information that puts your estranged husband at the base of a complicated array of criminal conspiracy including multiple murders. You are involved in his dealings all the way up to your diamond earrings." She continued in her stern terms. "It would behoove you to assist us briefly in gathering and verifying our information in an effort to clarify the case against him."

Shirley seemed surprisingly agreeable, or perhaps just impressed that Catherine had used the word 'behoove.' She gave it a few seconds thought, looked at Chad, and cleared her throat. "Okay then. We do need to talk." The elevator doors slid silently open. "Please come in. Chad, honey, would you please get us a bottle of wine and some glasses? That new bottle of Shelby would do nicely. We'll be out on the deck. And turn on the fans and the misters there as well, please." Chad obediently exited toward the kitchen.

Shirley targeted her next comments toward Catherine. She spoke quietly. "You listen to me. I have been held virtual prisoner by that asshole for over five years, and used in ways that you will find difficult to understand. Ms. Gadsden, if you can assist me in reaching my goals, I am certain that I can help you attain yours. Primarily I want my freedom from Bongelli, once and for all." Then she turned to me. "And if you, Mister Street, would like to topple his little fiefdom I can point you in all the right directions."

She did a great job of sounding really 'pissed' so I responded by acting unimpressed. "Goody. You might want to cancel your dinner reservations and order in. The examination of over thirteen years of criminal history is not a 'quickie'. If you're serious about talking to us we have work to do. A surface exam is not going to cover it."

She surprised me by looking me in the eyes. "Let's get started then. We have a lot to discuss."

43

I didn't like Shirley Parris very much. She came across initially as arrogant and rude on her own turf for no apparent reason, in the grand tradition of wealthy women whose every whim was addressed well, promptly and often. I'd encountered others of that type when I was a cop. Out in the world, who knows how she'd act?

Her best attribute right now was that she was anxious to speak loudly and continually about her hopefully soon-to-be ex-husband. She was already confident that she had ol' Bongelli by the short hairs. She was intimately familiar with all of his stunts. She knew where all the bodies were buried—literally. She was willing, able, and anxious to share her knowledge so she was temporarily my very favorite person.

For instance, she confirmed that both of the Connors' assassins, nearly a dozen anonymous alleged enemies of Grant Carty, and the six victims of the meth lab explosion at the block house were buried on the plot of land northeast of the house there in the desert. That explains the overgrown patch that Danny had pointed out from the copter. Carty had created his own 'potters' field' on that part of the property.

She prattled on about the aftermath of the meth lab explosion and fire. "It was awful," she told us. Three of the workers were killed instantly. The other three and Carty were seriously injured, but of course Vinny wouldn't allow anyone else to care for them, nor would he permit hospitalization. I had to sedate the others until they died from natural causes. They all eventually developed massive staph infections and died."

She was on a roll within a few minutes as Catherine and I shared the development of revulsion towards her. "Carty had been a machine. He was very scary. He'd identify a competitor of whatever aspect—even the car dealership—he would make an approach, be friendly and even congratulatory, and then when they arrived at the ranch he'd hunt them down like wild game. There may be close to two dozen buried on that one site. There may well be others elsewhere."

I asked. "Okay, what set him off about Rick Damarow?"

"That poor dumb kid was a competitor, plain and simple. There was a conflict over territory. He went against the protocol. They took the market away from him then Carty decided to use him as an example to other competitors. They had beat him up once before, then that last time they shot him in both knees, very painful, and dropped him out of an airplane over the eastern part of L.A. County. They were really sloppy about everything they did, though, and Arnie was a little slow on the uptake. He was caught red handed a couple of weeks later."

She continued, "Bongelli threw a fit when Arnie went down. He was scared to death that Arnie would spill the beans about the whole operation. After the conviction he made lots of promises. He'd fund Arnie abundantly for the term of his imprisonment and he would run appeals at every opportunity. Of course it was a great deal for Vinny and Grant, not so much for Arnie. That poor kid was totally unprepared for what happened to him."

I felt the need to balance the commentary a bit, though not in Arnie's favor. "Sutton was an easy mark for Vinny and Grant because he was scared and gullible. Bongelli promised to set up a trust fund for Arnie's daughter then he said he'd take care of the girlfriend and give Arnie a monthly allowance for the tenure of his sentence. That agreement, except for the stipend, ended a few years back when Vinny started crying poverty. The girlfriend and the daughter got 'zip'. The child is living with her grandparents in Henderson. She's lucky. The girlfriend is working in Pahrump's largest industry, in a brothel owned by a subsidiary of one of Arnie's corporations. He might have told you that he 'fixed everything' but that's not exactly true."

Shirley looked at me as if I'd grown horns. "What? Vinny into prostitution? You're kidding!" She seemed incredulous. "Really." She chuckled at the thought of it, and looked between Catherine and me as she laughed.

I offered, "It's one of the businesses held by a subsidiary of one of Arnie's corporations. As resident agent, Vinny has sole control of every bit of income at this point."

"Mister Street, you don't know Bongelli very well." She looked at Chad and chuckled, then she just shook her head. "You can't imagine what a surprise that is to me." Her facial expression was one of total surprise and great humor.

I felt like calling her joke to an end. "That's great. Tell me about the Connors hits."

"That was Carty and Carty alone. That was the first big hint that Vinny was going to have problems managing him. The soon-to-be-infamous Carty 'revenge motive' was in full flight. Connors was a marked man as soon as Arnie was convicted, a conviction that happened mostly on the strength of Connors' testimony. His justification was made much easier after the media and Connors' sister went after someone else as the sole suspect." She paused and took a sip of her wine.

This verified one of my theories, that the presumed villain Ray Cole drew attention away from them, and gave them security. Shirley nodded in agreement. "They used the blue truck at the ranch to transport the shooters..." I asked, establishing an element I already knew to be true.

"Yes. The truck still had the dealer plate on it. Had they been captured the dealership would have tied Bongelli to the murders. He was furious."

"How did the truck get wrecked?" I asked as Catherine took notes.

"That happened because Carty was 'wrecked' first. After the Connors killings, Bongelli demanded that Carty bury it on the ranch or somewhere. He did that for a while, but maybe 3 years later, about 10 years ago, we were in town for our anniversary. Bongelli took a call. Grant had hit a couple of cars in the parking lot of the Tropicana after dropping off one of their courier cars. He had a nose full, of course, and no license or insurance, and he needed to be rescued. I saw Bongelli again two days later."

I felt like she was on a roll. "What other killings can you attribute to Carty?"

"He swore revenge on the prosecutor in the Sutton trial. I'm not certain about that one."

I looked at Catherine. Her eyes narrowed at the comment and she said, "I am."

Shirley continued, "And I think that later on there may have been a couple of car dealers who caught on to the drug thing."

Catherine and I shared a glance. She nodded toward her laptop. I looked at my own and winked as she tapped a few keys.

After reading Catherine's note I said, "But if Vinny knows that you know all of this, how do you remain safe? Doesn't he have someone watching you, 24/7?"

"Oh, of course," she explained. "I control the progress of the situation."

"I don't understand," I said. "Because, well..."

"See, Carty was far smarter, far more diversified and far more—what's the word—devious, maybe, than he had ever given him credit for. There is money maybe twelve million dollars, that he considers *his own* money, secreted somewhere on that ranch. We don't know exactly where it is. Vinny is determined to find it."

I asked, "What's Carty's condition?"

"He's kept stable." She said. "He's in and out. He has his problems, of course. He's mute because his vocal cords are shrunken, due to the burns and his prolonged dehydration. A physical therapist works with him once a week to prevent further muscular deterioration, and we keep a close eye on it. He doesn't suffer and he doesn't know the difference. Frankly, I've lost interest."

I asked, "I saw evidence of skin grafts in his burn areas. Was all that work done at the ranch? Has he been away from there at any time in the last 5 years?"

Shirley answered, "No, Mister Street. He's been in that same bed for 5 years straight after the fire. Vinny brought in a mobile home until the addition to the house remodel could be finished. I was the primary care provider from the start. He showed signs of improvement for a while, so then he kept hired a medical crew from Mexico to try to bring him back, but their work was poorly done. We eventually sent them packing. They did as much harm as good."

I interjected, "So the bedroom was added after the fire."

"Oh yes. I insisted on that. There was a lot of cash lying around but the house was a total dump. We kept him in as good a place as possible until it was finished, and we used his money for the project."

Catherine asked, "Burn maintenance is a demanding regimen. Did he have other health issues as well? I'd heard that he was a user."

Shirley looked to Catherine. "You can't imagine. When he was injured he was filthy. He was such a dedicated and enthusiastic drug user that he was passing impurities for months. There were boils and sebaceous cysts and skin lesions. We had to call a dermatologist as well as the skin graft specialist to deal with him. It was so incredibly gross. We couldn't even keep hired help. The treatments had to continue because of the massive infections that were imminent." Shirley explained. "We had to have his teeth pulled and implants installed and there was another Mexican doctor brought in for the skin problems. My stomach still turns thinking about it."

I said, "You just keep him sedated around the clock."

"We do. He's on a regulated I.V. dosage of a mild sedative during the day, heavier at night. When we started he was a total wreck. He was badly addicted to cocaine. His nasal and sinus passages were collapsed. He had used meth to excess and he even had infections from his shitty tattoo work. His physical condition was horrible. His teeth were rotten, his gums infected. Like most drug attics, he didn't eat. He was burned at extremely high temperatures over 40% of his upper body. He should have been dead. He isn't. we have maintained and improved his condition for over five years. He should be grateful."

I responded, "Yeah, you're all heart. What are his chances for recovery?"

Shirley was cold, unconcerned. "He could be brought back. It would take a lot of work and dedicated care, but he could do it under the right conditions."

I picked up on the context. "He, not 'you'." There was no hint of recognition. "What would constitute the right conditions?"

"He'd require intense therapy for an extended period, but with the right attention I believe he could come out to start the process within a few weeks. We keep him on a minimum attention setting for the time being. He's in a good place—far better than the alternatives."

I was tiring at this and my attitude was not improving during the meeting. Catherine came to the rescue with a lateral. She asked, "So how long have you and Chad been an item?"

Shirley took offense, proving that she had been paying attention. "That has nothing to do with the situation at hand, does it?"

Catherine volleyed back, "We just wondered if you were aware that he's on your husband's payroll."

She looked at Chad. "Oh, but I pay him much more, and there are benefits here." She took his hand and squeezed it. I withheld the outward indications of a cringe.

Chad piped in now, still a bit too aloof and polished for my taste. "Trust me, pal, I'm on her side and yours. I want Bongelli taken down just as much as you and Shirl do. He's scum and he hurts people. I'm just in a situation where I can let him think I play both sides. The checks clear. What else could I ask?"

I was curious. "You're how old?"

"I'm twenty-six."

"Wow. You have a great future in the political field. I can tell."

He smirked the smirk of a seriously over-privileged kid. "Yeah I know. Snipe if you must, Mister Street. I'll survive quite nicely."

Catherine asked the next important question. "So Shirley, what do you want from this in the end? We need a deposition regarding your involvement in Bongelli's affairs and you will probably be asked to testify to a Grand Jury when the matter goes to court."

Shirley answered if she as if she had rehearsed the lines for years. "I am not yet divorced from Vinny. Six years this shit has been dragging on! It's a total pain in the ass. I want a final divorce decree in my hand. This is fucking Nevada! That should be easy! I have plans for my own future, things that I want and need to do but I'm bound by contract to take care of that dirtbag in that fucking dump. I gave up a strong career to deal with all this crap. I'll survive regardless but I do want out, once and for all."

"Fair enough." Catherine looked at me, then at Shirley, and said, "I think that's probably doable."

Now it was my turn. "There are a few more things. There was a P.I. following me last week, a Vance Boyd. Does he also watch you?"

Shirley smirked her dismissive smirk once again. "Vance? Of course. We let Bongelli think Boyd keeps us all at bay. Anybody can lose Vance."

I smiled. "Yeah, I know." I replied, "Is he based in Vegas?"

"He has a small property out off of Boulder highway in Henderson, and another place in Riverside. He visits the ranch a few times each week. He does his target practice there," she said with the bored tone.

I looked at Catherine as I explained, "Yeah, I got him on camera."

Shirley brought up a new point. "There's something you should know about Vinny. He is always armed. He has a small pistol secreted in his briefcase."

I said, "That's almost admirable considering his client load."

She continued. "Vinny has pull, Mister Street. He can get his aluminum briefcase in anywhere...prisons, police stations, courthouses, courtrooms, anywhere. Twenty pounds of custom carved aluminum alloy. He brags about it."

Chad piped up again, straining his welcome. "If I might add something here."

Curious, and less unimpressed than I had been a few minutes ago, I said, "Go."

"Vance is really suspicious of you, Street, and they intend to get in your road bigtime within the next few days, to keep both of you misdirected. As Sutton's sentence hearing gets closer, they're using operatives to watch your house and they bugged your car."

"I know that." I continued, "Vance is almost good enough to be bush league. I check the car every couple of days and I go deep when I clean it on the weekends. I have the model number and operational instructions for their spy stuff. I own some of the same items and now I own the one they used on me. No big deal, trust me."

Catherine took a breath then frowned. "Can we talk a minute, Street?"

Shirley took the hint. "I'll clear the table. Chad, honey, can I get a hand?"

Agreeable, and also on the clock, Chad agreed, "Sure, Babe."

44

Catherine and I stepped out onto the glass walled dining room onto the open deck. The view mostly consisted of the rear elevations of the hotel-casinos on the Strip and it would improve with each implosion. We sat at the patio furniture and consulted our background information and worked on the laptops. Shirley and Chad cleared the table and retreated to the kitchen. I kept an eye on them, still not all that comfortable with their cooperation. Shirley's tone indicated that she was solely devoted to ending her servitude to Vinny, and all of his minions. Chad, his image somewhat improved, had also shown that he was completely self-loyal and still clearly just along for the ride.

After a peaceful, informative and productive hour, Catherine and I made our way across the living room toward the opposite deck, where fans and misters lowered the temperature to a bearable level—maybe 95 degrees. Looking out over the skyline, I tried to gather my thoughts on our new alliance. I remain concerned about the increased interference and pressure from Vinny's operatives, and I still didn't trust these two all that much. So far and neither of them had jumped out from the kitchen waving a Tommy gun or throwing grenades. I took that as a good sign, but I still made sure that retaining strap on my shoulder holster was unsnapped.

I gave the situation some thought and spoke up. "Catherine, I have an idea. Let's get them out of here."

Catherin signed on instantly. "Moving to a remote location till the trial might be a good plan. Bongelli's probably going to catch on at some point, especially if the detective is watching. Do you have a destination in mind?"

"I do, and a method of transit." I explained the options to her.

"I love it, let's do it." We spoke to Shirley and Chad, they signed on as well.

The time to make the move was approaching, so I started making calls. I called the resort to reserve lodging for that evening and the next and to arrange the hire of a couple of off-duty metro officers for security. Finally, I called Danny Tanner to take Catherine and Shirley to the new digs. The Gold Strike casino at Jean, Nevada was located near a State Trooper headquarters alongside the I-15, dead center, middle of nowhere. Hey, I wouldn't think to look there, would you?

I still had minor trust issues with Chad, so I kept him with me. I needed to return Danny's 'Vette to the airport so I enlisted his assistance on the transfer, then he proved his worth. Chad had looked down from the southernmost deck of the condo onto the parking lot. He pointed out Vance's familiar grey Suburban, parked outside the perimeter wall of the tower. My opinion rating of Chad went vertical.

After consulting with Shirley and Chad and a bit of negotiation, I made the final set-up call and set the plan into motion. Danny used his tricked-out copter to pluck the slightly apprehensive Catherine and the ever-deserving Shirley from the rooftop helipad, slipping away without tipping off the allegedly-observant Vance Boyd. I received a call a half-hour later that the pair had arrived and were checked in at the Gold Strike.

I made some additional calls before Chad and I left the penthouse and we arranged a reunion with and a welcome of sorts for my old friend Vance. This time he was driving his own vehicle, a beefy old suburban that I recognized from the ranch images. He was parked just outside the exit ramp of the condo tower, perhaps unaware that we knew of his presence.

Chad and I regained the Corvette for the quick trip to Danny's Henderson airstrip. I hit the ignition and looked over at Chad's position as the engine began its steady throb. He had already tightened his belts and seemed to expect some action. I asked him, feeling like a distant relative, "So are you a car guy?"

"Yeah. I restored a 70 Chevelle SS 454 LS6 last year. It'll sell next January at Barrett-Jackson in Scottsdale. I also drove a Gen 4 Camaro and SCCA autocross for a season when I was in college."

His rating with me took another leap. "Cool. Keep an eye out."

As we encountered the ramp leading off the condo property I stopped on the driveway ramp to allow Vance to see who we were. I heard the tall gray 4x4 Suburban start and he began to follow us. Sheer bulk has its own pluses and the brute 'crush strength' of the three-ton behemoth was something I wanted to see only from a great distance.

With the truck 40 feet off my really pricey borrowed rear bumper I gave the gas pedal a strong push and the car squirted forward, hazing the rear tires. Danny had pull with the Las Vegas Metro cops and a friend of his in the Traffic Division had offered his assistance. By sheer coincidence there was a conveniently-positioned DUI checkpoint roadblock less than 2 miles from Shirley's walled high-rise fortress.

I caught the whine of a turbocharger as the truck's boost kicked in. He kept up with us surprisingly well for two miles as I took the Vette through side streets and one business park's approach road. One more left turn onto Tropicana and the trap was set. I pitched the car sideways with the Suburban a dozen car lengths back. After we passed a motor cop idling at the corner, the officer set off in noisy pursuit of our desperate vehicles for a fast half-mile.

A roadblock of Metro police cars flanked the restricted traffic lanes on the opposite side of the road as I approached the clot of traffic. Slowing from about 40 at the end of the row of waiting cars I initiated a hand brake turn that landed me square at the curb on the opposite side of the wide street amid a billow of Goodyear dust and vapor. That part was fun.

As the suburban barreled through the clot, Boyd tried to follow my lead to the opposite side of the flat divided six-lane street. He lost control from the truck's massive understeer and T-boned a parked L.V.P.D. Metro patrol Crown Vic a half-dozen spaces behind my curbside position. As the truck stopped moving, its front clip half planted in the driver side of the cop-spec Crown Vic, the group of somewhat agitated Metro officers converged on it, dragging the too-hesitant Boyd out of the truck through the window of the sprung driver's door and slamming him to the ground so hard that he bounced.

Vance put up something of a struggle for his freedom and was promptly tased for his troubles. After the predictable blue suit chorus of 'stop resisting!' from an army of Metro cops, he was transferred in handcuffs and shackles from the shadow of his mangled truck to the rear seat of yet another black and white Crown Vic. I slowly and calmly pulled from the curb unnoticed and we resumed our placid journey toward Danny's feeder airstrip. That stretch of travel was slower and calmer on slightly worn tires.

Danny walked out of the hanger 40 minutes later to take delivery of his next passengers and his car. I had stopped to top off the gas tank, then at a do-it-yourself car wash on Boulder highway to rinse the rubber dust from the flanks of the car as we drove to Henderson. Chad had handled the towels and the car was pristine from our efforts. Maybe he was okay after all.

45

Chad was driving his pristine dark green '70 Chevelle SS 454 out the new loop freeway toward Boulder city when his cell phone rang. The screen said it was her. It was 10:00 a.m. sharp so she was at the ranch. "Hey, babe. What's up?"

She sounded urgent. Chad, I'm at the ranch. I think someone's been here at the ranch. I see footprints from the house to the barn and I know we didn't make them."

Chad answered, "Probably that guy from L.A. that Vance mentioned. It's okay, don't worry about it. I'll go home and switch cars, and I'll head to the ranch in an hour or so. Don't worry, Babe. We'll get through it. I'll move what we found and start getting ready to leave for good. That sounds good, doesn't it?"

46

"Nice car, Danny!" I smiled as I flipped the key fob to him. "Oh, and I may owe you a set of tires." I walked past him smiling, hoping the potential damage to the friendship wasn't permanent.

"Yeah I heard. No sweat Street. I'll bill you. You guys ready to book?"

"Yeah, ready when you are."

We followed Danny to his copter and arrived at Jean twenty minutes after liftoff. Danny had earlier called a favor in from one of his friends at Metro and had an off-duty officer in attendance in the suite with two more in the wings for backup and shift duty. The officer stood near the door as Danny greeted him warmly and introduced him to me.

The Gold Strike was nowhere near 'fancy' but it was well-maintained and for our purposes very serviceable. Catherine had ordered a room service tray for the assembled horde from the restaurant downstairs. We started our planning meeting in advance of my pending trip back to SoCal. We talked and ate, then recorded the review of well-trod ground. Our latest advantage was the recent informal incarceration of Vance Boyd after his misadventure on

Tropicana Drive. After his arrest he was bound over to spend at least a few nights in the Las Vegas Metropolitan Detention Center. They 'lost' him for a few days after that too.

Note to self: Never total a LVPD Metro Patrol cruiser!

An hour later I looked out the window of the suite into the stark darkness of the desert. Our rooms overlooked a mammoth parking lot and we could see the trail of red tail lights on the northbound Fifteen. In the distance the faint glow of the lights of the Las Vegas skyline, 50 miles away, hovered on the northern horizon. I said, "This is great. What glamour!"

Catherine looked at me over the ravaged room service tray as I returned to the table. "Have a plan yet, Street?"

"I do. It will involve a bit of stagecraft and maybe some sleight of hand, but I think it'll get the job done. You game?" I lifted my eyebrows in a surefire charming gesture.

"Yeah, there you go again." I detected a slight sense of dread. "Tell me."

I did so. It was almost easy. All we needed to do was arrive at Sutton's hearing in the courthouse in Riverside, taking everyone not in this room at this time by complete surprise. To assist in the substance after the glitz, Catherine had a visitor, another one of her law school buddies who, luckily, was a Las Vegas attorney handling Nevada divorces. She consulted for an hour, filling in all the proper blanks and constructing a framework that would grant Shirley her freedom rapidly and finally. Once that was completed and Shirley's affidavits regarding Bongelli's operations were complete and signed by all the right pens, we just had to go to Riverside in time for the hearing in two days.

Our waiting game would soon have its own penalty box. The cosmetically-enhanced TV news reporter on the Las Vegas TV station earnestly reported a prime item at the top of her 7:00 o'clock news broadcast.

"In a crime related story, the Los Angeles County Sheriff's Department last night arrested sixty-three year-old Raymond Cole of Laguna Niguel for the brutal double murders of auto racing legend Ron Connors and his wife over 13 years ago. The couple was gunned down execution-style in the driveway of their fashionable Montego Hills home as they left for work that morning."

By mid-sentence I had already fired up the phone. "Street for Deputy Wallace, please."

The line was instantly connected. "Clinton? Street! What's this I hear about Ray Cole being hauled in?"

Clinton Wallace was still at his office finishing paperwork. "It is what it is, Street. We have a witness, swears she saw Cole and another man sitting near the Connors' home, in, let's see here, a dark brown late '80s Buick LeSabre coupe two days before the killings. Cole will be in a line-up tomorrow morning and we'll do a photo array with the witness in about an hour."

I spoke a little faster to emphasize the urgency. "Clint, he didn't do it! He wanted to, sure, and he planned to, as well. He may have even sat in a brown Buick once, but he's not the guy you're looking for. Cole was not in LA that week! We even have a statement from his ex-wife stating that they were offshore on their boat on the day of the murders."

The deputy sounded tired. "He's ours for now, Street. We'll take good care of him until this thing gets settled, and if you're correct he'll walk free once and for all. How's your search going?"

"We have enough to takedown a few of the majors in a mid-size do-it-yourself crime wave. Lots of layers, lots of players, lots of dead bodies, most of which can be traced back to a lawyer based in Riverside and one of his clients. We now know the identity of the pilot of the plane used in Damarow murder. Same person appears to be the mind behind the Connors hits. That was sheer revenge for the Sutton trial testimony. I'll get you a package when I get home, but in the meantime, I'll repeat, you arrested the exact wrong man for the Connors hits!"

"I'll keep that in mind, Street. You bring me another perp, Cole will take a walk. Till then, he's safe and secure as our guest at the

Twin Towers petri dish, in segregation, eatin' white bread, stale bologna and government cheese like everyone else there. He gets some of those little mustard packets too. We'll talk when you get back home. And Street, good luck!" He sounded as if he meant it.

47

If I'd listened to my folks I might have chosen a profession that wouldn't require that I spend so much time behind bars. Now I had to go back to the jail at Chino and harass a really dumb bad guy. I'd left Catherine, Shirley and Chad at the Gold Strike resort with a rotating trio of off duty and retired Metro cops sharing a day of security guard duty. I caught a red eye out of McCarran to Ontario, where I reclaimed my Tahoe. I drove directly to Chino to the state slam to continue my ongoing conversation with the resident genius, Arnie Sutton.

This time the Warden had offered his assistance along with a bit of official subterfuge. It was a little after eleven that night when a pair of uniformed guards brought Arnie from his cell to a secluded interview room in the admin office area of the prison. Arnie took a chair, turned it backwards and sat down. I tried to be all cheery as he was dropped into the room.

"Hey, Arnie! How's tricks? I wanted to come talk to you again, give you the facts of life speech like you should have gotten when you were twelve. I brought my 'Homie-to-English' translation guide and everything."

He feigned wiping sleep from his eyes as he looked around the room at the Warden. "Man, what the hell? It's fuggin' midnight! What do you want?"

I reminded myself of the importance of showing the proper respect. "Sutton, shut the hell up and listen. Your life is about to change!"

"How's that?"

"I'm going to save you a lot of trouble, Sutton." I leaned in close to him and ask quietly. "Where's Grant Carty?"

Smug, Arnie said, "I don't know. He ain't here, bro."

"Come on, didn't Bongelli fill you in? Man, if he hasn't told you what happened to Carty, he must not think much of you at all."

Arnie was defensive. "Whataya mean? Vin won't let Grant come here to visit, but things are crankin' along just fine. He's in good shape."

I countered, "Fraid not, Arn. Grant blew himself up in a meth lab a while back, the ranch operation shut down, Grant's in a hospital bed. Has been for five years. And Bongelli didn't clue you in at all. Man." I shook my head for emphasis.

The Warden said, "Bongelli's lying to you, Sutton. He running a number on you. He's stealing your money."

Arnie was faithful to his priorities. "How's he stealing money from me? How? I've seen the books. I get $2500 a month. I get out, I'll be nice 'n' fat."

"Arnie, that's not even a rounding error to him. He has worked his system to the point that you're worth well over a million dollars just for the property values. You're still behind bars because Bongelli is one of the worst defense attorneys in the history of the legal profession. He ropes you guys in and only his favorites get anything out of it. In your case that 'favorite' is Carty. He deserves to be in here with you, except that he got blown up in a meth lab explosion five years ago."

"You sure?"

"Yeah, Arnie, I am. Look, Bongelli's system is ripping you off big time. He lies to you every time his lips move. You want that? Man up and listen to what I'm telling you."

The Warden chimed in at this point. "Sutton, look... I know you're not some innocent waif, but you're a decent inmate. I've heard the inside gossip, about how Bongelli drains his clients then drops them like a hot rock. You don't want to be one of those. Listen to what Street's telling you, maybe you'll have a shot at getting out of here sometime."

The Warden had more cred than I did. Sutton looked at him, then at me. He said to me, "State your case, man."

I laid a makeshift spreadsheet on the table and pointed at various aspects of it. "We just recently uncovered his methods. Your name is on the corporate paperwork for all of these failed cover businesses. He's built up the corporate cash holdings, spending nothing on the operation of the businesses as they circle the drain. Thing is, he's seen the raw commercial property values rise 250% over the years despite the fact that all the business failed. He's become a real estate tycoon at your expense. When the cash value reaches the right level, he'll do a corporate bankruptcy on you to collect his legal fees. He'll sell your properties to one of his own businesses at fire-sale prices, just enough to cover his legal services invoices to you. You'll be on the hook for all of his paper losses. Bongelli will make million or two off of you, and you'll still be doing time, trading for smokes, and scratching your butt."

I took a breath. "He's charged you $400 an hour for 18 hours a month, including travel time, for 13 years just for visiting you. When he presents the invoice for his fees and you can't pay up, he'll drop you like a hot rock and cut you off cold. You'll be without your cash reserves, without your monthly allowance, flat-ass broke working for seventeen cents an hour like everyone else in here. You'll end up with some upstate hell hole like Corcoran for the next 30 years, and on the day you die you'll still be asking yourself what the hell happened."

Arnie took a breath and then swallowed. "Yeah. Okay. State your case, bro." It took another hour to explain what Sutton was up against and what he needed to do when court began. He was shell-shocked that his own attorney had set him up, but he finally understood what was at stake. He asked a lot of questions as we tried to explain all that proper terms for the forms from the Nevada Secretary of State's office.

Legal? By the book? Depending on who you asked, maybe, maybe not. Time was of the essence and this 'fast serve' ploy would take months for a bystander to unravel. Sooner than that it would help reverse the decades of harm done to Arnie and his associated victims by Bongelli and Carty. At some point in the murky future, it might also significantly help Sutton's situation. I tried my best to break it down for him. He was still having a hard time grasping multi-syllabic words not containing 'yo' but he gave it a good solid try. I was pulling for him, though more in the interest of Reanna and her daughter than for Arnie himself.

I avoided mention of Carty's near-death. "Look, this is your way out of this crap hole. If Bongelli's not your attorney-of-record, if he's not the sole signatory on your Corporation, if he's not your resident agent, he can't touch your money or your corporate holdings. Your daughter gets the trust fund you promised her, her mother gets the money you intended, and you get a better chance of getting out of prison before you eighty."

Sutton started actually thinking it through. "But when he comes to work with me next time, he'll find out."

Good point. Fortunately, we thought of that. I let the Warden do the honors. He looked at me and smiled an ironic smile. "Sutton, if Bongelli is no longer listed as your attorney of record, I have no reason to allow him a priority visit. He'll have to wait in line like everyone else. You'll be taken to court in the bus just like all the others. He'll meet you right before the hearing starts. No special treatment." He looked at me and continued. "We all know how messed up all the paperwork in our offices can get, but I'm sure we can get that little administrative problem straightened out just in time for Sutton, here, to put on this suit, get in the van, and get to court with only minutes to spare."

I thought about that and smiled. "See, Sutton? No problem. It's handled."

Sutton paused for a minute, then he nodded his head. I handed him the pen and slid the sheaf of papers beneath them. After the documents were signed, Sutton seemed more relaxed, so I decided to get more information. The warden sat in and observed as I continued the questions. "All right, Arnie, tell me more about Carty. You were there when he was building up the trafficking operation right after he moved to the ranch. He's one tough piece of work, right? There were some murders after that. Who did he kill back when he was starting out? What did he do with the bodies?"

"He's got a place at the ranch right after we started. He buried a few there. He called it 'the Patch'." Arnie paused, gave it some thought, and leaned back in his chair. "Take me up there, dude. I'll show you everything." He was starting to catch on. I was almost proud for him. Okay, almost.

48

February 20, 1996.

Rick Damarow was walking to his IROC-Z, parked at the rear of the parking lot at the Norms Restaurant in Corona when they came for him. A worn blue late '80s Ford Explorer that he'd never seen before was parked in the next space. As he approached, the front passenger door opened, and Arnie Sutton blocked his path. He looked angry.

Rick was surprised to see Sutton, but he wasn't worried...yet. He never felt threatened around Arnie. "Hey, Arn. How's it hangin'?"

Sutton looked uncomfortable as he spoke up. "Rick, goddammit I tried to warn you. You keep steppin' on Carty's turf, he's gonna get pissed!" He stood in Rick's path. "He wants to talk to you. Get in the truck."

Rick caught on, but surely he could talk his way past this. "No need for that, Arnie. I'll follow you in my ride. How far we gotta go?" Then he saw the gun in Sutton's hand.

"Goddammit, Rick, get in the truck!" Arnie loosely pointed the pistol in Rick's direction, showing an attitude never displayed in their dozen prior meetings. Rick went to the open door and climbed into the back seat of the truck. The interior smelled like wet dog hair. A chunky dark-haired young woman drove the truck. Arnie Sutton sat in the back seat, still holding the gun.

Within fifteen minutes the truck arrived at a single-story tract house a few miles north of Corona. When the doors opened the aroma of the nearby 'meat factories' swept into the truck. The young woman driver vacated immediately and walked to the house. Arnie leaned toward Rick and said, "Stay right here, Rick. Sorry, man."

As Arnie left the truck the closed door jerked open and Grant Carty looked in at the seated guest. Once again, they were only inches apart. Rick could smell the sour breath and see the sheen of sweat on the older man's face. "So, Rick Damarow, we meet again!" Before Damarow could respond Carty took the Colt pistol from the back of his waistband and shot Rick just above and outside his right knee...

As the white hot pain radiated through Rick Damarow's body, Carty continued to speak, louder over the shriek of pain. "See, man? You just didn't listen to what I told you to do."

Through the pain and nausea Rick felt himself being dragged by the collar from the truck. He shrieked in pain as he landed on the shattered knee on the gravel driveway, then again as he was pulled by his shirt collar around the front of the parked truck. He cried through the white-hot pain as he lay in the dirt and gravel trying to reach a fetal position.

Carty knelt down toward his victim. "You butt-wipe amateurs gotta be taught a lesson once in a while. I am NOT kidding when I tell you what to do! Do you think I was kidding, Rick?"

Barely able to comprehend the question through the pain and his developing lapse into shock, Damarow stammered to the blurry face looking down at him, "No! I'm sorry! Carty! Listen to me! You want money? I can get money!" He pleaded for the first time in his life. He had never known this level of crippling desperation.

Grant stood up, looked around, then looked again at the body writhing in the dirt in the dark. "Y'know, Rick? That's just not good enough." He kicked the kid in the wounded knee, bringing another plaintive shriek. As that shriek subsided Carty shot Rick Damarow above the left knee. Another shrill howl erupted before the wounded rick kid passed out from the pain.

When he next came awake Rick Damarow was in the back of the dog-smelling Explorer, bound and gagged, wrapped to his waist in what felt like a big trash bag. He was numb below the waist but for the throbbing pain from both legs and his vision was blurry from the tears and from an agony he had never before felt. He felt the truck stop and the rear hatch open before he passed out again as he was dropped to the pavement of the small private airstrip. In a final stroke of luck at the end of his short, privileged life, Rick Damarow didn't experience the rest of what would happen to him.

49

My first confrontation the next morning after four hours sleep was a little more pleasant than 'midnight at Chino', but potentially just as perilous.

Catherine had arranged to have Shirley's Nevada divorce decree ready in time for the next day's afternoon court hearing in Riverside. I drove to an affiliate attorney's office in Pasadena to obtain Certified copies for use in my next little stunt. I gathered the necessary documents in a nice vinyl folder, signed for the package and drove to Riverside.

I gave the documents a quick read before I pulled the Goat into the parking lot at Bongelli's office complex. I thought about storming into his office but reconsidered in favor of standing outside in the shade of a couple of tall, gently-waving palm trees. I saw no reason to waste even a few minutes of a beautiful southern California morning in the stuffy offices of a slimy lawyer who I didn't even like. I parked the GTO a few slots away from his shiny new silver pearl Mercedes S550 AMG coupe and assumed a very visible position leaning against the fragile front fender of the six-figure ride.

Momentarily a face appeared at the front door of the Bongelli

Law office and a sturdy-looking Caucasian woman opened the door. She stood there for a few minutes in the door frame, glaring at me. I smiled and waved at her and she shut the door quickly. Soon the door reopened, and Vinnie Bongelli, his own self, started huffing across the courtyard. His face was a nice rosy shade of pink by the time he came within hailing distance. "Boy, get your ass offa that car! Who the hell do you think you are?" By the time he was a few feet away I could see the sweat beading on his forehead. He had good voice tone considering how breathless he was.

I tried to be cheerful. "Hey, Bongelli! Is this your car? Bitchin' ride, dude! Do you still have the black one? I really liked those rims."

"Who the hell are you and what do you want?" He spoke through clenched, capped teeth as a bead of sweat rolled down his cheek.

I flipped him a card. "I'm him. Your dopey P.I. has been following me around for a while, so he's probably mentioned me to you. Frankly, I don't mind having him around. He makes me look good every time he turns a wheel. Oh, and he's gonna be indisposed in Vegas for a while. He crashed into one of their police cars. They get really pissed when that happens. Anyway, reason I'm here, it seems Shirley can't stand being married to you anymore. She wants out *really badly*. I can't really blame her, though I initially thought you two richly deserved one another".

Bongelli was listening, and he wasn't happy. "How does that concern you, Mister..." He looked at the card, "Street?"

"Well see, you ought to be concerned, because Shirley knows all about that little private crime wave you started orchestrating a while back with your buddy Grant... The Connors murders, the drug trafficking, the bodies at the ranch, all those business structures you set up to swindle your prisoner clients, even the brothel license in Pahrump. That one really surprised her. She thinks you're really not the type."

I took a breath and continued. "Anyway, the two of you have been together for a while, and she still has a soft spot for your fat crooked ass. She and my attorney friend, someone you've met before, prepared these documents for you to look over. To coin a phrase, you've been served." I handed him the folder. "There's some great stuff in there. Read it, give it some thought, and give me a call before the court hearing tomorrow. My number's on the folder, right there at the top. I am your sole contact for any of this, Bongelli. You have a little over twenty-four hours and I want a 'yes' or 'no'. Choose carefully and save yourself an immense amount of trouble."

I turned to walk away, then I paused. "Oh, and I really like your briefcase. Do you keep it loaded?" Bongelli looked at the documents, then at me, his face florid with rage.

50

I took a circuitous route around Riverside and Corona to ascertain that I wasn't being followed, then I drove back to Pasadena to Elizabeth's office. As I was ushered past the same impressively carved doors I saw Elizabeth at her desk. I spoke right up. "You're going to hate this."

She showed a thin smile and sighed, then responded, "What else is new, Mister Street?"

"You are aware that Ray Cole has been arrested for Ron's murder."

"Of course, Mister Street. How could I not be? The presumed suspect in the murders has been arrested at long last." She stopped just short of adding, 'I told you so.'

I raised an index finger. "That's right. You and I had this discussion a while back, didn't we?"

She was not pleased to have this conversation. "Yes, Mister Street. I believe you insinuated I was taking the path of least resistance."

"Yes I did. I would think you'd rather have the truth. We can have that if you're still interested."

She paused for a moment, pursed her lips, then said, "Very well, Mister Street. State your case. Again."

"Did Cole want to kill Ron? Yes! Of course, he did. He told everyone who would listen that he intended to do it, and he made plans to accomplish the feat. He tried to gather the resources to do the deed, but someone else had a better plan, more resources, and did it first. We found him."

"And that person is?"

"Guy named Grant Carty. He's also the pilot of the plane from which your son was dropped, and after Sutton's trial he acted on pure revenge in response to Ron's testimony. We have witnesses who were there from the very beginning and enough corroborating evidence to prove our point."

She looked at me and asked, "And you are asking what, my permission to proceed?"

"Absolutely not. My time is already paid for. I am simply advising you of our progress as I said I would."

She carried the thread further. "Surely you don't expect me to ask for Cole's release."

"Elizabeth, I know your animus toward him, and I know it goes back a long way. As I said before, his being a jerk doesn't translate to him also being a double murderer. You don't have to speak on his behalf, our evidence will do that. His release is not a priority right now. He's safe and sound in Ad Seg at Men's Central in downtown L.A. for a few days, and that may be an improvement for him."

Elizabeth pointed at the documents and pictures I had placed in front of her. "So, these people are responsible for my son's death, and this one commissioned and coordinated Ron and Annie's murders." She looked into my eyes, hers squinted slightly. It seemed that I had gained some traction. "You are certain."

"Yes I am."

She took a deep breath and held it for endless seconds, then exhaled. "Do not disappoint me, Mister Street. Proceed with your investigation as you see fit, but *do not let me down.*"

As I rose from my chair I said, "Understood. Thank you."

She rose from behind her desk and said, as I turned to leave, "And Mister Street. Good luck." She sounded as if she meant it.

51

From Elizabeth's office I drove home, did a couple of hours of computer work and updated the event boards, and then I gathered a few changes of clothes and packed for the next few possible days away from home. After the Tahoe was loaded I left it in the garage and took the GTO again. I was due to take a quick trip up to Hollywood Boulevard to the new studios of the TV network that employed Dierdre King.

From the reception area of the huge block-long off-white multi-story building I was directed through the cubicle farm to a third floor corner office bearing a freshly-embossed nameplate with the name D. KING. The aforementioned Ms. King rose as I approached the office. She was a striking young woman in her mid-to-late twenties, with long black hair and a trim, athletic 5-foot 7-inch frame. She wore no wedding ring. I'm trained to carefully observe such things. She smiled as she extended her hand. I handed her a card after the introduction and as I sat, she motioned for me to let the door shut on its stops.

I started the conversation. "Thank you for meeting me on such short notice. I appreciate the time."

"That's all right, Mister Street. I am pleased that someone

besides myself is interested in my father's murder. I tried for years to get official interest in his death, but the authorities have always written it off as a simple hit-and-run with probable connection to a nearby DUI crash the same evening. I didn't question it at first, I really didn't have time to think about it. Until my mom died a few weeks later I had plenty to keep me busy. As I started cleaning out their house to sell it I began reading Dad's notes and lots of questions arose. I started to question all the coincidences surrounding the 'hit and run' explanation. I no longer believe it."

I responded, "I think that my current investigation has uncovered information that not only *proves* that he was murdered but shows *who* was responsible. Coincidence has been a constant in this matter. What was your dad working on at the time of his death?" I knew what answer to expect.

Her brow furrowed. "He was revisiting an old case, something he did when work was slow. A few years prior he had tracked down a drug dealer who had thrown a rival out of an airplane. He had maintained that there were other people responsible other than that one who was convicted. He found that several people who had helped in that conviction had also been murdered. There was far too much 'coincidence' involved, so he was looking back into the same matter."

"Your father was a very perceptive man, Ms. King. He was investigating what I am looking into now, years sooner."

"Call me Dierdre, Mister Street. I'm just looking for some closure in this, y'know? He's been gone for a long time and it's been too many years without a solution. I feel like I owe him an answer."

I gave her a brief explanation of the current case, and how it pertained to her father's murder. The infamously unsolved Connors murders had been, partly, results of Grant Carty's response to her father's testimony against Arnie Sutton, how others had also been victims, and that at long last we had a line on Grant Carty, his show-runner Bongelli, and their backstory.

"All of this is coming to a 'thrilling conclusion' tomorrow at the courthouse at Riverside. You might consider assigning a crew there in the early afternoon. The fun should start popping off about two o'clock."

She was smiling now, and had made notes as I gave the details. "That sounds awesome! What do you need in return?"

Good question. "I'm glad you asked. I have been misquoted a few times in media over the last five years. Anything that involves me, comes through me first for proofing. Dumb mistakes and misquotes are non-starters. Let me guide your people through anything I'm involved with, and I will help you get a local News Emmy. Will that work for you?"

"Consider it done. Tell you what. I made copies of my dad's notes and files for his last work week, and I included archival material regarding his work with Ron Connors on the Rick Damarow murder case." She opened her desk drawer and withdrew a white plastic sleeve appropriate to a memory stick. "I have this one for you. It will probably take you an hour or so to get to the heart of the matter, but I think you'll find some interesting information there. Dad was on the verge of some important discoveries when he was killed, and I want him to finally receive credit for his work. Now that I have a serious media job, I can assure that happens and embellish it for him as appropriate."

"That'll work. Just pay attention tomorrow at the courthouse in Riverside. I can almost promise, that will be a big part of your story."

"Mister Street, you have my interest. I will be waiting for your call."

She smiled that smile again. She was a beautiful young woman, and I was certain that she was fully aware of that. Careful there, Street. Dazzled, all I could say was, "Thanks!"

"Where are you parked?"

I took the ticket from my jacket pocket and looked at it. "Third floor, two slots from the elevator."

As she rose from her chair she said, "Well, I'll walk you out and we'll get that validated. If you have a few minutes I can give you the cook's tour. This is quite a place."

"I wish I could. I'm back on the road to Las Vegas in an hour or two. May I ask for a rain check? This seems to be an intriguing place."

"Sure." We walked out of her department, she had my ticket stamped and we walked to the elevators. She explained her work, and related a few of the hassles she'd encountered in her rapid rise to an authority position in the heady world of network and major-market local news. It sounded as if she had sacrificed much of her personal life in the process. Oh, darn.

During the elevator ride to the parking deck she asked, "Are you married?"

"I'm not. Are you?"

She shook her head and smiled. As the door opened onto the appropriate level of the parking garage she said, "Well. We should go to dinner sometime. This place is full of metrosexual shitheads so it's good to encounter someone with their share of testosterone. That is rare in the entertainment industry unless they're on their third marriage and hitting on me."

"At the risk of being obvious, Dierdre, they have great taste." We were now standing next to the GTO. I hit the button on the key fob to unlock it. I'd brought the babe magnet again.

She looked at the car and smiled. "Oh, wow. I figured you might drive something 'killer'. This is beautiful!"

"Thank you. It's dirty right now. I'm usually really annoying about keeping it clean. I'll get back to it when this workload eases up a bit. You're into cars?"

She looked at me. "Oh, yeah. I worked my way through college doing detailing. I know the ropes and I have a few stunts of my own. Now that I'm making some money, I want a new Challenger SRT8. The dealers here don't want to stock the six-speeds." She leaned toward the GTO and wrote her cell number on the back of her business card. Magnificently.

Damn, this was getting good.

She waved the business card to dry the ink, then reached up to put it in my jacket pocket. I liked that a lot. "Ring me up when you get some time."

"Count on it." We shook hands and I watched her walk back to the elevator. I left the parking garage and drove home in a *really* good mood.

At home I spent the allotted hour studying the basics of Dierdre's father's activities prior to his death. The man had been dedicated in proving his suspicions. He had followed a 'young blonde', who sounded like Reanna, from the Sunset Auto Sales location to the Ontario Airport, had flown to Vegas and had tailed her driving one of the courier cars back to Jarupa on one of her work days. He had surveilled the dealer location for hours.

Looking at the attached pictures I surmised that his location was a stall at the coin-op car wash. A passing, and anxious, Carty would have noticed and become suspicious, and from what I knew of him he could have taken the same retaliatory action described in the accident report. Armed with the knowledge of the ownership of the car washes, his life could have been spared.

Detective King had also determined from the stock levels of Sunset Motors that something gnarly was occurring. The stock and the turnover of merchandise showed no competence when compared with similar operations. The 'nice' courier cars, usually upline imports, were brought into the operation after purchase at the Vegas dealer auction, then sold shortly thereafter at a Riverside or Orange County auction, often as a 'pure sale'—highest bidder gets it—and almost always at a loss. The other inventory at the lot was usually rolling shrapnel with values under $2000. Customer traffic was sparse at best. Other dealers in the area were baffled as to how and why the business remained open at all.

King had contacted the Riverside County Sheriffs with the information, and they had shown interest. Just as the ax was about to fall, King was run down, ending the official investigative operation from lack of information. I added 'lack of initiative' to the account myself and updated my event board, then it was time to hit the road.

I made the four-hour drive back to Jean in three hours flat, entering the suite to find Catherine at the desk by the window. Shirley and Chad cuddled on the couch watching an episode of 'Cheaters'. Odd justice there.

I entered with a cheery, Ward Cleaver-style, "Hi kids! I'm home!"

Catherine looked up, tired but smiling. "We made great progress today, and I have a game plan for tomorrow. You?"

I responded, "Sutton's on board, Bongelli's nervous, we have a significant new ally, and it looks good for court. We're staying at one of the Damarow properties in Riverside tonight, not far from the courthouse. You cool with that?"

52

December 11, 1996

Carty watched as Stacy finished the cabinet work in the barn. The place looked a lot better now, and as far as he was concerned Stacy's time was up. He had been an asset and a big help in 'civilizing' the house and barn, but he had seen a lot and had been marginally involved in far too many of the illegal operations at the ranch. While Carty didn't mind the company, he knew the hazards. Stacy had become dead weight and he couldn't be allowed to leave the property.

Stacy had asked that he be considered as a transport driver for the product shipments now that the routes were being expanded to include northern trips to Salt Lake City and Denver. No way! Regardless their care and attention to detail, were he ever stopped, even for a traffic infraction, they'd run his numbers, see his record, and the cops wouldn't let him go until something—anything—was found. Cons were bad news, dammit, plain and simple. No way around it. Dude was toast.

Carty watched as Stacy filled the dumpster, then he walked from his Bronco and spoke, "Lookin' great, Stace! You did good.

Last thing for today, let's go out east to the patch. You can help me move some dirt and smooth that top layer, then we're done." He walked to the old yellow Pettibone skip loader, climbed aboard, and started the diesel motor. Stacy hopped up onto the motor cover and sat sideways as the awkward machine bobbed along the rough two-track path toward the overgrown area a hundred yards from the house.

As they rolled along, Stacy called out, "So Carty, did you give any thought to me drivin' a route for you? If we ain't doin' business I need to cash out and book. I got stuff I gotta do, y'know?"

Ah, that. Over the roar of the engine Carty explained, "I'm sorry, brother. I just can't do it. It's damn near impossible to keep track of ever'body now. I'm not adding anyone anytime soon. We get done with this, we'll settle up and I'll give you a ride into town. That okay?"

Stacy was disappointed but not surprised. "Okay, Grant. I can dig that. I appreciate you answerin', anyway."

"No sweat," Carty called out. Ain't gonna matter for long, he thought. The skip loader coasted to a stop just short of the recently-hewn cavity in the sandy desert soil. Carty pointed ahead and called out, "Get down in the hole, Stace. After I drop a load, I'll use the bucket as a blade to smooth it out. You make sure it's spread evenly. I don't want any voids. Should take about four loads to get it done."

"Gotcha, boss." Stacy hopped off the engine cover and stepped down into the hole. Carty turned the tractor toward the piles of soil and loaded the bucket, turned back to the hole and made his dump, then repeated twice. As he prepared to drop the third bucket, he set the brake, put the tractor into neutral, and stood up beside the steering wheel. Behind the reduced engine noise, he called out, "Hey, Stace! Look at that!" He pointed beyond the hole as he pulled a pistol from the side pocket of his overalls and pointed it at Stacy, ready to finish his target off in his usual style.

As Stacy turned back to determine Carty's point, he saw the pistol appear around Carty's leg. He dodged the first shot as he rolled to a spot behind the upright shovel and fired his own pistol around the side of the bucket. His shot glanced off the tractor's tubular roll bar structure of the tractor, the ricochet missing Carty's head by mere inches. In response Carty resumed his seat, kicked the brake release, pedaled the clutch, and slammed the long shifter lever into gear. The transmission made a grinding noise for a second then the tractor lurched forward a foot, catching the would-be assassin at chest level as he aimed his next shot.

The angled bucket caught Stacy's shoulder, pinned his chest into the soft sandy dirt and the vehicle rolled its length and weight forward over the prone body. Carty then stopped, put the tractor in reverse, backed over the body again, and stopped a few feet away. After he shut off the engine, he hopped off the tractor, walked a few feet forward, and emptied the clip of his pistol into the lurching, broken body. Quaking in response to the first resistance any of his victims had ever shown, Carty emptied the corpse's pockets of a wad of large bills, a billfold, and a set of keys to God knows what. Minutes later he regained the skip loader, pushed the body into the hole, and pushed dirt over it. He finished by reversing the blade to level the fill, then he took the loader to the barn and went back to the house, still shaking.

53

Before we left the Gold Strike I put in a fast half-hour online studying the national crime registries verifying the situation of the dusty Denali parked in Carty's barn. I found it an easy 'get'. It had come back as a San Bernardino County stolen, connected to a missing persons case from six years ago. From that result I had sourced the San Bernardino County Sheriff's office and a veteran deputy, Ann Bond. Fifteen years on the job, the last five in Major Crimes with the cold case inquiries landing on her desk, made her an efficient and cordial contact. She promised a return call after the verification of my information.

My cell rang as we prepared to leave the resort for the trip back to Riverside. I stood outside the packed, idling, cooling Tahoe to take the call uninterrupted. "Yes, Deputy Bond, I appreciate the return call."

"No problem, Mister Street. I made a few calls and verified your inquiry regarding one of our cold deals. I'm all ears!"

"Thank you. In the course of one of my investigations, I located the light blue Denali in the image that I sent you. It shows up as a San Berdoo county stolen, connected to the disappearance of one Daniel Nathan Priess, who in turn comes up as a major Missing

Person case under your purview. I believe Priess went missing six years back with no trace of him or his ride. He and his family have, or had at that time, a few upmarket used car dealers in Riverside and San Bernardino counties. I found the Denali in a barn on a ranch north of Las Vegas. The VIN matches the stolen truck and the On Star locator has been disconnected. I re-attached the battery cable, got a faint tick on it so you may have gotten a 'ping' a few days ago. In my training that is the first step to determining a stolen with an OnStar."

"Thank you Mister Street. You are right on the money. I have gotten to know that family quite well, and that kid's disappearance really tore them up. You did the right thing with the battery but if the vehicle is in a barn a weak signal may not be sufficient to carry."

"That's good to know. There will be an interagency raid of that location sometime tomorrow. I will send you the contact information for the lead agency. If you have any questions, please give me a call."

"I will certainly do that, Mister Street. And let's get together out here at some point as well. If you can bring this 'missing' case home for us I know my squad will want to meet you."

"Sounds like a plan. Your e-mail is..." She gave me the address and we rung off. This was getting good. Happy at the progress, I regained the Tahoe and we hit the road south on the Fifteen. The fun was about to begin.

54

It had been a busy thirty-six-hour period with many tasks to be completed, mostly without an excess of planning.

Fly from Riverside to Vegas to uncover decades of criminal deceit: Check

Visit, confuse, attempt to terrorize and serve divorce papers to opposing attorney/crime lord: Check.

Visit State Prison to educate and correct path of corrupted incarcerated perp/victim with writing on his face: Check!

Visit and annoy my client: Check.

Confer with (hottie) broadcast news exec to gather archival material verifying suspicions and ensure accurate coverage for future events: Check.

Drive back to Nevada to retrieve my team: Check.

Return to Riverside to prepare for the Grand Finale/Showdown: Check.

And the real drama was still to come.

After I paid and released our private security all four of us piled into the Tahoe and made a fast run—no zucchini this time—across the desert to arrive at Elizabeth's 'professionally quaint' inn near the Riverside Mission a little over a mile from the courthouse. The reservation used one of my business names and a Damarow courtesy reservation so there was no public record that our cast of characters was in attendance on Bongelli's 'hood'.

You can't be too careful on potential enemy turf. I had figured that the Damarow name carried more weight all over southern California than Bongelli's handle did, but I didn't want to push my luck in the Inland Empire. Loyalties could still be in question and I didn't want to take any unnecessary chances with security. I called Zig and asked for a referral, knowing that he would send the best he knew for the task. I wasn't surprised at all when later that day he showed up himself. No surprise there, he is one of the toughest, most dependable people I know.

Everyone had been polite and personable to this point and I hoped that would continue. That night I took a couple of sleeping pills and caught a solid six hours of rest that I sorely needed after logging over 650 miles that day. The solitude would help in coping with the events of the next day and it would have been impossible if anyone but Zig had been on-point.

That next morning dawned dark and damp in the Inland Empire, with overcast skies and expected scattered showers. We stayed in a nice three-bedroom suite, killing time going over the game plan. We ascertained signatures, double checked legalities, and crossed our collective fingers. After a great early lunch ordered in from the Chilean restaurant where Catherine and I had first met, we took the inclement weather in stride and drove toward the Riverside County Courthouse, leaving at three minutes 'til one for a 1:30 start time for the Sutton sentence reduction hearing.

On the way to the courthouse my cell phone rang. The screen told me the caller, so I pulled into a strip mall driveway and took the call standing outside the truck in the mist. Catherine and the kids sat inside the idling Tahoe.

I opened the phone. "Street." Bongelli introduced himself, sounding a bit milder than during our last encounter. I said, "Well, Vin, what's your call? Yes or no?"

As he harrumphed toward actual speech, I realized who

Bongelli reminded me of... It was 'Boss Hogg' from the old *Dukes of Hazzard* TV series. I felt no intimidation whatsoever from then on. "Well, Mister Street, I wonder if we might be able to reach some common ground here. I sure do hope so. You seem to be a man of particular talents. I wonder if I could interest you..."

I interrupted his speech lest I toss my collective cookies. "You can't afford me, Bongelli, and I couldn't afford enough Simple Green to de-grease after each meeting. Here's the deal. You have exactly two options: One, toe the line, or Two: suffer the consequences. Pick one. Our T's are crossed, and I's are dotted respectively, and we are moving forward with the process described in the documents that you received. We can settle this easily. I don't need your money, and your hired goons will come up short every time against me. Don't you piss me off! Choose carefully, Bongelli." I listened for twenty seconds as he breathed into his end of the connection. "Time's up, babe. See you in court."

At Catherine's prompting I parked at the east side of the courthouse toward the rear of the complex. We entered through a coded side door and climbed to the third floor where we found an unoccupied conference room across the hall from 'our' courtroom. I opened the door to the Perry Mason Signature Edition courtroom and walked to the desk where the clerk was doing paperwork. I showed my credentials and explained our plans, finding the officer rather agreeable. Seems the court staff didn't care all that much for Bongelli either. We shook hands and I returned to the meeting room.

Catherine looked at me as I entered. "What's the deal, Street. Are we in?"

I looked at her as I answered. "We are indeed. We'll sit off to the left behind your witness table, in full view. This might be fun."

My cell phone vibrated, a sign I had been waiting for. I looked at the screen and smiled. At that very moment on the approach road outside the ranch property, a parade of official vehicles drove across the wide metal cattle grate and converged on the house and the ranch property. Officers prowled the grounds per our suggestions as two of

Danny Tanner's copters hovered at 5000 feet carrying local TV news cameras. A paramedic coach stood idling at the rear of the house until two doctors, flanked by a pair of Clark County Sheriffs' deputies, brought Grant Carty from the house on a stretcher. Carty was then taken to a suburban rehabilitation center just outside Las Vegas.

Early the next morning a phalanx of police cadets on loan from L.V. Metro, led by mounted Nevada State Troopers would take instructions and begin to grid-search and catalog the ranch property. It was a project that would last five days total. DEA investigators descended on the property and called in hazmat specialists to study the block houses.

I stepped to the window of the conference room when Danny's call came in. I could hear the hum of his helicopter in the background. "Street, it's a thing of beauty. State cops are all over the ranch. It looks as if they'll be busy for a while. The grassy area we saw last time seems to be of particular interest, a few Feds have shown up, too. The damaged cargo is on the road."

"Good to know, Danny! Thanks for the call!"

There was a tap at the door, Catherine opened the door, and an officer gave us the three-minute signal. Catherine turned to Shirley, smiled and asked, "It's almost time. Are you ready?"

Shirley was surprisingly warm in her response. "Ms. Gadsden, I have waited for this for years, a few minutes now won't make much difference." She looked at us and said, "I want to thank you both for your help in this." With that we rose and walked from the conference room to the courtroom and assumed our seats. Shirley and Chad sat in the fourth of five rows and I sat one row forward and toward the center aisle in clear view of Bongelli's defense table position at the front of the courtroom on the opposite side of the polished mahogany partition rail.

Catherine leaned toward me and whispered, "Street, does Bongelli know what's going down at the ranch?"

I whispered my response, "I doubt he does now, but he may soon. That call was from our 'guy in the sky', Danny. It's all starting to go down right now. The attendant at the ranch will probably contact Bongelli since Shirley is MIA. I'd imagine the office will contact Bongelli's office at some point, then they will contact him. That might add to the drama here sometime soon."

I looked toward the defendant's bench at the front of the room as Bongelli and Sutton entered the room and took their seats. The other seating in the courtroom were filling to about half-capacity. I could remember sitting in with my grandfather when his court dates coincided with my visits. I imagine he would consider the coming events 'interesting'.

After a couple of minutes my gaze met Sutton's and I nodded. Sutton turned to Bongelli and whispered at length. Bongelli reacted audibly, and we heard from three rows back as he said, "What? You can't do that!"

Just then the bailiff rose to his feet and called, "All rise. This Court is hereby in session, the honorable Walter C. Rothermel Senior presiding."

A tall, lean, dignified-looking elderly judge pro tem with a tall plume of pearl white hair entered the room from a side door and took his seat at the podium. He called, "All be seated" in a deep, booming voice. He looked at his paperwork for a few seconds then he looked out on the room. "In the matter of docket number 442, regarding a sentence reduction for one Arnold Sutton. Is Inmate Sutton present in this courtroom?"

Sutton looked shockingly civilized in his discount-store grey suit as he stood to answer in a high nervous voice. "Yes sir, um, Your Honor. And I want to hire a new attorney."

The judge paused, took the outburst in stride and smiled a crooked smile. He looked at Sutton over the top of his glasses and commented. "That may be easier said than done, Inmate Sutton. Is your new representative in the courtroom?"

A young attorney sitting two rows in front of us raised his hand and stood. "Arthur Waddley, Your Honor."

The judge looked at Waddley and seemed to recognize him. He

asked, "And your application and other materials are in order, Counselor?"

"Yes, Your Honor, and I'd ask a continuance in the hearing, perhaps two weeks?"

The judge looked at him, smiled thinly, and asked, "Are we asking the Court or telling the Court, counselor?"

The young attorney returned the smile, lifted his eyebrows and answered, "Just a modest request, Your Honor."

The judge responded, "Very well. Is there any other business connected with this request?"

Waddley answered, "Just the materials at hand, Judge."

The judge shuffled the papers into a neat stack and backed his chair from the podium. "Court will take a ten-minute recess." He motioned to Waddley and the clerk to accompany him to the side door of the courtroom.

At this point, Bongelli, sitting at an odd angle at his bench, looked back at me then recognized Shirley and Chad sitting a row behind me. He glared at Shirley and Shirley glared at him for seconds. Bongelli backed down only when his cell phone vibrated. He opened the phone and read the screen, blanched, and looked back at Shirley. Frowning, she stared him down again, then Bongelli abruptly turned to the front and opened his briefcase.

With a theatrical flourish, he took a pen and started searching the pages for the proper sites for signatures and initials. Each page was unfolded, initialed and signed a little quicker as his 'done' stack gained bulk. After five busy minutes, Bongelli took the stack of pages, straightened them and returned them to the original folder, then put his copies into his briefcase. He turned, his complexion a deeper red than I'd ever seen it. He signaled to one of the clerks, who took the folder, handed it to Shirley then returned to his station. Then Bongelli turned and looked back at Shirley, clearly enraged.

So far so good for all involved but this time when Bongelli turned to glare at us, there was a new element. An acquaintance of mine had joined us in the courtroom. Jack Wilkes had been another Atlantic City cop who had moved west in search of warmth and adventure, but he had taken a different path to the latter than I had. He now wore a Federal badge, having toiled for the last three years for the FBI in downtown L.A. He and I hadn't been 'friends' in A.C., but I knew him to be a full-on all-business professional. Catherine and I had spoken to him a few times in the recent weeks and he had decided that he needed some face time with Counselor Bongelli.

Now all six-feet, five-inches of Jack Wilkes stood behind Shirley's position toward the rear of the courtroom. He wore a black vested suit with his jacket unbuttoned and his thumbs hooked at the sides of his waist to display the nice big shiny FBI badge clipped to his belt. He absently tapped the badge with his left-hand index finger. The badge looked as if it was backlit and perhaps oversized. Really intimidating.

Black suit and silver badge. I'd have to remember that.

The Jack-sighting may have been Bongelli's first realization that our incredibly comprehensive paperwork didn't disclose *absolutely everything* regarding this situation after all. Well, damn.

The silent drama continued for a few minutes as Bongelli stared at us, and we stared back to no great drama or effect. I even smiled and waved. There was no real mystery between the players. I knew about Bongelli's secretly-armed briefcase and he didn't *know* I knew unless he'd paid attention when we met in the parking lot the day before. I kept an eye on his hands as we sat and stared at one another.

As I watched Bongelli, I was confident that his chubby little skull was buzzing with ideas for escape from his current predicament. And really, faced with the fast-approaching Bongelli Signature-Edition crapstorm, who wouldn't be tempted to make a run for it? I almost felt a little sympathy for the guy. He had lived the dream for a long time, controlling and benefitting from millions of dollars of other people's cash. Time to settle up was fast approaching, a time that Bongelli may have thought would never arrive.

His clients' inability to control their resources, or even complain effectively about the handling thereof, had made this a perfect 'racket'. For an operator of Bongelli's caliber, it had to be a dream gig, and I couldn't imagine that he would just lay down and let his empire topple, even in the face of the unique force being applied by his practically-former wife and a phalanx of authorities from numerous levels of law enforcement.

As silent seconds crept by, I saw him turn back toward his bench, pick up his cell phone and look at the screen. He turned back and glared at us again, his face now beet red. He put the phone into his shirt pocket, filled and closed his briefcase, straightened his posture in his chair, and moved the chair back a few inches. He stared straight ahead and sat bolt upright.

Within the allotted ten minutes the judge and the new Sutton counsel re-entered the courtroom as the clerk called, "All rise." We in the room rose and resumed our seats after the judge resumed his position. Fine, but as we sat back down, I caught sight of movement at the defense bench. Sutton was shoved out of the way as Bongelli made his way for the nearest side door. I saw the corner of his briefcase follow him out the door as it hissed shut.

Few if any of the attendees noticed until the judge pounded his gavel and called, "Is Counselor Bongelli still in the courtroom?"

Only then did the bailiff respond to the judge, "I think he left." Hizzonor was not amused.

For whatever reason I raised my hand and called, "I'll get him back for you, Judge!" I vacated my perch and dashed across the courtroom to the same side door as it finished its low hiss to full closure. As I took flight, I heard the judge start to bang his gavel but by the second bang I was already out the door. Contempt of Court, your Honor? Who, ME?

As I entered the hallway at the east side of the courtroom, I had the first realization that Bongelli was not only armed, pea-shooter though it was, but he also knew the inner layout of the facility in which he had done business for a decade or more. As I cleared the door, I looked in both directions and saw a door fifty feet away closing behind someone's exit. While there were relatively few people wandering that part of the courthouse, random civilian traffic and an escaping armed barrister were not a desirable combination.

As I readied my approach, Jack Wilkes appeared behind me at the corner of the hallway. "Street!" he called, before I looked at him. He pointed at the staircase near his position and I assumed from our shared training in A.C. that he would flank me on a lower floor. "Gun?" he called. I nodded to the affirmative and he slid a nice machine-finished Colt pistol toward me on the floor. I snagged it as it stopped at the toe of my shoe as Wilkes disappeared down the staircase.

Now packin' heat, I ran along the wall toward the doorway. I peeked into the window at the top of the door, seeing a simple, straight access hallway that ended at a similar door opening into the multi-story front lobby. Opening the door, I saw Bongelli as he reached the other end. He saw me as well and hit the light switch at his end, plunging the hallway into darkness. Attentive cat that I am I hit the similar switch at my end. The fluorescent lights flickered to full-on by the time I reached the opposite end.

I opened the door I to the lobby and looked to the left to see Bongelli racing down the curved stairway that wrapped that side of the tall glass-fronted lobby. Staircases on each side of the lobby serviced the various areas of the building. As Bongelli descended, he knocked those ahead of him out of the way, an element that slowed him down quite a bit. I ran to the top of the opposite staircase and gained on him, hitting the ground floor of the lobby about seventy-five feet behind him as he plowed through the front door and turned back to fire a shot in my direction. The shot went wide, chipping a flower pot off to my right.

My Bluetooth earpiece lit up and I tapped the prompt. Wilkes called, "Street, what's your twenty?"

"Front of the courthouse heading for the parking garage."

Wilkes had just exited his level of the lobby. "I'm on your six. I'll catch up."

Behind me I could hear Wilkes running, and ahead Bongelli was making the turn to the main entrance of the parking garage. We entered fifteen seconds later just as he made the right-hand turn to head toward the lower levels, probably priority parking for tenured visitors, a 'frequent flyer' area. On the sloping surface Bongelli picked up momentum as he passed the myriad of parked cars. Jack and I did as well.

As Bongelli made the left turn at the bottom of the garage he turned and took another shot in my direction. This one went wide as well, smacking a concrete piling that I was passing. Seeing him aim, I ducked a second late. A piece of concrete grazed my temple with a stout sting, and I felt my Bluetooth earpiece fly from my ear. Bleeding now, and annoyed as hell, I looked for a shortcut. I hopped over a low concrete wall just shy of the last turn and ran flat out toward the shiny new silver Mercedes I had sighted in the distance.

The problem, at least for Bongelli, was that there were maybe two dozen shiny silver late-model imports at the base of that structure, most of them indistinguishable in the low lighting. That slowed Bongelli down a bit and gave me my chance. I ran between two SUVs and used a half-height lane divider as a launch point for a flying tackle. A long second later I caught Bongelli at the left shoulder and the two of us went to the ground in a tangled heap. I gave myself a 5.8/10, deducting for age-appropriateness and an utter lack of style.

Okay, that kind of stuff works really well in High School football or on TV using professional stuntmen after three rehearsals and five takes from varying angles and a visit to the Craft Services table. It's not as artfully executed in a darkened parking garage on sandy concrete by a guy nearing middle-age wearing nice clothes. Bongelli twisted as he fell and I ended up under him on the concrete, my legs were under someone's silver Lexus SUV and my head against the rear tire of a big Audi sedan. I'd heard my jacket rip as we landed, and I could still feel my temple spewing from the shrapnel wound.

Bongelli was immobile for a few seconds, long enough for Jack to arrive at the site of the conflagration after I kicked my way out from beneath him. As I freed myself, I gave him a solid right to the jaw for good measure. His small silver semi-automatic pistol had landed in the middle of the traffic lane out of reach. I eventually rose from the tangle, rumpled and bleeding, torn and dirty from the journey. But we won.

Jack had arrived and drawn down on Bongelli as I went back to my feet. I was collecting Bongelli's gun and his fancy briefcase as the Riverside County Sheriffs' deputies arrived, guns drawn. Jack's Fed badge quelled their attitudes a bit as he sat Bongelli upright and cuffed him.

That task completed, Jack looked at me and smiled. "Street, you look like hell."

"Hey Jack, I been busy. Thanks for the assist."

He squinted and looked at the path of my acrobatics as he holstered his pistol. As I returned the one he'd loaned me he smiled and said, "I didn't know you could fly, kid." He smiled a little. It hurt a little when I smiled back. I sat back onto the lane divider, took it all in for a few seconds and let the guys with the badges finish the drama.

56

An hour later I sat at the back of a Paramedic Ambulance parked in front of the parking garage. A young black medic washed my forehead and temple with some clean-smelling clear blue antiseptic on cotton balls and applied an ever-so-stylish beige rectangular bandage—the kind that makes everyone look really well-tanned—to my right temple over a couple of butterfly bandages.

I could see the progress of the work by watching the mirror in the upper rear corner of the box ambulance. The medic handed me a bright blue fabric ice pack that I pressed to my forehead. It clashed with the bloodstain and road burn on my shirt and jacket.

Yeah, I know. I bitch a lot when I'm disheveled.

The medic and I chatted for a few more minutes until I saw Catherine approach the ambulance through a phalanx of media, and law enforcement. She pushed her way through the bystanders toward the ambulance. When she saw me she looked startled. "Street! Are you okay?"

I waved her off, "I have no idea. Ask this guy. I have a huge headache and my ears are ringing."

The paramedic looked at me and then at Catherine. "We got us a tough guy here. Just a few puncture wounds from flying concrete, a couple of scrapes and a bruise or two. We decontaminated the wounds and bandaged him up so he won't be scarred for life." He touched his temple. "He's lucky with this one. Half an inch to the left he could've lost an eye."

I smiled, looked at Catherine and said, "Yeah but half an inch to the right it would've missed me altogether." I had always wanted to deliver a classic Rockford line. The medic just frowned and shook his head. My head still hurt but I asked him, "Are we done here?"

"Yeah. You'll live. Go to the ER if you still hurt tomorrow and hit the Motrin when you get home. You know the drill by now."

"I do. Thanks, man." I started to rise but my head did a victory lap so I sat back down quickly. Catherine came to my side and after a few seconds. I took a deep breath and tried again, this time more successfully. She took my arm, and as we walked around the court-house toward the Tahoe she said, "Street, you look beat. That nice jacket is past tense."

"Remind me to invoice Bongelli." I tried to shrug my way out of it, with some difficulty from the bruised shoulder. "It's rough to maintain fashion sense when three hundred pounds of dirtbag lawyer land on you." I escaped the jacket and looked at it: Totaled. I asked Catherine as we rounded the corner of the courthouse, "So how did things go in there?"

Catherine smiled and looked at me. "Swimmingly! Let's see…"

"Shirley has her divorce papers signed, faxed to Carson City and filed twenty minutes ago."

"Grant Carty is under guard at the private hospital outside Vegas. Great play there, Street."

"Bongelli is in conference with your buddy Jack the Fed, and because of the paperwork you arranged he is out of Arnie Sutton's dealings for good. The daughter and her mother get what they were promised. He seemed remorseful about them. Oh, and you were right. The face tatts do him no good at all."

"Bongelli's law offices are set to be raided by the State and the Feds, starting right about…" She looked at her watch, "Now. It looks as if Bongelli had taken the cash value down to a half-million or so

The One That Kills You | 281

but with property values, the man is probably the wealthiest inmate at Chino. And Sutton has his new mouthpiece. Good work all around, Street. "

I looked at her and smiled. "That works for me. Thanks for all your help."

"So after all of this do you feel like a conquering hero? You don't exactly look the part right now. Sorry."

Listening, walking and comprehending at the same time had taken its toll. As we reached the Tahoe I opened the tailgate, lifted the top of the ice chest on the cargo deck and grabbed a quart of bottled water. I drank some of it and poured some of it over my head. "I'll be okay. It's been a long week. I think need a nap."

Catherine smiled and took the keys. "My office. I'll drive."

57

September 13, 2004

Vinnie Bongelli was pissed, more so than he could recall.

He couldn't count on anyone anymore. Though the inmate money machine was just starting to bear large succulent fruit he was still expecting a bigger take, soon. His biggest problem right now, besides Shirley demanding a divorce, was that the desert operation had stopped working. Carty had stopped kicking in his share of the earnings and had refused to provide any accounting for the money he was making. Worse, his ancillary businesses were a wreck.

Within the last week alone, the Riverside County Sheriff's department, the state Code Enforcement Department and the Department of Motor Vehicles had all called the law office about the Jarupa car lot. That operation had been Carty's idea, made fully operational through the law office. That operation was set up as a plug'n'play deal; any idiot could run it. A week or so ago word had come through the grapevine that Carty was running a ridiculous amount of money through the operational accounts, but with no justifying documents. An audit could be catastrophic.

Carty was going balls to the wall now with drug operation in the desert, and he didn't know when to quit. Added attention could bring the whole house of cards down in a heartbeat, and it would all come back to Bongelli. That couldn't be allowed to happen.

Stupid goddam Carty had to go. That's all there was to it. Bongelli wasn't going to allow some druggie POS screw up everything that had been constructed over a decade. Bongelli had taken a million-plus off the top so far this year for personal investments. Carty had seen that and decided to copy it and expand upon it. Eventually the cash payouts to the law office has dwindled to a trickle, while the actual production from the ranch facility had more than tripled. Only through Bongelli's pushback would the system remain uncorrupted.

Out of frustration, and because of Carty's refusal to communicate, Bongelli finally took a trip to the ranch in the desert. He tolerated Nevada, he treated Las Vegas as a necessary evil, but he hated the desert, with the heat and the wind and the grit. He had probably left that end of the operation to Carty for too long, though he had heard plenty of proposals for replacement operations. He tried to avoid thinking of the more attractive alternatives.

The wind that day was oppressive, unusually gusty, and the dust—more accurately, the grit—could be seen hovering in the distance on the darkened southern horizon. Heavy storm clouds cruised across the sky, hanging in groups against the bluest of skies, spitting out lightning every few seconds. The thunder was loud and getting louder.

Bongelli looked around as he drove slowly past the barn toward the collection of run-down buildings. The stark concrete blockhouses, crude when they were built, were really tacky-looking now. The side walls were stained from the extremes of weather but there were also urine stains, oddly within a few feet of a new working portable toilet. Great. The facility had been constructed at Carty's request by another of Bongelli's law clients, working off legal fees for a messy divorce. Carty had specified the construction after taking a trip to Mexico during which he had been shown a similar operation created to combine cocaine processing and meth cooking at one facility. As the buildings had taken shape Carty's paranoia had made him impatient. He had run the construction crew away somewhat short of the project's completion.

A thick black power line drooped between the power pole and the barn then ran along the eaves of the barn. It roped across the open space to the first blockhouse. The lines swung in a foot-wide arc that Bongelli just knew wasn't a positive, given the acrid atmosphere in and around the drug processing operation. Worse yet were the rough window and door openings, finish work that had been paid for but never completed. Old household window fans running at their limits attempted to draw the acrid fumes from within the shacks, giving the area a foul cat-piss aroma. That was the one thing the stiff winds actually helped.

'Someone is going to die here sometime', he thought aloud. Bongelli silently hoped for the right victims, then stifled the thought. He parked the now-filthy Mercedes at the end of the line of derelict cars, a few feet from the blue truck that had given him such stress a few years before. He left the car and walked across the driveway to the first of the blockhouses. He had to confront Carty today, once and for all. As he walked, he formulated his pitch, with Carty's preservation at the top of his concerns. He knew that if the proper connections were made by the authorities, he could face slam-dunk charges for racketeering. He would be disbarred and would face Federal time. He couldn't let that happen. He'd make an offer. They'd shut down the whole operation and let it cool off for a while. Carty could go to rehab, Bongelli could cover everyone's ass, as usual, then get back to real legal work instead of sweating these idiots all the time. That'd be good.

As he approached the first shack, he saw one masked, dust covered face at the window and called, 'I need Carty! Where is he?" The figure in the window pointed to the next shack, then held up three fingers. Bongelli walked down the line, knowing that his clothes would go into the trash after absorbing the disgusting odors...another expense. God, he hated this place! He pounded at the door of the third shack and the door opened a few inches. To the masked brown face he said, "I need Carty!" The figure raised an index finger and shut the door. Bongelli backed away a few paces to wait.

Momentarily the door re-opened and Grant Carty emerged. He was covered with a sheen of sweat and wore a car-themed T-shirt, a tattered pair of black cargo shorts, and a pair of thongs. He was covered with a pale white dust. No moon suit, still! He had been going from room to room, overseeing the varied operations. Aggressive and ambitious, yes, but too stupid for words as well. As he approached, Bongelli saw that his pupils were pinpoints. Carty wiped his face with a microfiber towel and smiled. "Hey, Vin. How's it hangin', bro?"

Excited now, Bongelli practically sputtered, "Carty, we gotta talk! I see you cut me off from our agreement, just as things were starting to perk! After all we been through together, Grant, why would you do that?"

Carty looked at the attorney and chuckled. "Bongelli, I guess I'm just playing my own game now. Whole different arena, babe. No more prison league for me. I'll be doin' my own thing now. Hasta la bye bye, babe!"

This took Bongelli by surprise. "That's not how it works, Grant! Let's talk this out. We can make this right! I have millions invested in you and this operation, and dammit, you owe me a lot more than that. I can't just let that go. I won't! Let's put our heads together and get back in gear. We can work a new deal. I have some new ideas to share with you."

Carty wasn't having it. He sneered at Bongelli and stepped toward him threateningly. "You got some 'new ideas'? Well, whoopie shit. I got a much better idea. How 'bout I just buy you out? That way I can do my thing and you can do yours. Ever'body's happy." A voice from inside one of the shacks called Carty and he turned to answer, then he walked away, calling back over his shoulder, "Gimme a minute, Vin. I gotta check the mix. I'll be back when

I'm done." He entered the third shack and the wooden door shuffled closed against its rough frame.

Bongelli was now seeing red. How dare this piss-ant turn his back and walk away! He stood back by the wrecked blue truck... that again... and waited. This crap had to end. He walked to his car, grabbed his briefcase and returned to stand by the truck. He laid his briefcase on the hood and popped the side panel to reveal his little silver pistol. If it came down to it, he would use that to force the point. He put the pistol into the side pocket of his suitcoat, and waited. Five minutes, then ten, as the sky darkened and the wind gusts increased. He could smell the aroma of the approaching rain. His rage smoldered as the odor from the blockhouses increased.

Then the worst imaginable event occurred. The approaching rain squall had darkened the skies to the extent that the blockhouse in which Carty was working needed more light. The shortened construction of the buildings had resulted in unfinished light switch boxes with twisted plastic caps joining the wires at the switches. Carty called, "Hit the lights" to one of the workers. A gloved hand reached for the switch. There was a bright blue flash at the switch then the whole room lit orange with a loud 'BDOOF!' The roof lifted two feet as flames spouted from around its base and through the door and window opening. The window fan, itself aflame, was launched from the window as the glass sprayed out from the opening.

A secondary explosion launched a screaming, flaming Grant Carty through the space formerly occupied by the window. As he was propelled through the opening his right foot caught on the rough concrete base of the space, throwing him into an awkward, twisting, flaming somersault. He hit the ground fifteen feet from the front wall of the shack, scorched around the edges but still aflame over half of his upper body. Bongelli, having been knocked from his feet by the blast, regained his senses to the extent that he grabbed one of Carty's arms and started to roll him on the dirt to douse the flames. He had no idea how long that effort lasted but later he couldn't rid himself of the vision of the screaming, smoking hulk of Grant Carty as the fat heavy raindrops started pounding the sandy soil moments after the blasts.

After 'his' fire was doused Carty passed out in the dirt. Bongelli, at gunpoint, arranged some 'assistance' from the workers in the other shacks and moved Carty into the house, then 'went for help', returning an hour later to wait for his wife the nurse. He had to come up with a game plan, fast, and it was going to cost him dearly.

58

So it all came down to a crooked lawyer...whooda thunk? As
crooked and ruthless as Vinnie Bongelli was, I was fascinated by
the complexity of his operation and the run-up to it. As I wrote the
reports and completed the paperwork for the various departments
affected I studied him a bit. It was fascinating in a criminalistic way.

The shakeout of the final solution to the crimes surprised and
confused onlookers and pleased few who were close to the situation. The impetus dated back to Bongelli's early law career. Like
many urban Law School grads, he was recruited into a huge downtown L.A. law firm and had subsequently been chained to a desk in
a dingy cubicle two floors down from the 'real' attorneys whose
names were on the stationery. While the near slave-ship conditions
of his work area made him resentful of both his employers and his
clients, they did inspire him to develop his clever system that would
eventually make him wealthy and influential.

Most of his early criminal work, assigned by jaded senior partners who were less than concerned with results, dealt with the
defense of cash-heavy narcotics traffickers and manufacturers. His
clients had been charmless thugs who, in the heady world of pre-
O.J. non-minority juries, saw little if any sympathy come their way.

His results there were mediocre at best, but his reputation had been planted with that small community.

Working with those defendants he found that they usually created ridiculous profits that were untaxed and rapidly wasted by the undereducated, undirected and undisciplined princes of the drug trade. This element folded nicely into his other legal specialty, the formation of California and Nevada corporate structures for small- and medium-size businesses.

With his plethora of cash-heavy and probably slammer-bound clients catalogued in his Rolodex, Bongelli's two areas of expertise —mediocre criminal defense and top-shelf organizational skills, were cleverly combined when he entered private practice.

For a handsome fee he would offer to manage the formation of Nevada corporations that in turn would own cover businesses that would launder the illicit income—sometimes millions of dollars per year—while lending an air of legitimacy to even the most cartoony drug dealers. The 'legal' protection of illegal funds, combined occasionally with a heart-to-heart talk about 'priorities' gained popularity within the industry of drug traffickers as more and more of his criminal defendants found themselves convicted and incarcerated.

Nevada's identity-shielded, largely tax-free corporate structures had been envisioned decades before to shield the phenomenal earnings from the state's legal gambling and prostitution industries. Organized crime was a large factor in the state at the time as well. No one ever told Bongelli, though, that smaller mobs could access them with similar success. If the client got nailed through simple sloppiness, Bongelli would go through the motions in defense. If the defendant lost his freedom Bongelli still profited handsomely after the miscreant entered the Penal system.

It all worked quite well for a decade as over two dozen convicted clients allowed Bongelli to run their corporate entities as his own. Everyone was happy. The prisoner received a healthy monthly stipend and, if applicable, family support as the property values of the corporate holdings escalated. A pretty picture of prosperity was painted for the inmates, so word spread. His client rolls grew, and an increasingly enthusiastic Bongelli profited richly. He opened a Las Vegas office after he commandeered a high-rise penthouse condo as payment for legal fees. He was a success.

Then along came Grant Carty, who became the model student for the Bongelli system for a few years. Carty's own methods were energetic and meshed beautifully with Vinny's. Carty's suggestion for a self-contained drug manufacturing/dealing/transporting system based through a licensed car dealer seemed to enable a perfect income loop, and his early to-the-letter cooperation made him a sterling example of the Bongelli system. Carty referred several of his friends to his buddy Bongelli for 'the fix'. Bongelli gifted Carty a new Corvette as an appreciation the same week he bought his first new Mercedes. Life was good for all involved.

When Carty hanger-on Arnie Sutton alone was arrested for the murder of rival drug dealer Rick Damarow, Bongelli did his thing again. The gripping, emotional testimony by the victim's uncle had turned the tide in that trial and Bongelli's mediocre defense ended in a stout prison sentence after the jury's verdict. No shock there.

Grant Carty had been inconsolable after his half-brother's conviction. He had pestered Bongelli for details of the trial and demanded a visit with Arnie after his incarceration had begun. Bongelli banned that idea, having just lost one client on a 'holding' charge while visiting his inmate father. Carty dealt with the ban by making a request, "Ask Arnie to dial me in with a coupla guys gettin' out of prison. I got a job needs doin'."

Unsuspecting due to his preoccupation with other work, Bongelli had passed the message. Less than a month later he was dumbfounded by the image of the star witness for Sutton's prosecution, Ron Connors, spread over front page of every newspaper in the U.S. after he and his wife were brutally murdered at their home. Bongelli made the connection a week later and was staggered by the thought that his favorite student had 'gone rogue'.

Still, a different prime suspect was sought for the murder and the flow of cash from the Carty operation was sufficient to assuage further concern or guilt. Other, later deaths, including Catherine's husband and the detective who had testified at the Damarow trial, as well as the disappearances of several rivals had finally raised Bongelli's suspicions again. Might *he* be the next target? Bongelli started keeping his distance from Carty, an early caution in the event that Bongelli had to cut ties for good at some point.

After an envisioned showdown with Carty, Bongelli assumed that he would regain control of the ranch and the impressive cash flow that its elements created. The events at the ranch that stormy afternoon upended the priorities permanently. Bongelli was forced to formulate a new plan instantly. The hugely resentful, thoroughly estranged Shirley was recruited to attend to the victims while caring for only one—Grant Carty. Her already-steep rates increased frequently.

In his mind, Bongelli had invested hundreds of thousands of dollars in the ranch facility and Carty's care and maintenance while he and his operatives occasionally searched for the imagined fortunes that Carty had squirreled away somewhere on the ranch. He commandeered over $100,000 in Carty's 'loose change' to procure a mobile home while the existing house was renovated. A nice slice of the missing money was secreted behind the front seats of the ubiquitous blue Chevy S-10 truck. Shirley and her boy toy Chad had first discovered that stash. I'd looked right at it and had missed it.

My arrival on the scene as the 'official' investigator of the Connors murders and my steadfast refusal to give up on a some-times-sketchy connection between Connors, Sutton, Carty and Bongelli introduced a new degree of difficulty for ol' Bongelli, one that eventually caused him to panic and try to make a run for it—a point of pride for me if ever there was one.

By midweek the next week I submitted my final report to my client, detailing the who, when, where, and why of her brother's murder as well as the corrected facts surrounding her son's demise. I didn't lapse into 'I told you so', even once. I received a call two days later setting a meeting for the following Thursday afternoon at her office. Waiting for me there were her sincere congratulations and a nice check...a single digit and a couple of commas that would pave more than one future path for me. There was no formal announcement, there was no media presence, it was just a simple business meeting between two respectful if not exactly 'chummy' professional allies. I was happy to see the matter come to an agreeable conclusion even though I came away with the feeling that Elizabeth still didn't care all that much for the final outcome.

In the next few weeks, many changes took place for many of the people I'd encountered along the way...

Elizabeth finally put Ron's house on the market, with a low seven-figure price listed. A bidding war ensued, and the home brought $110k more than the asking. Them that has, gets more. No extra charge for the vibes.

Jorge' and his wife moved to a nice house in Monrovia. I attended their housewarming party and had a great time. They're fine people and we've become good friends.

I paid Catherine a nice bonus for her above-and-beyond efforts. She and her fiancée were married on the beach in Cabo and started on their new life together. She and I have worked together a few times since. She's good people.

Arnie Sutton remained incarcerated at Chino while his new attorney attempted to deal with his client. The face tatts remain but the attitude is somewhat refined. Catherine promises to attend every sentence reduction hearing, ever. They better not make her mad.

After Ray Cole was formally exonerated for the murder of the Connors, he was released from Men's Central in downtown L.A. He walked to Union Station and caught a commuter train that took him home to the trailer by the beach. He greeted his dad, he took a shower to get rid of the institutional grime, then he took a nap on the screened-in patio, reveling in his return to the ocean breeze. After he awoke, he microwaved some Stouffer's Lasagna for dinner.

After he washed his fork and tossed his lasagna dish, he sat in his recliner in the cramped living room, hit the TV remote's 'ON' button and promptly suffered a massive stroke. After well over a decade spent under suspicion for a notorious double murder, he was free, then he wasn't. Maybe it's Karma.

Almost everyone is still looking for the missing money.

After Shirley testified against Bongelli at a preliminary Grand Jury, she took her shiny new divorce decree and her share of some money she'd found, offloaded the penthouse condo at a for-cash forty percent loss to Bongelli and moved to a small seaside town in South America. She's recently been seen in the company of a thirty-two-year-old dentist who looks like a male model. Chad stayed behind in Las Vegas, somewhat wealthier himself.

After a month Reanna received a mid-five-figure slice of Arnie Sutton's remaining funds and made her break from Pahrump. She bought a house in Henderson and opened a hair and nail salon in one of the new smaller casinos. Last I heard she was doing well though Lylie, her trust fund restored, still keeps her distance.

Vinnie Bongelli was taken to an undisclosed location—a nice condo in Thousand Oaks—for an indefinite period of time while Jack the Fed and his friends try to unravel decades of illicit operations in multiple states. The mostly-indoor sport of 'Racketeering' may have a new poster boy by the time they get through with him.

Grant Carty was taken from the ranch to a small private convalescent hospital near Las Vegas as the hearing in Riverside was starting that afternoon. Given actual medical attention instead of Shirley's cruel warehousing he regained consciousness within two weeks. He was showing significant physical improvement as well though he downplayed the differences to most observers. State and Federal charges were accumulating against him pending the outcome of a Grand Jury hearing centered around Bongelli. That would take a while as official attention to his security flagged.

Authorities examined the Potters Field at the desert ranch and retrieved twenty of Carty's murder victims as well as additional evidence regarding the drug operation. Much of the evidence other than the murders, the trafficking system and the 'hidden' manufacturing site, was murky regarding a time frame but the investigators called the system 'borderline brilliant'.

One Thursday morning thirteen weeks after his arrival, Grant Carty, along with a satchel of clothes and the teenage son of a Latina hospital worker, disappeared. The Law Enforcement community was properly embarrassed. I had made the occasional inquiry, watching the ongoing events from a respectful distance, and I had halfway expected the 'poof'. Carty's cagey like that. I have a line on his whereabouts, and I know many of his tricks. It's only a matter of time before he and I meet again.

Me? I finished my reports and filed them with any pertinent agencies, my client, and my referral attorney—whom I still owed a lunch. I banked my check, paid a slab of it to the tax guys in Sacramento, and took it easy for a few days. I had things to catch up on. so I stayed home for a week, not even answering the phone. I went to the beach a time or two, did some cooking and spent time with friends. Life is good but there would soon be new challenges.

ACKNOWLEDGMENTS

Many thanks to longtime friend Gary Schmidt for getting me started, Rob Lund (California Highway Patrol) for keeping me going, Attorneys Dave Beuoy and Bill Barrett for moral support and encouragement, and the late Mike Connors, (Joe Mannix to the rest of us) for the inspiration.

A LOOK AT BOOK TWO:
ENOUGH ROPE

NEW THREATS. SAME DETECTIVE.

When L.A. Private Investigator C. Street's close friend is brutally injured and nearly killed, he becomes an element in her protection—and she, an ally in his pursuit of a notorious and well-connected felon.

Grant Carty, the initiator of the auto racing legend Ronnie Connors' murder years earlier has emerged from his coma and is well on his way to a recovery after being rescued from his desolate Nevada desert hiding place. Singular of purpose, he aims to make up for lost time by arriving in L.A. with ample funding and zero scruples—looking for trouble around every corner.

On a desolate pursuit that takes numerous forms—from electronic surveillance to street racing—the strength of Street's resolve sees new challenges. Especially as Carty descends into a lethality that exempts no one...

AVAILABLE MARCH 2023

ABOUT THE AUTHOR

Tennessee native Rick Rothermel grew up in Huntsville, Alabama and lived in Southern California after a decade split between Alaska and Oregon. He was a columnist and freelance contributor for automotive magazines for twenty years and worked in the TV and movie production industry, specializing in automotive subjects. Classic TV and literature of the detective genre are hobbies that led to the creation of the C STREET MYSTERY series.